BODY A

Goldie

By the same author

Adult

Unjust desserts

For Children

Mavis road medley
My Story – Surviving Sydney Cove
(Published in UK as *My Story – Transported*)
Little Big School
6788
Email Murder Mystery
Astronet
Seawall
Killer virus
The Business of Writing for Young People (With Hazel Edwards)
Right or Wrong (With Hazel Edwards)

BODY AND SOUL

Goldie Alexander

Indra Publishing

Indra Publishing
PO Box 7, Briar Hill, Victoria, 3088, Australia.

© Goldie Alexander, 2003
Typeset in Palatino by Fire Ink Press.
Made and Printed in Australia by McPherson's Printing Group.

National Library of Australia Cataloguing-in-Publication data:

Alexander, Goldie
Body and soul

ISBN 0 9578735 9 X (pbk.)

I. Title.

A 823.3

Dedication

For David, and with many thanks to Hazel Edwards, Jennifer Dabbs, Vashti Farrer, Ruth Mushin and Ruth Alexander

Acknowledgements

News items and advertisements are quoted from the *Age*, the *Argus*, the *Sun* and the *Herald*, random editions between September 1937 and April 1938.

1

Father arrived home in such a foul mood I knew to keep out of his way. Over dinner he complained that we'd forgotten to change his table napkin, and that his rump steak was tough. All evening, even as we listened to the Classical Hour on the wireless, he scowled into his newspaper. Then he lowered it long enough to inform Julie that he'd invited a guest to dinner for the following night.

'Felix Goldfarb,' in reply to her startled glance. 'One of those migrant newcomers. What are you cooking?'

'Roast lamb, Father.'

He stared at his paper. An article on duck shooting caught his eye. 'How about ducks? And your excellent brandy sauce. No reason to be skinflint.'

'Certainly Father,' she calmly replied. 'But this week's housekeeping will never stretch to ducks.'

He took out his wallet and carefully unfolded a new pound note. I dropped my pencil and Ella had to scramble under the table for it. Father expects his weekly budget – two pounds, eighteen shillings and sixpence – to cover all Julie's housekeeping expenses plus any little thing we might need for ourselves. Mr. Goldfarb must be very special for him to be this generous. It's true that we are over the worst, and that Aarons and Marks has recovered from the

7

Depression, but 'take care of the pennies and the pounds will take care of themselves,' is still his favourite saying.

Though I never dare question him too closely, Ella is not easily put off. 'Father,' she cried amazed at his unexpected largesse, 'where did you meet Mr. Goldfarb?'

'A business connection,' was his brisk reply. Then he held up his paper to show her that, at least as far as he was concerned, this conversation was now over.

Nine months since we last had guests for dinner. Father's fiftieth birthday, and he invited his partner Morris Aarons and Morris's daughter Daisy to celebrate it with us. But that very afternoon he heard over the wireless that if there was to be another world war that the Americans refused to join in. 'Just like last time,' he yelled as if the news-reader himself was responsible. 'Those Huns'll come in as we're counting our dead.' He was so upset, just in time Julie stopped him telegraphing the Aarons not to come.

That night Julie cooked coq au vin with all the trimmings followed by a rich Bavarian pudding. I eat very little, and this meal was no exception. Instead I concentrated on my new project, noting how Father's lowered head, broad shoulders and strong, stocky frame are like a wombat's. But Morris is a Russian bear – as wide as he is tall with twinkling grey eyes and a full head of silvery hair.

The Aarons stayed on and on and it was midnight before Morris stood up from the table. Before they left, he congratulated Julie on the meal, then gruffly confided how Daisy couldn't boil water. If we expected Daisy to be embarrassed, we could not have been more mistaken. Instead she held up such soft plump hands, I'm sure she's never done a day's housework in her life. 'I could cook perfectly well if I tried,' she coolly replied. 'But if you, Daddy, are happy to employ a cook, why should I?'

Morris laughed, glancing around like the proud papa he is, and expecting us to admire his daughter's ladylike ways. Though Julie congratulated him, Father's face remained impassive. Ella smiled politely, but didn't dare catch my eye. Long ago we decided that Daisy is too spoilt to be likeable. Moreover she never stops talking about people we don't know, and parties to which she rarely invites Julie or Ella. And never, ever me.

Though Daisy and Julie were in the same class at school, their present lives are utterly different. While Daisy swans about doing whatever she pleases, Julie is responsible for the smooth running of Adeline Terrace. Ella is supposed to share all these chores. But she's such a dreamer, twice this month she let my bath run over, allowed the kettle to boil dry, forgotten to bring in the washing when it rained, or switch off the kitchen light before she went to bed. As for 'yours truly' – since I dropped a glass and cut myself picking up the shards, Father has given strict instructions as to what I can and cannot do. Sometimes the list seems endless.

Not that much has changed. I must have been about three when I went crying to Aunt Amy, 'How come Ella can run when I can't?'

She hugged me saying, 'Oh, my poor darling. You know that story by heart.'

'Tell it again, Auntie.'

She took her time settling me on her knee. 'After Ella was born,' she explained as I snuggled into a chest as firm and comforting as a bolster, 'your mother was very ill. When you, the second baby appeared, you were so blue and lifeless, Dr. Williams thought you were dead. Instead of helping you breathe, he tried saving your mother's life. So your brain suffered through lack of oxygen. Dr Williams later explained that this is called Birth Asphyxia, and often leads to damage.'

'That's why I hardly use my left hand?'

'That's why it curls inwards.'

'Why my left leg is shorter than my right?'

She sighed and then nodded. 'But if you ride your tricycle, Dr. Williams says this will strengthen your muscles.'

'But that's not happening, is it Auntie,' I wailed. 'My left side is getting stiffer all the time.'

'Ah well,' she said in the voice people use to hide the truth. 'You must pray to God to make you better.'

I like to picture a fairy godmother standing over us at birth. 'This first baby will be beautiful, courageous and artistic,' she decreed. 'Name her Isabelle or Ella. Her twin, though crippled and plain, will be prudent and discerning. So call her Elizabeth or Lilbet.'

2

ARE ALL AUTHORS SHY?
29th December, 1937
Fay Compton asks if all authors are shy? After interviewing Noel Coward, James Barrie, Somerset Maugham and J.B. Priestly, the writer and actress Fay Compton who is presently appearing in the J.C. Williamson production of "Victoria Regina" at King's Theatre, has concluded that some authors are warier of publicity than others ...

The clock struck ten. Father folded his newspaper, and Julie put away the supper things. Because Father hates Mitsy and Motsy, our old Persian cats, spreading black and grey fur everywhere, Ella shooed them out of the house.

She was helping me into bed when the subject of New Year's resolutions came up. It was the first time I dared mention my intention of writing a novel. I would have liked to tell her that this New Year's resolution was to complete my project by December the thirty-first. But wary about revealing too much in case they thought this too demanding for a cripple and therefore try to stop me, I didn't add that the subject would be my own family. Anyway, I knew Ella's response would be: 'Why bother? Nothing ever happens here.'

But this time she said, 'Good idea.' Absent-minded fingers ran through glossy dark-brown curls. 'Make it a romance.'

Not that she's interested in reading. Or books. Or literature. No, I knew she thought writing a novel would keep me occupied and give her more time to herself.

Maybe I could have said more, lots more in fact, if she'd shown the least bit of interest. For example, I would have explained why I have been scribbling for years, how I have always kept a journal, even mentioned Jane Austen, the Bronte sisters and Charles Dickens, my favourite writers, and why I reread their work; even gone on to how much I admire J.B. Priestly, Somerset Maugham and Pearl Buck.

Too late. By now her attention had shifted to the view outside our bedroom window. 'Just think,' she mused staring up at the clear night sky, 'those stars have shone over –'

'London and Paris,' I finished off.

She yanked the curtains together and the air felt thick with unspoken words. Twins are so close, she knew how impatient I was with her endless dreaming. However, not wanting or needing a quarrel and exhausted from the lengthy and sometimes painful process of changing out of my clothes into my nightie, I switched to our unknown visitor, saying, 'This Mr. Goldfarb. Wonder where he's from?'

She turned back to me. 'I think he's maybe German. Doesn't Goldfarb mean 'gold-colour'in German?'

I lay back on my pillow. 'Last month the *Argus* ran an article about German-Jewish refugees. Hardly any speak English and now there's a problem where to settle them.'

'Mr. Goldfarb must speak English or Father would never invite him. But where did they meet?'

'The Windsor Hotel. Or maybe the Parthenon Café. Those are Father's favourite luncheon places.'

'The Windsor Hotel? So expensive. How can a migrant afford to eat there?'

'That article said some had plenty of money.'

'Thought you only read papers for the crosswords,' she teased, though she knows that when I cut papers up to use in the lavatory, that I read and reread the news, cutting out any tidbits that I find interesting or might find useful, and pasting them into this journal.

That reminded me. I raised myself onto my elbows to add more vehemently, 'Another report said people are putting cisterns in their bathrooms. You know how slippery our back

12

steps get when it rains. If only Julie could persuade Father to put one in ours, at least I could manage that on my own ...'

'Oh, Lilbet' she pushed me down and tucked me in more firmly. 'You always ask too much of yourself. Of course we must help you whenever we can.'

Though I try very hard to contain my temper, I felt myself grow hot. I told myself that there was no point getting angry or disappointed. Ella would only get that tight blank look when something I say or do displeases her. She'd say, 'Without me and Julie to look after you, you'd be in the Carlton Home for Spastics and Retards.' Much safer to continue our conversation about tomorrow's dinner. I said, 'Thought Father doesn't like migrants. He says they shouldn't come here if they –'

'– can't act just like us.'

'Wonder what Mr. Goldfarb is like?'

She giggled. 'Probably young and looks –'

'– like Bunny Segal.' We both laughed.

Our good friend Bunny Segal calls into Adeline Terrace at least once a month. For reasons Father refuses to explain, he dislikes him coming here. Yet we girls think Bunny quite harmless – just a young man, an accountant like Father, who likes nothing better than a gossip over a cup of tea and a scone topped with Julie's special plum jam and cream. It's not as if he appears to be in love with Ella like some other men we know. If there is anything to criticise about Bunny, it's his weakness for food. He always says that Julie is the best cook in Melbourne, and jokes that if he had enough money that he would employ her as his personal chef.

Outside, a possum scrambled noisily up a tree. Inside, Ella collapsed on her bed and stared up at the ceiling. Dust motes floated in the glare of the overhead light. I knew she was thinking will nothing exciting ever happen? As if to confirm this, she said, 'Tell me Lilbet, don't you want more than this?' Her arm encompassed our room, our house, our very existence.

I tried not to sigh aloud. Ella is always desperate for romance, though not with anyone we know. If Julie should happen to mention that Charles Levy, Bruce Goldbloom, or even Ted Benjamin – though he's much too old for her – would be only too pleased to squire Ella around town, she gets that tight blank look. Besides, as soon as any man shows her a flicker of interest, she quickly chases him away. Instead she aches to travel overseas where, she insists, 'I'm sure to meet someone more worldly, sophisticated and exciting than anyone we know.' Sometimes, but only in the privacy of our bedroom, she threatens to stow away on an ocean liner, though she hasn't any money and only speaks English.

I broke into a cold sweat just thinking about it. Every newspaper carries reports that make me grateful to be in Melbourne, Australia.

> **HITLER REPEATS DEMANDS FOR COLONIES.**
> **7th September, 1938**
> Economic distress dictated Germany's claim for colonies,' said Herr Hitler in a proclamation which was read at the opening of the national Socialist Congress at Nuremberg today. Herr Hitler was given a tumultuous reception, both when he arrived by air to Nuremberg and when he mounted the platform at the opening of the congress ...

Adolf Hitler's avowed aim is to 'cleanse his nation of all Jews'. I can't help wondering how he will manage. Jews are such an important part of his country's culture, science and economy. Still, the BBC reports that demonstrators have been arrested, and there are rumours of labour camps no one is allowed to visit. Ever since the Enabling Act in 1933 – when he managed to rid himself of all the Social Democrats and Communist Delegates even though he had only 51 percent of all votes – Hitler does whatever he likes, and woe betide anyone who tries to stop him.

True that our lives are filled with what Ella calls 'boring domesticity'. But I quite like it that way. It's my experience that when our lives aren't dull, it's because of some unpleasantness that will be painful to endure. Rather, I prefer to perceive myself as different from the usual run of women. Though my external shell might be flawed, my mind is so charged, so alert, I am capable of taking control of whatever might affect me. Or put another way, if Ella is a leaf waving in the wind, than I am the stem on which she must rest.

So what does all this prove? That we are two sides of the same coin – irretrievably tied, but at the same time utterly different. I love books, dream of becoming a famous writer, and dread meeting new people who might comment on my spasticity. Ella adores animals, enjoys playing practical jokes on her family, craves to get into films and pines to meet someone urbane and exciting. Where I have never gone further by myself than to the end of Grandview Street, Ella can hardly wait to leave home and travel to foreign places. And where I find it hard to manage even the simplest tasks, Ella's dressmaking is so good, she could open her own first class salon. Even Julie claims that she has never met twin girls so dissimilar.

'Julie's life couldn't be duller,' I murmured. 'Yet she never complains.'

Ella rolled onto her stomach, her hair flopping over her face. She flicked it aside to say, 'Oh, Julie's such an angel, she can't imagine anything except looking after Father and us.'

'Not really,' I started to say, then changed my mind. Though Julie will be twenty-eight in June, by anyone's reckoning an old maid, I was convinced that she longed to be married. She was only eighteen, the exact age we are now, when she took over the running of Adeline Terrace. No easy task, for our father, Simon George Marks, can be very demanding. Yet there are times, such as when we listen to music, that I glimpse such longing in her face, my eyes and throat ache with unspilled tears.

Ella turned off the light and climbed into bed. She was not the only one to dream. I hoped that one day I too, would grow strong. Then together we would circumnavigate the globe. And our voyage would be as constant as the stars, as fixed as the planets, and as unwavering as the moon rising over our suburban backyard.

3

> **UNIVERSITY WOMEN MAKE BAD MOTHERS.**
> **20th December, 1937**
> 'University trained women have been proven to make unsatisfactory mothers because they consider a knowledge of domestic affairs as beneath them,' says a Mothercraft Nurse who asks to remain anonymous ...

If Howard Spring or Sir Walter Scott were writing this novel, they would describe their characters in some detail, and I intend following their example. First something about our background. My great-grandfather who sailed here for the 1850 gold rush, claimed that his father had walked all the way from Russia to France. An enterprising man, he managed to find a boat to take him across the English Channel where he eventually settled in Manchester. A weaver by trade, he soon found employment within a Jewish factory, and proved himself such a good worker and pleasant fellow that he changed his name from Chaim Markovitch to George Marks, married his boss's daughter and eventually inherited the business.

Twenty years later George died and his eldest son Maurice took over the factory. George's second son, also called George, had an adventurous streak that had him seek gold in far away Victoria. Here, he quickly found that the best way to make money was not by digging for it but by supplying the bits and pieces other miners needed. Needless to say, he made enough to build Adeline Terrace, open a drapery shop in Bourke Street – which he later sold for a very good profit – and marry my grandmother, Ruby.

Father was only conscripted in 1918 – too late to be sent overseas. At war's end, he was lucky not to catch the Spanish

Influenza, and in the December of 1919 he sailed to England on the P and O Line. On arrival he went straight to Manchester where he met his third cousin, Isabella Elizabeth Goldberg. They fell in love and were married within three months before sailing back to Australia. My sister Julie was born shortly after they settled back in Adeline Terrace, and Ella and I came ten years later.

Julie tells me that before Mother's death, Father was a joyous man who loved to tell jokes and tease his eldest daughter. Thinking about the dour man who controls all our actions with an iron hand, I stared at her incredulously. 'Joke? Tease? I find that hard to believe.'

Julie was all seriousness. 'He liked nothing better than a good laugh.'

As she rarely if ever jokes, and never ever lies, she had me almost convinced. Julie is so gentle, the worst she can ever do if something displeases her, is purse her lips into one thin line. Though she was adamant that Father was once 'the life of the party', this man has become so morose and dictatorial, I could hardly believe we were talking about the same person. Whenever I picture Father, my mind sees a man shaped like a wombat with balding hair, fiery dark eyes under shaggy eyebrows, swarthy skin, a tight mouth with very large yellowing teeth and a bullying, overbearing manner.

Julie insists that it was the double shock of Mother's untimely death and the effect of the Depression on Aarons and Marks that made him so bad tempered. But the business has recovered very nicely, and his partner Morris Aarons, also a widower, is both friendly and generous to a fault. No, I think it is something in Father's nature, something churlish and melancholy and depressive, that has made him such a brow-beater.

Given his many restrictions, it isn't surprising that Ella finds her life 'dull and boring'. Insisting that 'education is wasted on girls', Father refused to send me to Cambridge

Ladies College and even removed Ella as soon as she turned fourteen. (I pined a little less when I learnt that this College emphasised sewing, sketching, 'conversational French' and behaving in a 'lady-like' manner, rather than anything academic or vocational.)

Not that Ella was a 'blue-stocking', or that her mind ever retained any interesting facts apart from gossip. But she had rather enjoyed socialising with the other girls – her best friend Polly Partridge in particular. Perhaps if she'd been a keen reader like myself, had enjoyed analysing and retaining knowledge, even considered learning Latin, German or Italian, things might have been different. But at home she finds little to hold her interest if plenty to fill her days. She's fortunate in that she doesn't have to look for paid work. There's more than enough housework in Adeline Terrace to keep both my sisters busy from dawn to dusk.

Our day starts at 6.30 when Julie begins preparing breakfast. Only last year Father indulged her passion for cooking by buying a 'Kookaburra' gas-stove. What a relief it was to no longer have to light the old wood oven and keep it burning. It had been Ella's task to make sure there was enough wood, and somehow she always forgot to check that the bin was full.

Instead of our old ice-chest that constantly leaks, Julie longs for one of those new gas refrigerators that retails for thirty-nine shillings at Steele's Department Store in Bourke Street. Perhaps she would prefer an electric refrigerator, but their price is so astronomical, no advertisement dares mention it.

Back to Julie's day. Breakfast over, there is laundry, ironing, patching, dusting, sweeping, polishing, gardening, shopping and cooking; enough to keep Julie and Ella busy from sunrise to sunset. And myself, of course. Not that I am permitted to tackle too many household tasks. No, it's that Father insists they watch my every move in case I injure myself. He often speaks about me as if I'm not in the same room. Or worse still, as if I'm too much of a child to understand. It tells me with what contempt he holds me because I am a cripple and not beautiful. For example, he'll say in my presence, 'Just one moment of carelessness for Lilbet to slip on a too highly polished floor or trip on the stairs, and we will surely rue it.' Or, 'Make sure Lilbet takes her tonic, or we'll have her sick again.' Or 'Check that Lilbet's had enough to eat.' Or 'Don't let her become overtired. You know we must always keep a sharp watch on all her actions.'

What if I were to stand up to him? What if I were to point out that though my body might be flawed, that there's nothing wrong with my mind? Then I picture his wombat stance, yellow teeth and bellowing style, and change my mind. If I antagonise him too much, then he will surely decide to send me away. No, I'm best off remaining a mollusc and using my brain to prevent any change in our day to day existence.

Yet it's this same everydayness that drives Ella mad. She once confided that her only salvation was going to the movies and picturing herself far, far away in the arms of a dark-haired lover. Then she sighed and said 'Julie thinks my only escape is a good marriage.'

As the last thing I want is Ella leaving Adeline Terrace, I acidly replied, 'Isn't that changing one lot of domesticity for another? Anyway, you keep saying how all the men we know are boring.'

'Maybe,' she admitted. 'But there has to be something more than this.'

'Like what?' And watching her pretty face dissolve into tears, it was like looking into a clear pool clouding over.

Sometimes I think 'boring' is Ella's favourite word. 'Dull' is the other. According to her, our house is boring, our lives dull, our suburb uninteresting, life in Melbourne Australia, grey and depressing. But boring can also mean non-eventful. Dull can mean shielded. Uninteresting as needing to find one's own intellectual stimulation. And grey and depressing, safe and sound.

How differently we see the same things. How hard I must work to ensure that nothing changes.

4

INFLUENZA VACCINE DRAWS A LITTLE CLOSER.
16th December, 1937

The possibility of a vaccine for one of the world's most feared illnesses, influenza, has come closer this year through the work of an Australian scientist, Frank Macfarlane Burnet. Burnet has found that there is more than one strain of influenza virus, and this has created a path to discovery for researchers looking for the possibility of a vaccine for the disease ...

Woke to a hot northerly bringing swirls of dust into our backyard. Julie barely gave me time to finish my tea and toast before she fastened my leather and metal caliper onto my left leg and helped me into my wheelchair. Lips one thin line, she showed the effort of preparing a formal dinner with too little warning. 'Ella, we'll start with chilled fruit soup, so make sure the peaches aren't green. And check that the ducks are fresh. Buy a small bottle of brandy for the sauce. Here,' she thrust a shopping list and her purse into my lap, 'don't forget the oranges.'

Though Julie encourages me to walk short distances, today with the heat and rush, I stayed in my chair. Once we got inside the market, Ella wheeled me to Mr. Brumby's fruit and vegetable stall. Here Ella bought all the vegetables on Julie's list, and Mr. B. – who always has an admiring gleam in his eyes for Ella and a pitying glance for me – handed us two juicy plums as our morning tea.

We thanked him very nicely, then headed on to 'poultry' where a line of dead chooks and ducks hung from the rails. The stink of singed feathers and bloody entrails made my head spin. But Ella's stomach is far stronger than mine, and she poked her finger into each duck's breast until she found two plump and young enough to buy.

Ducks plucked and wrapped in last week's *Herald*, we set off for the other side of the market. Ella pushed me around stalls filled with pots, pans, cups, plates, buttons, rolls of material, clips, bits of ironwork, tools, second, third and fourth-hand clothes, and anything else you can think of. But with the sun beating down on the tin roof, it was so hot, so much dust and noise, so many last minute shoppers, I felt my head swim. I wondered if I mightn't be sick. 'Ella,' I cried. 'Let's go home. We've bought everything on our list.'

But no, all week she'd been planning to edge the collar on Julie's second best dress. We cut through several stalls selling boots and shoes, took another sharp turn through to the back until she finally paused in front of a table covered with haberdashery. We were sifting through various laces when I heard a man say, 'You like my stock?'

I glanced up to see a young giant with olive skin and a halo of dark frizzy hair. His gaze on Ella, he cried, 'Plizz give your name, little bird?'

'Mind your own business,' sat on the tip of my tongue. But the young man's eyes, round and black as coffee beans, were so admiring, it was hard to take offence. To my amazement, he quoted Keats, crying, 'A t'ing of beauty is a joy forever.'

All this passed over Ella's head. Her looks are the kind people goggle at. Though some might consider her a little too short for true beauty, her figure is as perfectly proportioned as the statue of the Venus De Milo. Ella has milky skin, one of those long swan necks you see in Victorian portraits, a perfect oval face, thick masses of chocolate-brown ringlets that cluster around her cheeks, teeth white as milk, and full wine-red lips that curl up at the corners. Her only flaw – if it is a flaw – is the high-bridged nose she inherited from Father. She often moans about its shape, but I think this gives her face strength and without it, she would be just another pretty girl.

We rounded the corner, and I glanced back to see the

stall-holder watching our retreat. In those thick woollen trousers, heavy collarless shirt and rough waistcoat, he seemed quite oblivious to both the heat and his surroundings.

I thought I knew where he was from. Though most of the Jewish families we know settled here last century, lately there's been a small influx of Jews from Northeastern Europe. Hard to believe that we are all of the same faith, these migrants are so different. Father says it's because they come from tiny *shetels* – villages with no made roads, and where people and animals cluster together in huts with no running water or electricity. Some were driven out by murderous pogroms. More left to better themselves financially. As Father once explained, 'Most want to go to America where they expect to make their fortune.'

'Least both countries speak English,' commented our ever-practical Julie. 'So they can't be too different.'

'But to sail here they must travel so much further,' he replied. 'After two months on a ship, Australia feels like another planet. It's as if a serf has been lifted from medieval times into the twentieth century.'

'But Father,' I butted in. 'Grandfather Marks was once equally foreign, and he was able to adapt.'

Bushy eyebrows met as he glowered at me. 'Since when Lilbet, did you become an expert on family history?'

However much I longed to answer back, I knew better than to argue. Long ago I leant that any attempt to reason with Father, no matter how wrong he might be, is like putting my hand inside a hot oven and expecting not to get burnt.

Presently, because I was tired, irritable, still felt ill and above all wanted to go home, I gestured towards the stall-holder and said tartly, 'What a gawk!'

Ella just laughed. I try not to be unkind. But people are always ogling her, as if her loveliness can be cut up and shared like an apple or an orange. This is most obvious at Passover or Jewish New Year when we three sit upstairs in the lady's section of the East Melbourne Synagogue. I can't help noticing how the men seated in front of the Bima look up and stare, and how the women in the upper gallery make silent but unflattering comparisons. Julie and Ella pretend not to notice, but my reaction is to glare rudely back until I shame the gazer into looking away.

By now it was so hot under the market's tin roof, even Ella agreed it was time to go home. She pushed me through the doors at the back of the markets into the street, and we headed towards 'Paddy's Pub' to buy a half bottle of brandy for the orange sauce. As we rounded the corner, we walked into a group of children with dirty faces and ragged clothes. I shrank into my chair, hoping none of them would notice me. Thankfully, none did. But as they surged past, I did so wish I had their strong limbs and sturdy bodies – though not their worn boots and dripping noses.

The bottle-shop is up a steep flight of steps. Ella left me in the shade after promising to be quick. So the morning would have been a success if I hadn't overheard one middle-aged woman in a floral frock and straw hat as she walked past say loudly to her companion, 'There's another o' those spastics. Shouldn't be kept 'round normal folks.'

Her friend – pale blue frock and matching straw sunhat – nodded. 'Oughter be put away in a 'ome where you'se can't see 'em ...'

'Too right. Those spastics're just a trouble to us an' themselves. Don' the professors say they didn't ought to be left alive? Eugenics, they calls it.'

'Uhuh. All the rage in Europe and America.'

'In the Mother Country, too.'

'I 'eard of this spastic girl 'oo were taken advantage of. They'se had to take 'er aways to somewhere's she couldn't be got at.'

They moved out of earshot. If only I could have run after them to cry that not all spastics are retarded. That spastics, no matter how poorly they might look or seem, have feelings too, that are easily hurt.

Those learned professors who advocate eugenics claim that this science will purify the world through controlling unfortunate characteristics that should be eradicated. Needless to say, there was a great outcry at the last Olympic Games in Berlin when Adolf Hitler declared that the American Negro's ability to win so many sporting events was due to their inferior racial background which, he said, makes them more akin to animals than people. He also intends to rid the world of anyone as disabled as myself, as well as Gypsies, Jews and homosexuals. When I asked Julie what homosexuals were, a pink spot appeared on each cheek. 'Those who prefer their own sex,' she said and changed the subject.

In some ways I can understand that Herr Hitler wants to rid his country of useless people like me. But what if cripples can be made to feel useful? What if they can triumph over terrible adversities? Only this month, the *Argus* newspaper featured a story about a heroic man who managed an amazing swim:

DEFORMITIES, NOT HANDICAPS.
3rd December, 1937

Charles Zimmy who has no legs, swam down the Hudson River from Albany to New York, a distance of 143 miles in 148 hours. His feat is an addition to the achievements of men and women, famous and obscure, who have triumphed over physical deformities ..."

We arrived home hot and tired. A quick lunch of cheese and tomato on brown bread, and then Ella set about cleaning and polishing Mother's best silver. Father insists that we use the correct number of knives, forks and spoons for every course, plus our crystal wine-glasses, so this task can take forever. Because we were running late, Ella asked me to fold the linen napkins into swans. Two hours later she was still setting the table, and Julie shelling peas and whipping cream. They left me to scrub the potatoes, a task I can manage without any help. By five o'clock, the temperature in our kitchen was well into the century, and I felt sorry for Julie who was bent over a hot oven and for Ella who was still halfway through ironing our best summer frocks.

The front gate creaked open. First thing Father did was check that the table-setting was correct. Next, he marched into the kitchen to demand, 'Who laid the table?'

Julie was standing over the stove, stirring. 'Why Ella,' she said, her mind on her sauce. 'It's always her task to fix the dining room.'

When Father gets cross, his head seems to darken and swell, and then he reminds me of an angry hippopotamus or a raging boar and we'd all better look out. I'm sure that one day his hot temper will be the death of him. He barked, 'Those napkins look dreadful! Redo them immediately.'

Ella glanced up from her ironing. 'Lilbet did the napkins. I think she's done rather well.'

'How many times must I remind you that Lilbet is a cripple?' His eyes under those shaggy brows seemed to burn right through her. 'You might think those napkins are fine, but I don't agree. Redo them immediately.'

Ella's cheeks crimsoned. She's nearly as hot tempered as Father and I half expected her to refuse. Then she stalked into the dining room to do as she was told.

I limped into the passage to hide my tears. There are times when Father's need for excellence over-rides any sensitivity. I tell myself to be more understanding. However unintentional it was, he can never forgive me for what he perceives as causing Mother's death. Somehow he never manages to blame Ella. Nor can he ever forgive me for being a cripple and not beautiful. If only he could love me half as much as he loves my sisters. Though he frowns whenever Ella speaks to him, I notice, when he thinks no one is watching, how his eyes linger on her.

How different Father is with me. I remember when I was

small, peering up at him hoping to see some recognition in his eyes. Yet whenever I come within his sights, his expression turns sour and his mouth turns down. 'Hullo Father, are you there?' I sometimes want to cry. 'It's me Lilbet, your daughter. Please talk to me.'

Someone knocked on the door. Behind the lead-light roses, I glimpsed a man's outline. My scalp prickled. Something told me that Ella's wish for excitement was about to be granted.

5

The shadowy figure on the other side of our front door tapped once again. I rubbed my eyes and opened the door to a young man with a shock of gingery hair. 'Miss Marks?'

'Yes.' I limped back to let him in. 'I'm Elizabeth Marks.'

He removed his hat. 'Felix Goldfarb. How do you do.'

He put out a hand. I looked at it uncertainly. Thinking he wanted to shake mine, I went to take his. He bent forward. Next, his moustache was tickling my skin. Astonished, I pulled my hand away. Too late, and realising what I had done and how offensive this might seem, once again I put out my hand …

'Mr. Goldfarb …' Thankfully Father was already half way down the passage. 'Good of you to come. No trouble finding your way here?'

'None at all, Mr. Marks. Your directions were very clear.'

'Simon, please call me Simon.' Father insisted.

'And you must call me Felix,' his guest replied as they shook hands and Mr Goldfarb handed Father a bouquet of the most exquisite long stemmed red roses I have ever seen.

Father garrumphed his thanks over the flowers, managed to look embarrassed as he juggled them from one hand to another, meanwhile insisting that they were quite unnecessary, far too expensive, and then handed them to me. While I carried them into the kitchen, he hung our visitor's hat on the hall-stand and shepherded him into the living room.

When I returned I saw, in the late afternoon light, that Felix was not at all what we had expected. He was young, no more than twenty-two or twenty-three, slim and short, not much taller than Ella, though several inches taller than myself. His hair was a blaze of orange curls, his eyes were an unusual olive green, his nose well shaped with a sprinkling of freckles. He wore a pencil-slim gingery moustache like Ronald Colman, and his smile showed straight white teeth. Beneath his rather fleshy lower lip was a small firm chin with a marked cleft in the centre.

Just as Father had finished settling our guest into his own favourite chair, Julie walked into the room carrying the roses in a vase which she placed on the mantlepiece. This done, Father pushed her forward. 'Felix, meet my eldest daughter, Julie.'

He sprang up to brush her hand with his lips. Though she didn't pull away, she couldn't help giggling.

Father's expression didn't change. He turned to Ella, 'Meet the twins. This is my daughter Isabella. We call her Ella.'

Felix kissed Ella's hand. I waited for her to be equally embarrassed, but she smiled as if hand kissing happened to her every day.

'And our youngest, Elizabeth,' Father said turning to me. 'We call her Lilbet.'

I thrust both hands into my pockets. To my relief, Felix reminded Father that we'd met already.

We waited for Father to offer Felix a sherry. Instead he steered Felix into the dining room and told Julie to bring in the soup.

With Ella beside me, Father at one end of the table, Julie the other, and Felix directly opposite, now I could study him at my leisure. Julie says that I have a writerly eye for such things, so I took in his appearance very carefully – noting that his suit was fashioned from the finest wool, his tie was pure silk, his shirt Egyptian linen, his hair cut by a master barber, and his hands as soft and white as Daisy's.

Because I had never met anyone like him before, all I could think was, surely he would find us too unworldly and wish that he were somewhere else. One glance at Ella, and then Julie, and I knew my sisters thought the same. So imagine our relief when he praised everything he ate to high heaven. 'This is as good as anything I have eaten in Paris,' he declared between mouthfuls of duck 'Not many have skin as crisp as this. Nor do their sauces compliment the palate as well ...' He went on like this for so long, I wondered if we were both eating the same dish. But Julie, pink with pleasure, picked at her food as if his compliments fed every need she'd ever had.

I am convinced that my sister Julie must be the best cook in the whole of Australia. When cooking for a guest, she always makes sure that her menu is European, only using the finest ingredients she can buy. For example, she would never serve mutton, only lamb. Never pumpkin, only new potatoes. And she would certainly never use suet in her pastry, only the best butter. Unsalted, if she can find it.

SUGGESTIONS FOR A FESTIVE MEAL.
30th December, 1937

Mutton pie.
Mashed pumpkin.
Baked Fruit Pudding.
For the Suet Crust: 10 ozs. flour. 1 large teaspoon baking powder. Pinch of salt. 5 ozs. shredded suet. Cold water.
For the filling: 1 lb. Plums. 3 ozs. Granulated sugar.

Between the duck and the tomato sorbet, Felix told us something about himself. He'd attended an English Public School (he didn't say which) then studied philosophy at the Sorbonne University in Paris. That's why he speaks English and French so well. And Spanish and Italian, I later discovered. Only a faint lisp on the letter 'V' hints that English isn't his mother tongue. Seems that his family own a steel foundry outside Frankfurt, and as they are extremely wealthy, they can afford to overcome the usual entrance problems for one who is Jewish.

Soon Ella forgot her shyness long enough to ask him which cooking he likes best? 'Why, there's no beating the French,' he cried leaping out of his chair to help her out of hers. 'Little better than a slice of camembert in a crisp *ficelle*.'

'A small crusty bread containing a soft cheese,' Julie cried. She has always collected recipes and I think if Father were not so dependent on her, she might have trained as a chef, perhaps even travelled overseas, as in France great chefs are sometimes women. And right through her special dessert – almond cake with a dark chocolate and rum topping surrounded by our home-grown passion fruit folded into thick cream – Felix insisted that this dinner was equal to all the five star restaurants in France he'd ever visited.

Over brandy, the men discussed the latest events in Europe. Father said, 'In spite of Mr. Chamberlain's efforts, there seems little chance to prevent another war.'

Felix agreed. 'All for one man's overwhelming ambition.'

'Think what he has achieved.' Father's tone was ironic. 'Abolished unemployment. Boosted business. Occupied the Rhineland. Got rid of so many bankers and confiscated their property for the good of the Fatherland.'

Felix nodded ruefully. 'Just before I left Frankfurt, he was removing Jewish children from their families.'

Ella's eyes widened. Unlike Father and myself, she rarely bothers to listen to the news. 'I don't understand. How could he do that?'

'He argues that as these Jewish parents are opposed to Nazi ideology, that the state should take over the education of their children.'

Julie's jaw dropped. Her greatest failing is that she always believes that everyone is good as herself. 'Surely some Germans will stand up to him?'

'Indeed some will. But most are far too frightened of Hitler's blackshirt larrikins. Particularly since Martin Niemoller, a most highly respected cleric, was arrested in August.'

BRIEF CABLE NEWS.
2nd January, 1938

Berlin, Tuesday – Judgement in the trial of Dr. Martin
Niemoller, leader of the Evangelical Confessional Movement
which is protesting against the 'Nazification' of the Lutheran
Church is shortly to be given. It is expected that a heavy sen-
tence will be imposed on Dr. Martin Niemoller who is
accused of subversive acts ...

Felix went on to tell us how once he crossed a bridge on foot
to see Herr Hitler being driven towards Bechtesgarten,
'Where,' he said helping himself to more dessert, 'he has
built a monstrous castle for himself.'

'Why does no one stop him?' Ella hotly demanded. 'If I
were a man I wouldn't let a bully like Hitler terrify me.'

His spoon stayed in mid air. 'Indeed, some have. Even I,
in my own modest way. When Hitler's Mercedes passed by,
I called to him that he no matter how hard he tried, he
would never manage to conquer the world. To my dying
day I will never forget the hypnotic look in his eye.'

'But the mongrel still prospers,' Father said darkly.

The table fell silent. We hadn't bothered to switch on the
overhead light, and now there was only the soft glow of the
Shabbat candles to see by as Father went on to talk about
various commercial opportunities that might interest a newcomer. But Felix was so busy smoothing his moustache whilst
admiring our twin candlesticks, saying how real the silvery
flowers looked, he only half listened. We waited for Father to
lose his temper – he so hates for anyone to be inattentive.
Instead he interrupted himself to tell Felix that those candlesticks were nearly fifty years old, then went on to explain how
his father had brought them from Manchester during the gol-
drush. 'Imagine what that voyage was like,' Father mused.
'Grandfather was probably lucky to find a hammock.'

Felix helped himself to a macaroon. 'A two month journey can never be a pleasure.'

Father said, 'Surely things have improved.'

Felix's gesture covered a world of discomfort. 'You cannot imagine how difficult it is to begin life in a country so far away.'

Father offered Felix one of his precious Havana cigars. 'Tell us a little about your journey.'

Felix waited for Father to light up. 'Before leaving Europe,' he said, 'I had spent several months in Zurich handling family business. While I was away, the Nazis took over the house, the foundry and the country estate. I returned to find everyone gone and my life in danger. Hans, our oldest servant, helped me escape. He smuggled me out of the country in an old farm lorry under bundles of hay.'

Though I rarely open my mouth when strangers are present, I was so entranced by his story, I forgot myself enough to cry, 'Why, that's just like *The Scarlet Pimpernel*. Baroness Orzy describes smuggling aristocrats out of France exactly that same way.'

He paused for a moment to study me. What was going on behind that pleasant but bland smile? What was he thinking? Then he gave a little bow and said, 'Exactly that same way.'

In the ensuing silence, the cicadas' song seemed to rise, and we heard the distant sound of rowdy New Year revellers, and a dog yap at the moon.

Ella gave a little cough. Felix glanced up and caught her gaze. For a long moment, they stared into each others' eyes. As they stared and stared, my breath caught in my throat. I could have sworn that the air was stilled … that all sound ceased … that the Earth stopped turning on its axis …

Then a gust of wind came through the window. The candles flickered and the spell was broken.

Recollecting that his audience was waiting for him to continue, Felix turned back to Father. 'On board the smell of tar plus the rolling of the ship made many of us seasick. We felt slightly better if we stayed on deck. One night there was a terrible storm. I had wedged myself beside the wheelhouse to watch the rolling, heaving sea when a wave started to carry me away. Yosel, one of the passengers, hung on to me until we could make our way inside.'

'Goodness!' Julie exclaimed. 'What a giant this Yosel must be.'

'He's certainly big,' Felix agreed. 'Six foot four and fifteen stone of pure muscle. Still ... you'd never find a gentler soul in all the world.'

Everyone fell silent. Father pointed to the piano and asked Felix if he had ever learnt to master a keyboard. 'Of course,' Felix cried, ' I have even had lessons with Master Pagliacci.'

Father blinked. 'Pagliacci?' He glanced at Julie who also shook her head. 'Surely you mean the opera? No, well ... afraid we've never heard of him.'

'Never heard of Rachmaninov's best pupil?' Felix shook his head at our collective ignorance. With this, he settled himself on the piano stool. He adjusted its height, tested fingers and keys, then launched into the Chopin *Mazurka in B flat*. He made many slips of the fingers, but to counter those, there was much tinkling and splashing of chords and rolling tremolos. When he finished playing, every one cried 'Bravo,' and clapped very loudly.

After several encores – Schubert and Debussy – he changed places with Ella. She chose to play Mendelssohn's *Consolation*. Though she has practised this piece many times, as the melody rose and fell, it was as if I'd never heard it before. Felix stood by the piano and I couldn't see his face. But from Ella's fiery notes I knew how taken she was with him. And how, if it hadn't been such a hot night, he might have warmed himself on her glances.

Oh, I understood why Felix, like every other man we have ever met except perhaps for Bunny, responded to Ella's loveliness. Still, it was disappointing that he was no different from anyone else who fails to see Julie's inner strength and beauty. Or even my poor self.

Finally Felix talked Julie into taking a turn. Julie barely finds time to practice, yet her ear is so good, she can play almost anything. So to 'Down Mexico Way' and 'Tea for Two', Julie played, we sang and Father beat time. At midnight we heard fire-crackers, so we linked arms and sang 'Auld Lang Syne'.

That night in bed, Ella and I were too excited to sleep. Usually we chat about the day's events. But when I asked what she thought of Felix, she rolled onto her stomach saying that she was far too tired to talk. Yet I heard her tossing and turning so I knew she was awake. In the end I slid my hands under the blanket and holding my breath, I stroked myself *down there* until my body quivered all over. Then I too fell into a dreamless slumber.

6

HUGE FIRES CAUSED BY BURSTING SHELLS IN CHINA
15ᵗʰ September, 1937
Shanghai: Having driven the Chinese back at various points the Japanese claim that they are now within two miles of the Nanking Railway. They are still bombarding the Kiangwan arsenal where they hope to trap the forces that are retreating ...

All yesterday Julie was busy cleaning up from last night's dinner. Ella was supposed to wax the dining table, chairs and sideboard, and with a little help from me, polish the silver. However the day was so sultry, we were so hot and tired from last night's excitement, Ella promised Julie that we would tackle the furniture tomorrow. Even then we were too listless to do more than wipe the cutlery and pack them into their felt-lined drawers.

I woke early, all sweaty from the hot muggy night, and threw off my sheet. Lying awake in the darkness, I heard Mr. Grimes' horse clip-clopping down our right-of-way. Every morning at about five o'clock our milk is ladled into the billy-can hanging by the side gate. What must it be like to walk the streets when everyone is in bed, your only companions prowling cats, bushy-tailed possums and the rats that frequent our alleys? Does Mr. Grimes ever get lonely? Or does he enjoy the freedom of having only his horse to talk to? What is it like to wake so early when the rest of the world is still slumbering? I pondered these questions before turning onto my other side and going back to sleep.

The storm broke mid-morning, bringing down a branch of our old apricot tree. It fell across the tomato and cucumber vines, and made Julie throw up her hands and threaten to give up growing vegetables. She rarely gets cross, but I always know when she does because her forehead wrinkles and her lips pleat into one thin line.

After breakfast Father inspected the debris, then sent Ella to fetch Mr. Moloney, the odd job man, to clean the mess away.

'Come Lilbet, an outing will do you good,' Ella ordered. I mostly leave the house in my wheelchair. But ever since Dr. Williams has warned that unless I exercise daily, the muscles in my left leg will contract even further, Julie insists that I take a walk at least once a day.

Hat and gloves on, we made our way down the street. Instead of using Mr. Left and Mr. Right (my iron-frame walking sticks) I pushed my wheelchair, and Ella strolled alongside. In the storm's aftermath, even the shadows seemed more sharply etched, the air cool and clear, the few clouds on the horizon soft and fluffy.

Grandview Street is wide enough to have a strip of grass running down the centre. One side of the road contains dwellings built shortly before Queen Victoria died. These are mostly double story with elaborate metal lace-work and fronted by gardens filled with climbing roses. The cottages further down the road are far smaller. Mr. Moloney, his wife and their eight children live in the tiniest. Peering down their hall you can see into their lean-to kitchen and laundry, and it is hard to imagine how Mrs. M. manages to remain calm, but she has since told us that none of her older children still live at home.

Though Father employs Mr. Moloney, he hates us having anything to do with his family. When Ella was younger, she would sneak out to play with the Moloney boys. I hated it when she did because invariably, I was left behind. The last time this happened, Father found me crying in the garden, and of course he made me tell him what was wrong. Then he was furious. 'Those boys swear like troopers,' he said grimly to Ella when she returned. 'And those elder daughters, what are their names ...?

'Mary. The other one is Judy.' Ella's voice was very small.

'Have you see how that Judy dresses? I suppose you intend following in her footsteps?'

Ella looked up at him. 'I think she looks quite nice,' she managed in her bravest voice.

'Trousers? High heels? Face plastered with rouge? Ella, I despair of ever turning you into a lady.'

Ella chafed at this restriction. But shortly after we heard Mary had gone to a Home for Unmarried Mothers. Worse still, Judy had run away to the Tivoli Theatre to pose as a 'living statue'.

Back then Aunt Amy was still living with us in Adeline Terrace. I asked her what this meant. Our good aunt was too appalled to answer. So it was only years later that I read in the *Argus* that as 'living statues' these girls go on stage bare-breasted. Once there, they must remain perfectly still or be prosecuted for indecency, and the police check every performance.

On our way home we called into Brant's Grocery. Mr. Brant's walls are lined with sacks of flour, rice, sugar, tins of fruit, bully beef, dried peas, *Nestle* condensed milk, and *Swallow and Ariel* biscuit tins. No wonder all these delicious smells have seeped into the woodwork. Ella bought a pound of cheese, and a pound of butter from the slabs inside the counter, plus two pounds of demerara sugar that Mr. Brant carefully measured into a brown paper bag. Then I climbed into my chair and we were home just before lunch.

Our bread is delivered every working morning, but today the baker was running late. Ella fretted, 'What if Sport is ill?' She hates anyone to be cruel to animals and Sport was getting old. Because Julie is keen on gardening, sometimes she gets Ella to follow the carthorses and collect their droppings in a bucket. She claims that this manure does wonders for our garden beds and that's why our roses bloom so well.

Sometimes Ella and I would meet Sport as we set out for our daily walk. Ella always carried a carrot, or an apple, or a lump of sugar, and Sport would open his mouth and gently pick the tidbit off her palm with his strong yellow teeth. Once or twice she allowed me to offer them to him, though I was always nervous that he might mistakenly chomp his teeth around my hand. One night I even dreamt that I was holding out an apple and he did indeed bite off my hand. Only as I held out my bleeding stump, the horse disappeared and I was looking up at Father's yellow horsey grin.

Anyway, lunch was our usual cheese and tomato sandwiches, only this time Julie popped them under the grill. Because they were so tasty, just this once I managed to clean my plate. 'Lilbet,' Julie couldn't resist saying, though she knows how much I hate her going on and on about my poor appetite, 'if only you would eat more, I'm sure you'd have more strength.'

I just shrugged. Long ago I realised that if I am stuck in a chair or a bed, that I have little hope of ever feeling hunger. Yet each time I argue that I would like to help with more of the housework, even manage the lavatory by myself, they get that tight blank look. Perhaps they have some hidden need to keep me powerless? Of course this can't be true. More that they believe it is their duty to look after me. And then there are Father's strict instructions as to what I may and may not do.

This afternoon I watched Ella change the bed linen, and Julie bake scones and queen cakes and our favourite almond macaroons. After a while I wandered into the living room where for the second time I browsed through yesterday's *Argus*. The editorial argued that foreign doctors shouldn't practise here for their techniques might be harmful, though no more harmful than the three operations I have been through. That last one stiffened the muscles in my left leg even further. Dr. Williams has warned Julie that in time they will distort my bones, and that I must always wear my leather and metal caliper no matter how much it scrapes and chafes.

If only Father had sent me with Ella to Cambridge Ladies College to complete Grade Nine. Riding there and back on my tricycle might have made me stronger. When I was little and went to weekly Religious Instruction classes, I used to wonder about God. Why, if He is all seeing, why has He given me this affliction? What might He hope to achieve from a young girl's pain? Perhaps God is not Jewish or Christian after all. Perhaps He is Buddhist or Hindu. And if, as the Hindus say, we are reincarnated to atone for sins committed in a previous life, in my last I must have been very proud to make this one so painful.

THOUGHT FOR TODAY: IS LIFE A GAMBLE OR IS THERE A PLAN?
3rd January, 1938

It is well that Christmas and the New Year are nigh on one another for the flight of time would make us shudder without the light which Christ has thrown. Hasn't Christ said that every life is fraught with a divine purpose ...

Father often reminds us that we descended from a proud Jewish family that can be traced back to the Spanish Inquisition. He says that it is up to the Marks women to preserve the sanctity of the Sabbath, to attend the East Melbourne Synagogue on High Holy Days, and to celebrate the Passover. In that way, he says, we will do our best to preserve our identity. 'There are four key values,' he often repeats for his daughters' benefit. '*T'zedka*, to look for what is just and right. *Chessed*, or kindness. *Derech eretz*, respect for all. And *Michpacha*, caring for the family environment.'

If I was asked if we keep to those four values, I must honestly reply that it is only Julie who attempts to follow them. Ella shows little respect for Father, or for many of the people we know. And I suspect that I can often, if only in my mind, be quite cruel and judgmental. Just like Father. Perhaps the only value we all keep is Michpacha. Even Ella, who says she would like to run away, is held by these powerful family ties.

I suppose we are fortunate in that Father doesn't expect Julie to maintain a kosher kitchen as that would certainly mean more work for her – particularly when I think how hard it is to maintain the separation of meat and milk. 'In these hard times,' I once said to Julie, 'it is so much easier to be Christian rather than Jewish.'

'Perhaps,' she gravely replied. 'But too many of the old Jewish families have married out and lost their religion. You wouldn't want that for us, would you?'

Though I quickly agreed, deep inside I wasn't sure. After all, what has religion ever done except make me feel even more unfortunate? Not only am I set apart because of my spasticity, but my background doubly emphasises this difference. Like so much else in my life, it seems most unfair.

Late this afternoon Julie and Ella spent an hour in the garden. As I'm halfway through *The Good Earth* by Pearl Buck, how I long to see the film. Yet I'm sure it won't be nearly as good as the book. I settled on the verandah where I could both read and keep an eye on things. How good it must be to bend and kneel without a thought. The roses and hydrangeas are in full flower. I called to the others that this sultry weather has turned our yard into a veritable paradise. It was altogether the wrong thing to say, as Julie – usually the kindest person you can imagine – thinned her lips and dryly replied, 'Also helps the weeds to grow.'

We talked about the garden, but our thoughts were elsewhere. Hadn't Father actually thanked Julie for making New Year's Eve such a success? Hasn't Julie spent all last night reading and rereading her recipe books? As for Ella – though I suppose one day she must marry, I intend doing everything in my power to prevent this.

So this was my dilemma. Here was I, caught by this newcomer's charm *almost* as much as everyone else, at the same time praying that he will never bother us again. I remembered how, as we sat around the table and the last of the sun caught his hair, turning it into a fiery halo, he seemed to command more space and light and air than us ordinary mortals. We have never met anyone half as interesting. Because he has travelled as far south as Portugal, east as Russia, and west as Ireland, his stories held us spellbound. It was as if he was giving us our own 'grand European tour', but without the bother of having to buy passports and visas, pack cabin trunks and sail overseas.

Yet recalling how gentle Father became in his presence – rather like a tame wombat – how Julie blushed when he praised her cooking, and how Ella smiled into his eyes, I am convinced that I must find a way to prevent whatever might happen next.

7

MANY NOTABLE ACHIEVEMENTS BY WOMEN IN 1937.
3rd January, 1938
Women may look back to 1937 with some pride. All over the world women's names were well at the top of the list in adventure, art, politics, education and business. Amongst them are Princess Elizabeth, Madame Kai–Shek, The Duchess of Windsor, Mrs. Eleanor Roosevelt …

Last night was again so hot, too hot for peaceful sleep. A night for uneasy dreams. In one I came across Ella packing a metal trunk, the kind used for long sea voyages. 'Don't get in my way,' she cried as I limped into the room. 'I'm running late. I've only minutes to get to Princes Pier.'

I stared at her in dismay. 'Where are you going? Who are you sailing with?'

'What does it matter? Can't you see I'm running late? If I miss the boat, I'll be stuck here forever.'

At which I flung my arms around her neck.

She tried to wriggle free … she was impossibly late … I was holding her back … but the more she tried to free herself, the more limpet-like I clung and the harder it was to tear me away …

Half strangled, I woke to find that the bed-sheet had wrapped itself around me, and dawn was seeping through the window.

I stared at the shadows playing on the ceiling. I loved Ella, and I knew she loved me. There are ties between twins that no one else can begin to understand. But sometimes twins can feel something that is so close to hatred, even thinking about it makes me shudder. Once when we were very young, Ella told me about a recurring nightmare. In it we had changed places. She was Lilbet. And I was Ella. I can imagine her overwhelming relief to wake and find this only a dream. And I always knew when she dreamt this because after, she always showed me a little more patience. Still, she too often says, 'If only you could be more assertive, even display a little independence, you would be far less irritating …'

'Ella, it doesn't do to be too harsh with Lilbet,' I once overheard Julie scold. 'Just remember that the least we can do is make her life as comfortable as possible.'

But Ella frequently complains that looking after me takes up too much of her time and certainly too much energy. Sometimes when I have been particularly clumsy – dropped a glass, spilt my tea, or needed help putting on my boots – she'll yell, 'Just remember that any time we can send you to that Special Home in Carlton.' But I know that after one of these explosions, she always feels horrid.

Lately however, since I started work on my book, she seems to miss my company. She peered over my shoulder. 'What are you writing? '

I placed my hand over the page. 'Notes for a novel.'

'A novel?' She barely hid her yawn. 'So why are you cutting out all those bits from the newspapers?' I shrugged and didn't answer. She didn't seem to notice. 'I hope it's a love story. Doesn't love make the world go round?'

I frowned and half-nodded. I wasn't worried that she'd try and read what I'd written. When I first began these notes, I had thought – just like Leonardo Da Vinci – to use mirror writing to keep my musings private:

?etavirp erom seton ym edam evah siht dluoW

skraM edialedA htebazilE yb

Or I could invent my own language where every letter becomes another:

Dbo zpv sfbe nijt?

But it would take up too much time. Anyway my handwriting is so bad, so much like a drunken spider's meanderings, I suspect that it would be too much effort to delve into my notes. Besides, Julie has no time for reading, and after deciphering the first page Ella would soon get bored.

If only she would let me get on with things! But no, now she was on about Felix Goldfarb. 'Isn't he the handsomest man you've ever seen? So well travelled and sophisticated. So urbane.'

'You're right.' I tried not to sound too dry, 'We've never before met anyone like him. Certainly not in real life.'

Not knowing quite how to take my meaning, she frowned slightly. 'Not even in the movies?'

'Not even in the movies,' I agreed.

WILL FLY HERE FOR FILMS.
Hollywood's Plans
5th January, 1938
'When the large clipper planes are flying from America to Australia in four days, Hollywood film companies will fly units over here to obtain background material about Australia,' said Mr. John. O. Blystone, a director of films who arrived in Sydney today ...'

8

Spent all morning help Julie cook jam. One task I can manage is cutting apricots in two and removing the stones. Julie makes the best apricot jam in the whole world. Her secret is to add a great number of lemons, grated ginger and sugar. Once she has brought the apricots and sugar to a simmer, I settle beside the stove. Then it's up to me to skim off the froth. Once the jam sets, Julie pours the mixture into jars that we sterilise by placing in a hot oven. Those jars are then covered in hot wax and carefully labelled with their contents and the year. By lunchtime, we had twelve jars cooling in the larder.

I think that we could survive on the contents of our pantry alone. Father often laments that Adeline Terrace has no cellar. But as well as all the fruit, vegetables and pickles Julie puts by, at the back are a dozen bottles of French wine; these only to be opened at a celebration such as Ella's wedding.

Whenever I recall that one day Ella must get married and leave, I suffer such severe stomach cramps, I can't stop crying. How I dread that day. Life is so unfair. If Ella leaves, who will then look after me? It would be too much for Julie to both run Adeline Terrace and care for a crippled sister. My secret terror is that they will send me to the Carlton House for Spastics and Retards. What will happen if Felix Goldfarb falls in love with Ella and he carries her away? Why could I not be equally beautiful? Why did I have to be crippled? Even thinking this way made me hot enough for Julie to feel my forehead to see if I was becoming feverish.

She decided that I wasn't, so the rest of today went as usual. Julie baked minced beef and grated carrot rolls for lunch. Though Julie's pastry melts in the mouth, I could only manage one. Mitsy and Motsy eyed them greedily, so when Julie wasn't looking I fed them my second.

After lunch I placed a book in my bag and using Right and Left, made my way to the park where I settled next to the playground. Two small boys were squabbling over the slippery-slide. Both were in knee length grey pants, cotton shirts and knitted vests. I watched the bigger brother push the smaller off the ladder. The little one burst into tears. I would have liked to comfort him. But of course I couldn't. They would never listen to a cripple. How sad to know that if I was more ordinary, more like everyone else, that they might have asked me to settle their fight. Instead I pretended to read, and watched the smaller lad race out of the gardens towards his house.

Now I waited to see what the older boy would do. He used the slide several times. Then as being all alone offered little joy, he too, took off for home.

All this reminded me how when Ella and I were little, we often played in this very same garden. Back then Aunt Amy, Father's sister, lived with us. Having no children of her own, she made a very good substitute mother for three orphaned girls. Like those small boys, Ella and I were always dressed in identical frocks and pinafores. I remember Ella playing on the slide while I sat by watching. How I longed to be able to race up the ladder and slide down. Sometimes Aunt Amy would lift me onto the swing. I loved the feel of the wind in my hair and the trees bobbing up and down. Back then, I could never really believe that a miracle mightn't happen and that one day my spasticity would be cured.

Other children had hopscotch, hide and seek and catch-if-you-can. Of course I couldn't play those games. Instead, Ella would invent wonderful plays where the central plot – explorers, travellers, spies – was hers, and I would add all the details. Her plots were always improbable and romantic and involved a lot of running around and shouting while I sat by watching. My details were carefully based on books like *Robinson Crusoe*, *Voyage to the Bottom of the Sea*, *Oliver Twist* and *Seven Little Australians*.

We owned few toys, but our favourite was an enchanting doll's house with miniature wooden cupboards, beds, table and chairs. Even a tiny bath and sink. This house once belonged to Julie and as we grew older, it became our most prized possession. Our other favourite was a china doll with yellow wool hair and a cloth body. We called her Mavis after the cleaning lady who helped Aunt Amy look after Adeline Terrace. But one day my bad leg slipped from under me and I dropped her on our concrete path. She smashed her head so badly, even after Father took her to the Dolls' Hospital in the city to be fixed, she returned with a twisted face that reminded me too much of my own.

Ella never liked dolls half as much as animals. She was still quite young when she created a hospital for caterpillars out of leaves. Since then she's rescued countless baby birds by feeding them honey using an eye-dropper, and even now when grey shrike thrushes nest in our garden, she feeds them by lining our kitchen windowsill with cheese-rind. The year we turned twelve, she managed to bring home two white mice. I never did find out where she got them. Julie is terrified of rodents, and she demanded that Ella get rid of those mice. 'As if we don't have enough vermin in the alley-way beside the house,' she scolded. 'What will Father say?'

Ella's solution was to hide her pets in the back of the garden where Motsy and Mitsy couldn't reach. She fed them on scraps she foraged from the kitchen, and spent hours playing with them, hoping that they would breed. However one after-noon, she discovered that one had died, and the other had eaten off half its head. It took her days to recover and Julie was far from sympathetic, 'Told you mice were dirty, horrid animals,' she scolded, upset that Ella's eyes were so red.

I think it a great shame that we are now eighteen and can't play with toys anymore. Instead I make up imaginary games where Mr. Left and Mr. Right become characters in my latest adventure. Mr. Left is usually bad, though not always, but Mr. Right is always good. Today Mr. Right has become a film star like Douglas Fairbanks Jnr., though with gingery hair and olive eyes. Mr. Left envies him intensely for his ability to get the girl. I had just reached the part where Mr. Left's devious plot is overcome by Mr. Right when Father came home and Julie called me into the kitchen.

9

WOMEN SHOULD HAVE VOICE IN PUBLIC AFFAIRS.
5th January, 1938
"For twenty years important matters brought forward by
deputations from influential woman's organisations have
been under consideration from certain Government
Ministers," Mrs. Clarence Weber said last night. She was
addressing the Melbourne Women's Club after dinner meeting at the Young Women's Christian Association rooms. Mrs.
Weber will be a candidate in the forthcoming state election ...

This morning Father warned Julie that he would be late
home as he was off to see a client after work. Ella
grabbed the opportunity to fiddle with the wireless until she
found some dance music. Then swaying around the living-
room, she sang, *'Night and day, you are the one ...'*

I settled on the piano stool and hummed along with her.
This Cole Porter song is one of our favourites. Only *Body
and Soul* is better. Ella moves so well, such a pity Father
refused to send her to dancing school. I remember Aunt
Amy pleading with him to let her take ballet classes. But at
the height of the Depression, money was so tight he was
forced to say 'No.'

Sometimes I wonder if ballet would have satisfied her
need for excitement? Would Father have allowed her take it
on as a career? He has such fixed ideas on what his daughters can and cannot do. Ella has always dreamt of becoming
an actress. Certainly she has the looks, though I'm not sure
about the talent. But Father has long made it clear that this
would never be acceptable. 'Over my dead body. So every
larrikin could stare at you?' When she gets really cross, she

threatens – but only to me – that she'll run away to become a Tivoli showgirl like Judy Moloney. 'I'll be a Living Statue,' she'll add, smiling from ear to ear.

'Nothing else you could do would estrange you from Father,' I was quick to point out.

'Nothing?' She laughed at my shocked face. 'Don't you believe it. I'm sure there's something.'

Julie goes along with everything Father says. I wish she would sometimes argue back. Even when he's at his most impossible, his wombat stance so threatening, his yellowish teeth so alarming, she'll find him an excuse; even tonight when after such a late start to our dinner, he was too crotchety to let us eat in peace. Over the dishes, she reminded us that he still misses Mother most dreadfully. Ella and I often wonder if he mightn't have been happier if he had remarried.

When Ella and I were thirteen, Mrs. Ruby Goldstein, an attractive childless widow, invited us to several Shabbat evenings at her East Melbourne mansion. I remember Father ordering a bespoke suit from 'Levy & Sons Tailoring' – which he could have bought much cheaper ready made – even though at the time Aarons and Marks was struggling to stay solvent.

We were all impressed with Ruby Goldstein's house. Decorated in the style known as 'art deco' it had a grand central staircase leading to an upper floor with four bedrooms and an ornate room tiled in green and cream mosaic with taps shaped like shells. Ella was most impressed by this bathroom. 'Imagine being able to see yourself all over.'

I shuddered. 'Why would anyone want to do that?'

'What a prude you are, Lilbet,' she sang. 'Anyway, don't you pine for an internal lavatory like Ruby's?' and to this I had to agree.

Off the downstairs hall was a smaller bathroom called a 'powder-room' with a lavatory and handbasin, a very large living room with glass doors embossed with fish and mermaids, and a separate dining area with a polished dining table large enough to seat sixteen people.

I recall the sitting room very clearly. I had never seen such a pretty room before. There stood a magnificent concert piano, though I doubt if anyone ever played it. Also a white marble fireplace, delicately patterned chair coverings and many precious china and crystal ornaments on the mantlepiece. But everything seemed too neat and unused. So in the end I decided that it was a cold room, almost as cold as the owner herself.

Ruby's husband had owned many properties in Collins Street and East Melbourne, and she could afford to employ a cook, two maids dressed in black with white lace pinnies and caps, and a gardener who doubled as chauffeur. I remember that her table shone with the most expensive napery money could buy. Not that this made me like her any more, as whenever her gaze fell on me, her nose wrinkled as if she'd just smelt something horrid.

Nor did the conversation interest us as it mostly centred on Ruby's finances. Back home I said to Julie, 'Do you think she only invites us to get Father's advice without having to pay for it?'

Julie looked astonished. 'Lilbet, you are so suspicious. Isn't she just trying to be nice?'

Ella giggled. 'Father has little else to talk about than his work.'

'Except for our short-comings,' I said dryly. 'Though I agree that he has nothing but praise for Julie.'

Julie blushed and shook her head. Back then she was

going out with Carl Brown. Carl was tall and thin and his sleeves and trousers were too short for his arms and legs. He reminded me of a bumblebee as he could never sit still, always hopping up and down to fix or collect something he'd forgotten. Trained as a lawyer, he was about to join a firm of solicitors in Adelaide. He was as keen on Julie as she was on him. With Father so obviously interested in Ruby, Julie was delighted to set up her own home with a clear conscience. Ella thought it a fine idea to have someone as pretty and wealthy as our stepmother. She hoped Ruby might take us overseas, as her conversation was filled with all the European cities she had visited.

I was less enthusiastic. Pleasant as she was, I knew Mrs. Goldstein would insist on certain changes. And I was pretty sure that none of those changes would be good for me.

Things went swimmingly for three months or so, then the invitations to her Friday nights suddenly ceased. Julie sent Carl away. Though Julie remained as gentle and caring as ever, something in her withdrew, and I often wonder how deeply hurt she was. Perhaps a different girl would not have sent Carl away. But Julie is such an angel, it would never occur to her not to feel responsible for Father's and our well being. Though I wonder if she doesn't wish Ella to be a little older and certainly more reliable.

After dinner, I got started on yesterday's crossword. Ella was laying a pattern on the dining room table. 'What's a ten letter word meaning lover?' I asked her.

'S W E E T H E A R T,' she counted on her fingers. 'Ten letters.' She went back to cutting out material.

Father glanced up. 'Ella, what are you making?'

'Slacks, Father.'

'Only loose women wear trousers,' Father growled into his newspaper.

I held my breath, but for once Ella didn't answer back. Instead, she picked up the fabric, pins and scissors and took them into the spare room where Father hardly ever enters.

Julie put down her book. 'Lilbet, you ready for bed?'

I made my way to our room and waited for Julie to check my under-sheet for wrinkles. Examining her mild face with its high forehead, soft brown eyes, thin lips, and squarish chin, I thought how beautiful she is, only so different from Ella and myself, a stranger could hardly tell that we're related. Where Ella is as stubborn as Father, it is Julie who looks most like him. Then our smiles. So dissimilar. When Ella smiles, she seems dreamy and self-contained. I smile and my mouth falls into twenty to two. But when Julie smiles her forehead wrinkles, as if the world is too painful for her to endure. I said to her, 'Why is Father so strict?'

'He wasn't always like that.' She plumped up my pillows. 'Only losing Mother, and then the Depression ...' She sighed pensively. 'He used to be so different.'

'In what way?'

'I remember him always laughing and teasing.'

'Truly?'

Father so rarely laughs. And when he does, his eyes narrow and seem almost oriental, and he shows off those teeth that remind me of Sport, our bread carter's horse.

Juie nodded. 'Mother and he were always hugging and touching.' She went to draw the curtain.

'Please tell me about her,' I pleaded. 'All you ever mention is her beautiful white neck and the smell of tea roses.'

'Elizabeth Isabella Marks. That was our mother's full name. You two were called after her.'

'What did she look like?'

'Very beautiful. Ella looks like her.'

'Is Ella like her in other ways?'

'Not in the way she behaves. Mother always tried very hard to please. To tell the truth, I don't know who Ella is like. Perhaps she's most like Father.'

I slid further under the blanket. 'Tell me about Mother.'

'Our mother? Ah ... she was always so warm and patient.'

'Wonder if mothers have a special way of being warm and patient,' I said without thinking.

'I wish I could be half as patient as she was,' Julie said calmly. But I knew I'd cut her to the quick.

'Oh Julie, forgive me. You are far nicer to us than any mother. We could wish for no one better.'

'It's nothing, dear. I understand. After Aunt Amy and Uncle Bernard went to Sydney, I tried to be both mother and sister. Perhaps I wasn't successful.'

'But you were, you are. The best mother and sister in all the world.'

'Lilbet, calm down. You'll get feverish.'

'How can I when I've hurt you so badly ...'

She left shortly after still protesting she was fine. How typical of Julie to blame herself for other people's shortcomings. Sometimes her ability to only see the world through rose coloured glasses can be infuriating. Last month she visited Judith Cohn, an old school friend. 'What scandal did you hear?' I demanded when she came home. 'Who's getting engaged? Who's getting married? Who's having a baby? Come on, tell.'

Julie was shocked. 'Lilbet, how can you say such things. The food was delicious and Judith looked wonderful.'

'Was she nice to you?'

'Of course.' But her voice wobbled.

Huh, I thought. I could just imagine their conversation:

'Darlings, you'll never guess where we're going next Autumn?'

Squeal, squeal. 'No Judith, do tell.'

'Well, Daddy says I'm looking tired, so I made him promise Doug and me a trip OS.'

'Lucky, lucky you. Will you go Home?'

'Where else? Then we're going on to Paris and Rome ...'

And:

'These days you can't get any decent home-help.'

'Know what you mean. You'd think with so many people looking for work, they'd try a bit harder to please ...'

'*Please? All they do is steal anything they can lay their hands on …*'

We hear enough from Daisy Aarons to know how Julie's old school friends live. Julie's existence is so opposite, there is no way that she can relate to them or that they would accept her. Things are different for Daisy. Her father spoils her so outrageously, she somehow manages to keep up.

Soon after Julie left, Ella came to bed. She fell asleep immediately. I lay there listening to her breathe. Though we are twins, I can't think of two girls who are less similar. Though I try my very best not to aggravate Father, from the time Ella was able to stagger about, she has always defied every attempt at discipline.

She should have been a boy. In Primary School, she was always in trouble for dipping girls' plaits into inkwells, and twisting the arm of any boy she didn't like. Though Aunt Amy combed her hair into rags every night so it would curl next day, by the end of the afternoon, she looked as if she'd never seen a hair-brush.

She spent a lot of time in the corner with her back to the class for 'insolent behaviour and lack of discipline'. Sometimes I think it must have annoyed those teachers very much that while I topped the class in most subjects, Ella did splendidly at Art and Needlework.

She was always beautiful, so beautiful that our women teachers nicknamed her Shirley Temple. Boys would do anything to get her attention. Our grade five master Mr. Beacham had been wounded in the Great War. He came home with bad lungs and a worse temper. Once when he left the room, Spotty Hogarth called Ella a rude name just to get her to notice him. She'd jumped onto the desk to yell at him to repeat it when Mr. Beacham caught her. 'Isabella Marks,' he cried. 'You're to write an essay entitled 'The Inadvisability of Walking on Desks' before you leave tonight.'

'Help me, Lilbet,' Ella whispered. 'What'll I say?'

'I'll think of something,' I promised. Weren't we the Marks twins who did everything together? Weren't we Siamese twins? So this is what she handed to Mr. Beacham:

The Inadvisability of Walking on Desks.
by Isabella Marks.

Desks are made out of wood. Wood comes from trees. Trees grow in forests. Forests are filled with wild animals. Those animals were once hunted by primitive man for food. Without food, primitive man would never have survived. Neither would his children, grandchildren, great grandchildren or great great grandchildren. Without those great great grandchildren and their descendants, you and I would not be here. Therefore it is inadvisable to walk on desks for without those desks none of us would be here.

Mr. Beacham read this, and said, 'Very fine Ella. But I seem to detect your sister's clever touch.'

At home, Ella is no better. She clashes with Father, sometimes with dramatic results. When we were twelve, they had a terrible fight, though to this day I cannot remember what it was about. Perhaps Ella was insisting on visiting a friend alone. Or refusing to help Julie with the washing up. Or openly disagreeing with Father. His opinion of young women is very low. 'Impetuous to the point of acting dangerously,' he'll tell anyone who cares to listen. 'With little or no intellectual capacity worth mentioning.'

If only I was a tiny bit braver, I might have challenged this by reminding him that I read all his newspapers and that by the time I'd turned fifteen, I'd gone through his entire library. But when it came to Ella, there were so many things that could lead to a clash. What I do remember is Ella running into the rain and staying away until morning.

Julie and I were terribly worried. But Father refused to fuss.

'Ella will come home when she's cold and hungry.' And that's exactly what happened.

Afterwards, I asked her, 'Where did you sleep?'

She stared at me through red-rimmed eyes. 'Who said I slept?'

'Well … what did you do instead?'

'Walked to the city and back,' she said defiantly.

My eyes widened. 'But we don't live all that far, less than two miles. Why did it take all night?'

'Oh Lilbet, I camped out there. Lots of people camp out in Flinders Street Station,' she said impatiently.

'I suppose that's where the homeless go.'

'Those. And others.'

Her tone was such that I glanced up. What was she keeping to herself?

'Julie always warns us to watch out for strange men. Wasn't that dangerous?'

She laughed and didn't answer. Not even later when I teased her about keeping things to herself. What did she see that she refused to tell me about?

If ever I look back, it seems as if Ella has spent most of her life defying the world. I recall the rumpus Father created when she shingled her lovely hair, even though she knows he hates short hair. And she often wears the kind of clothes – like slacks and figure defining frocks – that she knows he'll hate. In fact, she's always doing things to annoy him. While I stay out of range, she will deliberately flout all his rules, then laugh when he gets upset. Therefore it was so unjust that after Grade Eight, Ella was sent to Cambridge Ladies College, but I had to stay home.

'But Father,' I wanted to cry, 'I enjoy reading, writing, analysing.' Yet all he ever comments on is my poor penmanship. Ella finished her sub-intermediate year. Then Father decided that the school's fees were too high. And anyway, 'Everyone knows that education is wasted on girls'.

In the early hours of the morning I had a dreadful nightmare.

This house is full of locked doors hiding shameful things. Everyone insists on keeping secrets. I usually dream in black and white, but this time my dream was in colour. As I floated through silent rooms, the threat loomed large. Just as I was about to test the final door, I woke up. My heart was thudding as if it might break out of my chest. What was it that could be so threatening? Even wide-awake, this house seemed too risky to stay in.

'Lilbet, you asleep?' Ella whispered.

I moaned slightly. 'It's too hot to sleep.'

A flicker of light came through the open curtain. 'Let's go into the garden.'

'Right now?' I cried, alarmed. 'What time is it?'

'Who cares. Shhh. Don't wake the others.'

Ella helped me down the passage. Not a breath of wind, the night still and hot, only the faintest outline of trees against the sky. She settled me on the ground right at the back behind the fruit trees. Then she stripped off her nightgown and while I hummed softly, she danced naked into the night. A half moon came out from behind a cloud to spotlight ivory limbs, dark nipples and jet-black hair. Through half closed eyes I pictured myself dancing alongside Ella, saw each action as shimmering and languid as a mermaid's dream.

Eventually, our actions became less restrained. My eyes half closed, still humming, I imagined other girls joining in. Two … four … now a dozen. Holding hands, we wove in and out of the trees and bushes, the blood pulsing in our ears, our bodies trembling with desire. From behind the tree, a man appeared. I couldn't take my gaze away, he was so beautiful; his skin white as snow yet with a light powdering of freckles, his hair forming an orange halo around his head, his green eyes boring into me. I reached out to him and running my hands over his body, I could barely contain my excitement.

Right then a possum rattled the branch above us. I returned to my senses. What if a neighbour saw us? What if Father heard a noise and walked outside? We'd never hear the end of it. I stopped humming and cried, 'Ella, get dressed. Let's go back to bed.'

She paused in mid step. 'Oh Lilbet,' she cried impatiently, 'why are you so sensible? Why do you always stop me from doing whatever I want?'

But I am sure she would be less inclined to fantasy if our everyday existence was a little less pedestrian. As we wandered back inside to our airless room, I couldn't help recalling how Julie keeps saying, 'What we girls need is a decent holiday.'

10

> **A SUGGESTED SUMMER MENU**
> 9th **January, 1938**
> **Breakfast:** Chilled raspberries in pineapple juice. Steamed brown rice with cream. Scrambled eggs with rolls of crisp bacon. Toast. Tea or coffee
> **Luncheon:** Tomato soup with Melba toast. Nut and celery salad with cheese dressing. Brown bread and butter. Cherry tart. Tea or coffee
> **Dinner:** Alligator-pear canapé. Clam bouillon. Crown roast of lamb. Mint sauce. Baked potatoes. Peas. Mushrooms. Lemon ice on squares of watermelon. Tea or coffee.

So hot! I spent most of today on Julie's bed as her room faces south. Couldn't face breakfast or lunch. Halfway through dinner, Father noticed I wasn't eating. 'Lilbet's arms are like match sticks,' he said to Julie. 'Must be sickening for something. Get Williams to prescribe a new tonic.'

'Nothing's wrong with me,' I cried nearly in tears. 'It's just too hot to be hungry.'

Father glared at Julie from under his eyebrows. 'Not hungry for this delicious lamb?' He forked a fatty bit like a yellow slug into his mouth. 'You girls don't know when you're well off. In the war we lived on black tea and bully beef ...'

He went on and on. Rather than have him continue to rage, I managed a mouthful. Then nearly vomited. Though Father never saw action overseas, he often describes his army days as if they were his best two years ever. He'll talk about Bluey, Will and Tommy, those boys who never came back, as if they were closer to him than his own daughters. A framed photo in his study shows a dozen lads not much older than us, some even the same age or younger, in khaki uniform, the slouch hat hiding most of their features. Mostly it was those like Father who didn't sail overseas to fight because of poor eyesight or flat feet that still meet once a year to relive the war.

GREAT WAR HAS COST AUSTRALIA 840,000 GUINEAS.
10th January, 1938
This statement was made by the Treasurer, Mr Casey, in the House of Representatives to day in reply to the deputy leader of the Opposition (Mr Forde) …

I once dared suggest to him that the War had been nothing but an excuse for the Great Powers to gain more economic benefits, and that we had come out of it very badly. What's more, that we seem to be heading the same way again.

Father gave me his coldest stare. 'Tell me Lilbet, since when did you become a Socialist? Does Bunny Segal teach you these notions?'

'I … ah … course not,' I protested in the face of his irrational hatred of Bunny. I could have explained that my ideas come from listening to the radio and reading newspapers. But I didn't. If I wasn't a cripple, he wouldn't treat me like a half-wit. Or if I was half as beautiful as Ella. Nor would I have to work so hard to gain his approval. How unfair it all is!

When I asked Julie why he hates Bunny so much, she looked at me quizzically before saying, 'Because Bunny is a fairy.'

Bunny a fairy? Picturing his portly frame in a frilly skirt with gossamer wings and a twinkly wand, I burst out laughing. Bunny has kind brown eyes, a wide mouth, prominent teeth, and much to his dismay, he is losing his hair. What with his plump tummy and out-turned feet, he's more an over-grown elf than a fairy – all he needs is a pointy hat and toe-turn up boots. 'Rather a gnome,' I decided. 'But as he's an accountant like Father, why call him a fairy?'

She shook her head. 'Not the kind of fairy that lives in the trees and grants magic wishes. I mean Bunny likes men rather than women. And ever since the Aubrey Maddocks scandal …' she broke off. 'You know who that is?'

'Wasn't he sentenced to eighteen months gaol?'

She nodded. 'If such an important man, once New South Wales head of police and then Commissioner for Transport can be sent to gaol for being a fairy, no wonder Father disapproves of Bunny.'

'But Bunny is always nice to me,' I said, puzzled. 'What do fairies do that is so terrible?'

Her lips thinned. 'Really Lilbet, you wouldn't want to know.'

That was all I could get out of her. But I keep wondering … why must other people tell us how to lead our lives? Bunny is the kindest person – apart from Julie – that I know. Admittedly his conversation usually revolves around Bunny himself, and I can hardly ever get him interested in politics or world affairs. Then there are those jokes he tells, those I have such trouble understanding. Curious how he often refers to himself in the third person, and then as a 'naughty boy.'

What does he do that is so naughty?

But then, he is so good-natured. So caring. No task, no matter how insignificant, is too much trouble. He always makes sure things are within my reach, and if he can ever save me the trouble having to walk somewhere, he always does. Surely whatever his 'naughtiness' is, it can't be too harmful.

Father is so difficult to please. Sometimes I wonder what he would have been like if Mother were still alive. Would she have made him less prickly? What if I have inherited his tendency to shout others down? Whenever Ella and I quarrel, I accuse *her* of being most like him. But it's only her refusal to accept his domineering ways, her stubbornness, and her facility with numbers that strike me as similar.

This night she waited for him to go into his study before saying, 'Lilbet, why let him treat you like that?'

'I'm sure he doesn't mean it. He worries if I don't eat …'

'Missing a few meals never hurt anyone,' she angrily interrupted. 'It's because you don't answer back. He never tries it with me.'

I stared at my feet. Why go into the differences between us? Though I often hear Father complain to Julie about Ella's contrariness, she can be as difficult as she pleases, and still he'll watch her with loving eyes.

I said, 'I'm not brave like you.'

'Maybe it's time you were,' she said briskly.

She doesn't understand that if I were to lose my temper, answer back, that he would despise me even more than he does now. If only I was beautiful. If only I wasn't a cripple, then surely he would love me as much as he loves her. Why is life so unfair?

Dishes washed and dried, we three sat on the verandah staring at a fingernail of a moon and listening to the frogs and cicadas' songs. Summer is the time for picking mulberries, and I saw that the fruit on our tree was turning purple. In another few days, Ella will put on her oldest clothes and climb up to fill tins and billy-cans while Julie and I warn her to be careful. When we were younger and I could move about more freely, I would stand below and Ella would aim mulberries straight into my mouth. By nightfall our faces, hands and clothes were covered in juice, and Julie would get so cross. Mulberry stains are hard to remove.

Our backyard is very long, and the area behind the vegetable patch was a wonderful place to play. Ella loved pretending we were in moving pictures. No matter what story I invented, whether it be cowboys and Indians, adventures in space, or even putting on a musical, she was always the star while I directed the action and filmed her using a small brown case as my camera. Once when we were playing at being shipwrecked, Ella got stuck in the pear tree and Julie had to run down the street to ask Mr. Moloney to fetch his ladder to bring her down.

But all this was before our bodies forced us into adulthood.

How much simpler things would be if we could have stayed Peter Pans forever. I think my darkest hour was when I realised that through no fault of ours except for growing up, that I must lose Ella forever. I remember thinking that I would be better off dead; even wondering how I could manage my own ending. Almost too easy to borrow Father's cut-throat razor and run it across my wrists. Or even slide under the bath water and stay there until my breath gave out.

Would they miss me? Would I leave a hole in their lives? Or would they secretly feel some relief that the tiresome business of caring for a cripple was now over, and that 'poor Lilbet' was no longer in pain.

Around seven thirty the cool change blew in bringing goose pimples to our arms. We settled back in the kitchen and Father came in shortly after. Ella was darning, Julie writing a shopping list. I was reading the evening *Herald*. Halfway through the crossword, I asked Ella if she knew an eight-letter word ending with T meaning tyrant?

She glared at Father. 'How about martinet?'

Father kept on reading.

'M.A.R.T.A.N.E.T.,' Ella spelt out firmly.

Only then did Father glance up from his paper to say that her second A should be an I.

I filled in the squares. Julie poured milk into a saucepan. Father turned on the wireless. Half way through 'The Classical Hour' someone knocked on the front door. Julie asked, 'Father, are you expecting a visitor?'

'No,' he said and went to answer the door. We heard voices. Then Father popped his head into the kitchen to tell us that Felix Goldfarb had come to thank us for that wonderful New Year's Eve dinner.

The effect was electrifying. Julie pinned loose hair into her bun more securely. Ella ducked into our room to find her lipstick. I limped into the living room where Felix, very smart in tweed sports jacket, linen trousers and silk cravat, his orange hair and moustache shining with cleanliness, and smelling strongly of 4711 Cologne, was waiting to greet us. He handed Julie a splendid bunch of pink long stemmed carnations, kissed her and Ella's hands, and remembered to only shake mine. 'I must apologise for troubling you,' he said to Father. 'But I came to request a small favour.'

Father sent Julie to put on the kettle. The next ten minutes were wasted finding a vase deep enough for the flowers, and our best teacups, silver spoons, milk-jug and sugar bowl. Why had he come in person? Surely he could have sent Julie and Father a thank you note. By now I was nearly dead with curiosity. Meanwhile Father gave Felix *his* account of the latest events in Spain. Father loathes fascists and communists alike, while I mostly hate General Franco. I would say so too, if I didn't know this would bring on another angry outburst.

SEQUEL TO CIVIL CONFLICT
12th January, 1938

'If the Spanish civil war lasted throughout the following European summer, Italy and Germany would become so desperate that European conflict was inevitable,' said the Spanish Prime Minister (Senor Negrin) today.

Somehow or other, Father went on to talk about travel and the explosion on the Hindenburg that happened last May in New Jersey, and how many people had died. There are lots of theories as to why this happened, but as Father's favourite is sabotage, he ended with 'Serves those Nazis right.'

Felix listened politely, nodding every so often. But I noticed how his olive gaze took in the high-backed couch and armchairs; the piano's elaborate scrollwork; the mirrored dresser with the crystal goblets and silver tea and coffee set. Suddenly it struck me that he was assessing our worth. But Felix was Father's friend and surely I was mistaken? Father interrupted himself to say, 'Now Felix, what can we do for you?'

A little sigh echoed round the room. He said, 'As you know Simon, I am presently staying in a boarding house in Princes Hill run by a Mrs. Finklestein.'

Father's eyebrows shot up.

'I have not come to criticise her establishment,' Felix continued. 'My room is clean, and the food most adequate.' He patted his stomach. 'None of this would worry me except that my gold cigarette lighter, the one my father gave me for my last birthday, is missing. So I came to ask if you know of another, a more *gemutliche* guest house?'

Father frowned. 'Not really. Of course, the girls won't mind putting you up until you find something suitable.'

I watched the blood rush to Ella's cheeks.

'No, Simon. I think this would be too much trouble.'

'Nonsense, old man. Your family would do the same for us, eh Julie?'

Julie remembered to close her mouth. 'Yes. No trouble at all.'

'Most grateful, I'm sure.' Felix rose and gave her a little bow. 'I will write to my wife tonight to tell her what generous people I have found in this new country.'

Father helped himself to a macaroon. 'I didn't know you were married.'

Felix looked annoyed, as if this had slipped out unintentionally. 'My wife, Sylvie. From your Shakespeare.' And he sang in a pleasant tenor, '*Where is Syl-via, who is she?*'

A wife called Sylvie? I glanced at Ella. Her cheeks had gone from pink to white.

'Your wife,' said Julie. 'Where is she now?'

'In Switzerland. The way things are in Germany, we decided to take an apartment in Zurich, and I would commute to Frankfurt when necessary.'

I cleared my throat. 'Wasn't this rather complicated?'

'Indeed it was.' His glance was shrewd. 'Far too complicated to be successful. Also, who knows what will happen at home? That is why we decided I should settle here. I plan to find work and somewhere to live, then send for Sylvie.'

'How about your family? Aren't you worried about them?'

'Of course I am. But what can I do?' His freckles stood out like inkblots. 'I dare not return. The minute I set foot in Germany I could be sent to a labour camp.'

Julie sent me a warning frown. 'Dear Mr. Goldfarb,' she cried, 'you are only too welcome to stay here.'

'Felix. Please call me Felix.' Then he softly added, 'I will never forget your generosity to this poor outcast.'

Julie reddened. Then the subject of payment came up. Before you could say 'eenie, meenie, minie, mo,' Father decided Felix should give Julie seven and sixpence a week. Julie protested, then quietly backed down. As mentioned before, Father keeps us on a tight budget and anything extra is always a blessing.

Felix left shortly after, promising to return the following Saturday afternoon with all his belongings.

An unusually silent Ella helped me into bed. I lay there, imagining how disappointed she must be. Half asleep, I fell into a dream where I was staying in a house right on the beach. Through the open door, the moon goddess trailed her silvery path across the sky. Mermaids rose from the deep calling to me in liquid tongues 'Lilbet, come … come to us.' Though I had never heard their watery tones before, how well I understood what they were telling me. Plunging deeper into my dream, I cried, 'But after all I'm not yet ready …' and disappointed, they fell back into the sea.

I surveyed my surroundings. This house was made of rough wood and half the roof had fallen away. Through the gap I could watch stars sail across the sky and the passage of the moon. How primitive it all was; no floor, no windows, no furniture except for my bed. I looked back through the open door. A huge wave was heading our way. It flooded over me. I suppose I should have felt angry, but all I knew was a wonderful sense of release.

11

No time for filling in crosswords, or creating roles for Left and Right. Instead I helped the others slave away preparing the spare room. 'Hope he isn't planning an extended stay,' I said to Julie.

She stopped halfway rolling up the rug. 'Lilbet, do you have any idea of what it's like for those poor Jews still living in Germany?'

'Not all of them,' I declared. 'According to the *Argus*, some seem to move about quite freely.' I held out a cutting, 'Look at this.'

EASIER FOR GERMANS TO TRAVEL.
11th January, 1938

Olive skinned, dark-haired and speaking excellent English, only slightly tinged with a German accent, Miss Yvonne Frankel-Cohen was photographed on arrival on the Nestor yesterday morning.

Another arrival, Miss Mona Hardt, described her interests as domestic like many other German girls who do not wish to take up a career but prepare themselves to be good wives by learning household work and studying at a domestic science school in Berlin ...

She read it through very carefully. 'Do you really believe this?'

I slowly shook my head. 'How can we? Look at what happened on Krystalnacht. And then the book burning, all books by Jewish authors destroyed.'

I inwardly shuddered. What if I had finished this novel and it had been destroyed?

'So you see why we must make an extra effort to be kind to Felix?'

'All the same,' I insisted. 'We go to all this trouble. Then his wife sails into town and he'll leave.'

Julie's lips tightened as she drew herself up to her full five foot four. 'Felix is a homeless refugee. Besides, it's good for Father to have another man about the house.' Not a word about the extra work this would give *her*.

Julie is overly kind. Word has got out that at our back door there's always a hot cup of tea and a thick slice of bread and jam. Lately, things are a little better. But I once counted as many as twenty homeless men and women within three days.

Julie's housekeeping is meticulous. Nothing is ever thrown out. Every bit of string or paper is carefully stored. If she has a little extra soup or stew, she feeds it to the tramps. Stale bread or leftover porridge go to next-door's chooks. In return our elderly neighbour, Mrs. Otway, gives us eggs when her hens are laying.

Mrs Otway loves her birds like other folk love dogs and cats. Her rooster is such a handsome bird, all shiny ginger and charcoal feathers and the most splendid red comb I have ever seen, though I often wish he crowed a little less. When Mrs. Otway's rheumatism is troubling her too much to bend over, she'll ask Ella to collect the eggs. I always go too, as I like to watch the hens pecking the ground. What stays with me for hours is the acrid smell of hen droppings, damp straw and rich earth.

Both Julie and Ella would very much like to keep hens, but Father forbids this on the grounds that they encourage rats. Soon as he mentioned the word 'rat', Julie blanched. The rats that wander our alleyway often feature in her nightmares. Ella thinks that a rat must once have bitten her, though so long ago she doesn't remember it.

I once mentioned this to Bunny, who is very interested in Dr. Freud's theories. Bunny bit into a queen cake as he thought this over. 'Very possible,' he said dusting the crumbs off his bulging waistcoat. 'But according to psychoanalysis, those rats may simply be a metaphor for Julie's subconscious fear of sexuality ...'

'Oh?' I was dying for him to say more. Only right then Julie came into the room and he changed the subject.

Mother and Father moved to Adeline Terrace when they were first married. The spare room holds all Mother's clothes Father couldn't bear to throw away. Plus our old pram, shelves of dusty books, Ella's sewing machine and nearly two dozen boxes of fabric, patterns, cottons and buttons. All this to be sorted and stored. Then curtains to be washed, floor polished, mattress beaten, blankets laundered and bed-sheets aired.

I found Father and Mother's engagement portrait in the back of the wardrobe. Mother is only sixteen two years younger than we are now. Her hair is a tower of burnished curls, her waist no more than a hand span. Father too is thin, with a narrow face, a pleasant smile and a full head of curly hair. Even his nose somehow looks shorter, his ears less crinkled and his lips fuller. Instead of his usual wombat slouch, he stands tall and straight.

Several drawers were filled with Mother's linen. Julie once mentioned that she plans to add those beautifully worked table-cloths and tea-towels to Ella's glory box. I think Julie has given up hope of ever finding a husband, and it's taken for granted that 'poor crippled Lilbet' shouldn't even think of it.

Sometimes I daydream that my fairy godmother appears and changes me into someone taller and beautiful whom a handsome red-haired, olive-eyed prince decides to marry.

Enough. Back to today's events. In Mother's cupboards, Ella also found damask camisoles and nighties, all scented with lavender and smelling faintly of musk. As we plunged our faces into the finest linen, I had the curious sensation that we were garnering Mother's essence, and that one day this would give us strength.

Another drawer was filled with baby clothes. Nighties, booties, jackets, caps and a wonderfully fine crochet lace shawl. Mother would have knitted and sewn those clothes herself. I pictured her stitching, ironing the finished articles then wrapping them in tissue paper. If I try very hard I can imagine her happy chatter about the new baby she was expecting. She had no idea that she was carrying twins and that they would result in her own death. I often ask myself; had she survived, would I have been less timid? Perhaps she might have persuaded Father to send me to college so I could further my education. Perhaps I might even have found a profession.

ADV.	**AMBITIOUS GIRLS**
	13th January, 1938
	ANNUAL SCHOLARSHIP EXAMINATION
	METROPOLITAN BUSINESS COLLEGE

Every year on our birthday when we visit Mother's grave in the Carlton cemetery, I silently ask her what future she might have planned for me. Though I wait for a sign, so far all that has happened is the wind whistling through the trees and once, an unexpected squall.

Friday, Julie called us in to inspect the room she had prepared for Felix.

'Perfect,' I cried, and Ella added, 'Almost perfect.'

Julie grimaced and held out the curtains. 'Are they too worn?'

We inspected where too much sun had frayed the material making it almost transparent.

'Then Ella will have to make more,' Julie decided and she immediately sent us to Foy and Gibson Emporium to buy fabric. I wouldn't have minded walking with Left and Right, but Ella decided our shopping would be that much faster if we took my wheelchair.

We caught a cable tram into the city. She helped me into the cabin, then lifted my chair onto the steps. The elderly conductor didn't bother lowering his voice to complain about 'useless cripples 'olden' up traffic ...'

Ella was about to tick him off, when an elderly man sprang to my defence. As the tram rounded a corner, he grabbed the conductor's lapels and roared, 'Ap-pologise to the young ladies.'

'Good on ya luv,' cried a motherly woman in a shabby black hat and coat. 'You tell that bugger where to get off.' And she sent me such a pitying look all I wanted was for the floor to open up and for me to disappear forever.

'He's only doin' 'is job,' another woman protested. 'Ain't none of your business.'

'Come on. Ap-pologise or else ...' the elderly man insisted.

'Got no right to 'old up public transport,' the conductor retorted. But finding opinion generally against him, he quickly backed down and did what he was told.

I accepted his apology, then spent the journey in a mix of anger and embarrassment. Perhaps that conductor would have agreed with the ancient Spartans who left their imperfect babies on a mountain top to die so as to prevent them from becoming a burden to their families, the State and themselves.

Five minutes later we were standing on the corner of Swanston and Bourke. Five minutes to nine, and the streets were crowded with cyclists, Gladstone bags strapped to their backs, and office workers rushing to their various destinations. Foy and Gibson was holding its annual sale, and we had to push our way through a motley crowd of shoppers to get to the rear of the store. Haberdashery being on ground level, we could avoid walking through the shoe department on the First Floor, and I was grateful not to be reminded that all I can wear are specially made lace-up boots, the left made even more hideous by its two inch sole.

'Fabrics' had so many wonderful materials to choose from, I could hardly get Ella to concentrate on curtains. Eventually she found a pink and blue flowered cretonne at three-pence a yard. We managed ten yards for one and six-pence, which we both agreed, was a bargain.

Just as we were heading back to the main doors, I heard 'Yoo hoo, Ella ... Ella Marks.'

Daisy Aarons. In a purple hat and beige suit that made her look plumper than ever. 'Fancy running into you.' Her cow brown eyes widened in curiosity. 'What are you doing in Foy's?'

'Why Daisy, shopping,' Ella said brightly. 'Same as you, I expect.'

Daisy hooked an arm under Ella's and insisted on treating us to morning tea. Nothing for it but to be pushed down Swanston Street. The footpaths were crowded with men in business suits and hats, and women shoppers dressed in their best hats and gloves. I couldn't help being irritated by the admiring looks Ella collected, even in her second best frock and hat. She is such a bright light, no one sees me behind her.

Daisy led us to new tearooms in Block Arcade. She grabbed the best table, ordered their most expensive dish, lit a cigarette and blew smoke in my face. At the same time she kept up a running patter about her New Year's Eve party to which, I might add, she hadn't invited Julie or Ella. Nor of course, yours truly; she hates me so much I'm never included in anything. She dismissed us all with 'The theme was Roman, and I know you Marks girls are far too serious to dress up in sheets.'

Our sandwiches arrived. No ashtray, so Daisy butted her cigarette on my plate, whipped off her hat and smoothed her frizzy hair. All this without pausing to take breath. 'I ordered vol-au-vents from Stewarts, and Daddy made champagne cocktails. By midnight everyone was so sloshed. Bunny Segal took us for a spin in his new MG, and we ended up at the Green Mill where we fox trotted until dawn. Everyone said the evening was sooo chic.' She pronounced 'chic' like in chicken.

I asked, 'Did you do the Turkey trot?'

'Turkey trot?' Daisy squeaked. 'No one does the Turkey trot any more.' She turned to Ella. 'Hear Felix Goldfarb's staying with you.'

'You've met Felix?' I was dying to know what she thought of him, but as usual when I speak to her, she pretended to be deaf.

'Felix Goldfarb?' Ella said casually. 'Oh, him! Father met him at Masonic Lodge and suggested he stay with us till he gets his own flat.'

I finished my smoked salmon sandwich. It was delicious.

Daisy signalled to the waitress. 'I don't know why they employ these girls, they're so hopeless.' She jumped up to inspect the pastry. 'Don't suppose you twinnies feel like a cake?' We shook our heads. We especially hate being called *twinnies*. Daisy's face fell. 'Maybe not. I am putting on weight.' I silently agreed. 'I haven't met Felix,' she continued,' but I do so like European men. They know how to treat a girl. And everyone says Felix is handsome and sophisticated. That'll be something for our boys to swallow.'

'They won't have to swallow much,' I butted in. 'Felix Goldfarb is married. His wife's called Sylvie.'

This, Daisy heard. 'Married? But she's still in Germany, isn't she? I'll bet he doesn't know if she's alive.'

'Sylvie's in Switzerland. She's waiting for him to send for her.'

Daisy shrugged this off. Then we had to hear more about the best New Year's Eve party ever; how good the food was, how smashed everyone got, how she and Bunny Segal entered 'The Green Mill' tango competition and won a vase in the shape of a naked lady.

Half an hour later, Ella had a tussle with her over the bill. We let Daisy win, thanked her and left. Ella waited before saying crossly, 'Wouldn't have gone to her Do if she'd sent a Rolls Royce to pick us up.'

'Spoilt rotten!' we said in unison. Then linked little fingers and wished.

As we waited for the tram to carry us home, I watched Daisy pause in front of a shop window to pat her hair and adjust her hat. Something in her demeanor suggested that she was planning more than a shopping excursion. I'd lay odds she was meeting a man. Who was he? Knowing Daisy's reputation for being 'fast', I knew it had to be someone unsuitable.

What will they do together?

I closed my eyes to picture Daisy descending a long iron staircase into a cellar where *he* was waiting impatiently. Hat pulled low, I couldn't see his face. But his lithe body was clearly outlined in a tight suit, and he wore a bow tie with large polka dots – much like a gangster. My mind's eye saw him swoop Daisy into his arms and bend her backwards as they moved into a kiss. While they kiss, his fingers unbutton her blouse and stroke her nipples …

Though I would have dearly liked to picture what happened next, our tram clattered towards us. In the resultant crush and bother of lifting my chair into the cabin, my daydream vanished.

12

> **SPIRIT OF PROGRESS: A TRAIN FOR TODAY.**
> **14th January, 1938**
> Roaring along at speeds up to 79 miles an hour – an Australian record – the new Sydney Limited express train, *The Spirit of Progress* completed its first official trial between Melbourne and Geelong today. The majestic blue and gold train, built in Victoria was watched by more than 1,000 people as it glided out of Spencer Street Station …

Felix arrived this afternoon with a large metal trunk packed to the brim. I did wonder how he'd managed to bring so many possessions from Germany when he'd barely managed to escape in one piece, but he assured me that every article in there had been bought since his arrival.

I helped Ella settle him in. There was much laughter and to-ing and fro-ing to find enough hangers for his beautifully tailored suits and tissue paper to lay between that gorgeous Egyptian linen.

Three quarters of the trunk unpacked, the others went off to eat lunch. As Ella was leaving, she asked, 'You coming, Lilbet?'

'I'll just finish unpacking these ties.' Soon as they were out of earshot, I held a singlet to my nose to establish his smell in my mind, then searched through the trunk for any photos or documents, something that would tell me more about him. What was curious was not what I found. But what I didn't. No photos, no documents, no sign that he'd ever had a life before he turned up here. As I limped towards the kitchen I told myself that this was not unusual. People escaping from harsh regimes would hardly bother with personal belongings. But not even a photo of Sylvie?

How very, very strange!

Father returned from the office earlier than usual. On Saturdays he often works until dinnertime. As a special celebration Julie produced a roast sirloin with all the trimmings (roasted potatoes, pumpkin, parsnip, minted peas, all covered in a thick rich gravy) followed by her special almond, rum-chocolate and passion-fruit and cream cake.

Felix insisted on drying the dishes. Then we gathered around the piano for a singsong. By bedtime Father's arm was around Felix's shoulder and he was smiling broadly, not at all his usual bleak self. This is what he must have been like before Mother died. If only he would stay like this forever. Though I'm sure that it's unwise for Felix to be living here, I'm grateful that he has shown me how happy we can be.

So all would be well, except that last night I dreamt that the devil himself – horns, forked tail, cleft feet – came to tease me with his ginger hair and amazing olive eyes. We were just getting acquainted when I woke with a start to find myself soaked to the skin with my own perspiration and feeling prickly and quite wide-awake below the waist. Somehow I knew this feeling was wrong, as Julie sometimes mentions that I should never, ever touch *down there*, no matter how much I long to. However, there is sometimes a world of difference between what one is told and what one actually does.

13

> **HOUSEWIVES SCOFFING AT REDUCTION IN PRICE OF BREAD.**
>
> **15th January, 1938**
>
> Bread is down a farthing a loaf, but as there are no farthings, and the lower price is in respect of cash purchases only, the situation is further complicated. Officials of the women's organisations demand that the government should either provide farthings or the bakers make a cut that that can be availed of ...

Saturday nights were when Julie and Father went over the week's housekeeping. Also when Julie brought up any little worries that had built up over the previous week. Browsing through yesterday's *Argus*, and cutting out bits and pieces that interested me, I waited for her to put the dishes away, walk down the passage and tap on his closed door.

'Come in,' I heard Father growl. A methodical man, I knew that he would have already brought out the ledger in which he kept their accounts.

She went inside, leaving the door slightly ajar. Because I like to stay ahead of any changes that they might be planning for me, I crept into the passage to listen.

'Ah ...' I heard. 'Felix settling in? No problems there. Not too much work for you?'

'Not at all, Father.'

But she was not being quite truthful. It had taken a huge effort on all our parts to ready the guest-room in less than a week. And though Julie enjoys the challenge of cooking for a more discriminating palate, I knew that it would pull on all her resources to vary our menu without boosting her budget.

79

'Well, good,' Father grunted before she could elaborate. He probably didn't want to hear all the ins and outs of running Adeline Terrace. He said, in some gruff attempt at humour, 'Hope you're not going to ask me for extra housekeeping.'

Holding my breath, peering through the crack, I watched him jot figures onto his blotting pad. He said, 'I have just made a little investment ... well, more of a gamble I suppose. So funds are low ...' he gave a little cough, 'You know how we just managed to survive the Depression.'

We certainly do. Father never stops talking about how close Aarons and Marks came to bankruptcy. I think that it is why his already morose nature grew so much worse. And why his partner Morris makes a better 'front man' for the office than Father ever could. I suspect that it has always annoyed him that Morris seems unnaturally optimistic when it comes to investing, or as he calls it 'speculating'. But, as he so often says, 'Morris spends too much on day to day living for the firm, or for me, to take any more risks.'

Before I had time to wonder at what this 'new investment' might be – or how come Father had broken his golden rule and involved himself in something risky – Julie coughed gently. He said, 'Can always rely on you Julie, to keep things going in Adeline Terrace.'

Though I couldn't see her face, I'm sure she blushed at this rare compliment. I know she was thinking, because she has mentioned this several times to me, 'Since Felix came to live here, Father's moods are so much better. It proves to me that he needed the company of another man.'

'And the twins?' Father was saying. 'No problems there?'

A faint pause. 'Lilbet's new project. Did you know that she has set herself the task of writing a whole novel?'

'Oh? Did you ask her what it was about?'

'She says ... about life.'

His laugh was more like a grunt. 'What would she know about life?'

'That's not what worries me, Father. But she tires herself out too much.'

'Do you want me to tell her to stop?'

My breath caught in my throat. I am forbidden so much 'for my own good', surely not this as well …

'No, no.' Julie said hurriedly. 'It keeps her occupied.'

I had to close my eyes, I felt so faint with relief.

He garrumphed awhile. 'And Ella, I suppose, is being Ella.' A short pause. 'Time she found herself a husband. Her mother was a year younger when we married. Sometimes I feel too old and tired to cope with such a wayward young woman.'

I peeked through the crack. Julie had picked up a pencil and was playing with it.

'I'm sure Ella doesn't mean to annoy you.'

'No?' I could just glimpse Father's sardonic look. 'Then what else is she doing, pray?'

Julie found it best to change tactics. 'But wouldn't we miss having her here?'

Though he frowned and shook his head, I knew he was lying. I knew he would miss having Ella's lovely face to gaze upon.

Julie glanced at the clock on the wall and brought him back to the ledger. As he picked up his reading glasses and they settled down to work, I made my slow way back to our room to think things over.

14

> **FREAK WAVES CAUSE HAVOC IN SURF AT BONDI**
> **20th January, 1938**
> Five people died when waves up to 35 feet overwhelmed hundreds of swimmers at Bondi Beach yesterday afternoon. Thirty lifesavers risked their lives to save nearly 200 bathers who had been swept out by the backwash. About 40 bathers were treated on the beach for shock and immersion ...

All this week has been such a scorcher, the house so breathless, our garden yellowing in the sun. Today Julie decided that we should go to the South Melbourne Baths to cool off. At the very last minute Felix joined us, then suggested that we catch a taxi there.

I think we have been in a taxi only once, and that was bringing me home after my last operation. Julie said, flustered, 'But we always go by tram.'

Felix gestured impatiently. 'Four tickets will cost nearly the same.'

Julie shook her head. But Ella totted it up and Julie had to agree. Nor would he allow us to pay our share, arguing that he never haggled over coins.

Our taxi driver was a young larrikin. He called Felix 'mate' and didn't bother getting out to open our doors. Then he wanted to know what kind of bathing togs we wore. Felix thought him too impertinent to answer – I think he finds it hard to accept our lack of class distinction. But Julie is far too kind to be rude to anyone, even a cheeky taxi-driver. She said 'Why, the usual.'

'Watchout them wowsers don't fine you for no neck an' knees,' he said, grinning.

Felix frowned. 'My good man, what are you talking about?'

But we nearly split our sides laughing. Last year several men were prosecuted by the council for letting down the shoulder straps of their bathing togs. It's a great joke that we're expected to wear neck to knees when the stores no longer stock them. The compromise is that all togs must have an extra half skirt, and the council patrols this very strictly.

We explained all this to Felix. Then *he* spent the rest of the journey laughing at our out-of-date laws and promising to appear topless.

At the baths, we changed our clothes in the tiny and uncomfortable cubicles inside the ladies' dressing-room. As it was the weekend, the red and blue flags that signified mixed bathing flapped in the breeze. Wooden walls lined with wooden decks protect three sides of the sea-baths. People sunbathe there even on the hottest days. The fourth side leads onto sand and the sea. Julie helped me over the pebbles to where waves splashed against my legs until I felt brave enough to wet myself all over.

FOUR SWEPT TO SEA. DRAMATIC SURF RESCUE
17th January, 1938

Overwhelmed by strong seas off the back beach at Portsea yesterday, four bathers were brought ashore by lifesavers …

When Felix eventually joined us, to our secret relief his togs were quite respectable. His arms and legs were well muscled, the skin as soft and white as a baby's. While I attempted a little dog-paddle, Ella splashed him so thoroughly, he threatened to pick her up and drop her into the deep end.

At this she dived into the water and swam off. He plunged in after her. Though Ella is a self-taught swimmer, she has a strong over-arm crawl, and she beat Felix's European breaststroke very easily. On their return he challenged her to another race. At the far end of the baths they paused for such a long time, heads bobbing up and down, I wondered if they were having trouble swimming back. But no, seems that they were building up more steam. Back only a few minutes, they swam off again, this time staying away much longer.

I closed my eyes and lost myself in weightlessness. How good it was to feel the sun on my face sending orange flashes to the back of my eyes. I was no longer sad, crippled Lilbet. Floating, I became one with the gods. Buoyant, I flew through the skies like Diana, goddess of the rising moon.

Soon the wind livened up, pushing tiny waves over my cheeks and making me sway up and down. Towels hanging from the promenade flapped in the breeze. I looked around to see Ella and Felix back on the sand, and pretended not to hear Julie calling to me to come out. Finally Ella came to fetch me, saying I'd best return as Felix had gone to buy everyone an ice-cream cone.

Back on the sand Julie was murmuring 'So generous' as we waited for him to return. When he finally reappeared, but empty-handed, he told us he'd run into two old friends. They'd been so busy reminiscing, he'd quite forgotten what he'd gone to buy. All the same, this reunion can't have been happy because immediately he started pressuring Julie to leave. 'Not as if there is anything to do here but swim.'

I asked, 'What do you do on a European beach?'

One ginger eyebrow shot up. 'Why Lilbet, you could holiday on the Riviera all summer, and never tire of everything there is to do.'

'Even on a beastly hot day like this?'

I looked up to see him staring uneasily towards the street. I followed his gaze to where two men in tight suits and bowler hats seemed to be watching us. Were those his friends? They seemed unlikely companions for someone as class conscious as Felix.

Now he couldn't wait to leave, hurrying us back into the cubicles to shower and change. No more taxis. Instead he helped me into my wheelchair and Julie bustled us up the road and onto the tram. We arrived home around five, hot and dusty and tired, and rather wondering if all the effort to cool down had been worth it.

GERMAN TENNIS STARS IN S.A. TRUNKS CONTROVERSY.
22th January, 1938

The German tennis stars, Baron Gottfried von Cramm and Henner Henkel, swam in topless bathers at Glenelg this week, thereby infringing a by-law that has aroused keen resentment. They were not seen by the police, and thereby escaped the mortifying experience of having their names taken. But the incident directs attention to the fact that the weight of public opinion is against the ban ...

15

Last night a change in the weather, and Monday dawned bleak and wet. After yesterday's excursion, I couldn't help sharing Ella's need for something exciting to happen. Then feeling let down because nothing did.

Father left at 8.05, as punctual as Big Ben on the wireless. Though Ella can do little wrong in his eyes even when she questions his authority, his attitude to me has always been one of distaste. I was nearly sixteen when I overheard him ask, 'Lilbet got her monthlies yet?'

Julie sighed loudly. 'The poor thing should have the curse right now.'

I skulked behind the door, wanting to know more, yet dreading what I might hear. His newspaper rustled impatiently. 'Does she know how to look after herself?'

Julie spent the next few minutes assuring him that 'the poor thing' did. Ella's name didn't crop up. But then, Ella isn't a cripple.

Every twenty-eight days, as regular as the moon rising, I think how unfair it was of God to make my insides normal, but to distort those bits of me everyone can see. What use is it to me to have a womanly cycle? How much better if I'd remained a child both inside and out. Then I think that if God had to turn me into a cripple, why couldn't He have made me as beautiful as Ella? Whenever we meet someone new, I know they're thinking, 'Twins? One so fresh and beautiful. The other so sad and plain.' Before my last operation, in that split second before losing consciousness, I remember half hoping that I would never recover. Yet when I did – maybe it was the sun pouring into my room, the pigeons cooing outside my window, the other children in my ward – I found that after all, I was happy to be alive.

MIRRORS IN SICKROOM HELP TO INTEREST PATIENTS.
23rd January, 1938

Half the trouble with convalescent patients is to keep them cheerful. Once their interest in things around them shows signs of waning, so does their recovery. And yet, to keep the patient's interest is not such a difficult task ...

When I am low, I have a recurring dream where I am lying on a trolley being wheeled into the operating theatre in the Women's Hospital. The sickly-sweet smell of ether fills my nostrils. Before I can explain that this is a mistake, that I shouldn't be here, doctors in surgical gowns are peering down at me. When I try to sit up, they clamp a mask over my mouth and nose.

Now I can no longer breathe. The smell is overpowering. I fall into a giant kaleidoscope. Colours swirl around me. I sink ... I'm sinking fast ...

When I open my eyes, at first I don't know where I am. Pain overwhelms me. It has a life of its own ... Everything is pain ... My world consists of suffering and pain. Pain colonises me, quickly replacing my innermost being with more and more of itself.

I hear someone cry out as from a long distance. A needle pricks my buttocks. Soon my mind distances itself from my body. All that pain and suffering is happening to another girl. It has nothing to do with me. After a while I fall into blissful unconsciousness.

This happens so many times. Just like it did in real life. All I ever want is the sweet relief the morphine brings me.

It's then I find myself sitting up in bed in a cold sweat. It was all a dream. A dreadful, dreadful dream. But such little things can bring it on; Dr. Williams opening his briefcase;

visiting any hospital or doctor's surgery where the sickly anti-septic and chloroform smell has seeped into the woodwork; even some of the bitter-tasting tonics they force me to swallow. How tiresome it is to always be sick. And how fortunate those young people are who have found relief by being treated by Sister Kenny. If only that could happen to me.

POLIO TREATMENT HOPE
23rd January, 1938

Sister Elizabeth Kenny arrived in Melbourne today at the invitation of the Victorian government to explain her method for treating the virulent disease of infantile paralysis (poliomyelitis). Her method is claimed to be 20 percent more effective than other treatments in use.

If reincarnation really exists, all I can pray is that I will come back as someone bursting with rude health. I often joke that in the next life I shall return as one of Ella's cats. Though Mitsy and Motsy are growing old, they lead very happy lives. Much happier than mine.

Whenever I feel this low, Julie tries to boost my morale by mentioning how lucky we are to be living so very far from the worst effects of the Great War. Just to be contrary, I reminded her that so many of our young men died in Gallipoli and Flanders, and that as a nation we also had suffered.

'But we haven't had war in our front gardens,' she pointed out.

'Maybe not,' I replied. 'But remember the great flu epidemic. Wasn't that brought to us because of the war? Doesn't it prove that war creates world-wide chaos?'

Julie smiled briefly. 'Oh Lilbet,' she said dryly. 'Best not let Father hear you speak like that, or he will forbid you to read the newspapers.'

My eyebrows shot up. 'Surely he'd never do that!'

'If he thinks you are taking on socialist ideas. Lilbet, how often must I warn you to watch your tongue.'

I must remember to be more careful. But it is hard to watch every little utterance in case I am misinterpreted. This is like being in a never-ending war ... a war with one's own family where I am general, soldier, spy, and correspondent.

16

WOMAN'S WORLD. HAIR TO BE STRAIGHT.
24ᵗʰ January, 1938

After we have all had our curls renewed for the New Year, it is decreed that hair is to be straight and smooth and drawn back from the face with an old Victorian pinchback comb ...

Last night soaking in the tub, I watched Ella clean Father's shaving mirror with her towel, then stand on tippy-toe so she could see more of herself. 'Hopeless.' she muttered. 'Why can't we have mirrored walls like Ruby Goldstein?'

'Father says he can't afford it.' I sank further under the water. 'Anyway, mirrored walls ... Wouldn't they just fog up?'

She breathed heavily on the shaving mirror, then rubbed the mist away. 'Wouldn't you like to see yourself all over?'

'No, not really.'

She didn't hear. 'Don't you pine for an indoor lavatory?' She opened her towel to inspect her body. 'Lilbet tell me honestly, do you think I'm pretty enough to get into movies?'

'Course,' I said, because she really is. 'People are always saying how beautiful you are.'

Satisfied with this assurance, she returned to the mirror. 'I hate my nose. Why isn't it more like Marlene Deitrich's or Claudette Colbert's? Maybe I can get it fixed.'

'There's nothing wrong with your nose,' I said, already bored and annoyed. Why does she have to keep on emphasising the difference between us? 'Just be grateful not to have Julie's chin ... or my mouth.'

She held up the towel and tried a few dance steps. 'What about my legs?'

My eyes rolled. 'Your legs are fine. I wish mine were as strong as yours.'

She giggled. 'Do you think they are long enough to be a Living Statue?'

I turned to look at her, laughed, then shivered. I can hardly imagine what it must be like to stand perfectly still so every man and his dog can stare at your breasts? While mine are more like pimples they are so small, I knew Ella liked hers – round peaches with pale pink tips. She stood tall to examine them. 'Polly Partridge says that after you marry, your breasts droop and the nipples darken.'

She now had my interest. I sat up and steepled my chin in my hands. 'How does she know?'

'It happened to Polly's mother. Because of what Mr. Partridge does to her.'

'Did Polly tell you what he does?'

'Not really ...'

'Julie keeps advising us about men, how we shouldn't ever stay alone in a room with one, no matter how much we trust him.'

'Oh Julie, she's always warning us against something,' she said, tossing this aside.

'What about Felix?' I said slyly. 'She doesn't seem to think him dangerous.'

Ella giggled. 'Course not. Since all he can talk about is what a great cook she is, he can do nothing wrong.'

'What about you? Can he do nothing wrong with you?'

She smiled and continued rubbing herself with the towel.

A shadow passed by the window. I sat up abruptly. 'Someone's out there.'

She had to lean over me to pull the curtain aside and peer outside. 'Only Father.'

I frowned. 'Why was he looking at us through the window?'

'What makes you think he was? This house is so hot, he probably went outside for some fresh air.'

'But I saw him looking in at us.'

Her smile was mischievous. 'Oh Lilbet, don't you know that men like looking at women's bodies?'

'But we're his daughters,' I protested. 'Why would he want to look at us?'

All she did was laugh.

Nothing shakes her self-confidence.

17

This morning over breakfast Ella pumped Felix to find how he intended to spend his day. 'Maybe the Stock Exchange,' he said smoothing that pencil-thin moustache. 'Maybe I will spend the morning there.' His smile was disarming. 'They might even offer me a job.'

Thinking about Felix, and work in general, I suspect that most men would find it hard to be as organised as our Julie.

Today is Monday, wash day. Tuesday we iron and put clothes away. Wednesday, Julie dusts and sweeps and polishes. Thursday, she bakes and Friday we prepare for the Sabbath. No housework on weekends as Father is very emphatic that there should be no noise when he is home from the office. Between all this, there is the garden to keep shipshape – even though Mr. Moloney does the heavy work, there is still weeding and trimming, maintaining our vegetable patch, and in a hot, dry summer, daily watering. It makes me wonder how most men fill their time? Certainly Father spends long hours at work, often not coming home until well after dusk; even though his office closes at 6.00. I know that he attends a weekly Freemasons' meeting. But what of those other nights? Where does he go? What does he do? Sometimes it seems to me that men live totally different lives from us women. No wonder Ella gives me her constant cry: 'Why does nothing ever happen?'

In our next life we must try very hard to come back as men.

THE WORLD OF WOMEN.
28th January, 1938
Everyday Problems.

Will you please repeat in your columns the directions for stiffening a crochet basket with sugar. " Newly Wed." Camberwell.

To make stiffening for six baskets take one half cupful of icing sugar and enough water to make a thick syrup. Cook this mixture until it is thick, then place the baskets inside. Stir them around with a fork until thoroughly saturated. Then run a string through the handles and hang them in a cool place to dry ...

Hat on, umbrella unfurled, shoes shined to mirror perfection, Felix left us to our usual morning drudgery made even worse by the increasing rain. Mrs. McInerny our charlady attacked the washing. Managing our laundry is a full day's work for three women. I watched Ella sort the washing and Mrs. McInerny fire the copper. Finally Father has agreed with Julie that using a wood copper is too labour intensive. He has promised to look into the cost of piping gas into our laundry. Recently, he bought a mangle, and asked Mr Moloney to attach this to our laundry sink in the hope that this will save our hands and wrists from too much wear.

Once the water was hot, Julie threw in enough soap-powder to make it frothy. First they boiled the whites. Then the coloureds. Using a long wooden pole, Mrs McInerny hoisted the washing into a trough, and rinsed everything in two lots of cold water. Finally Ella helped her dip the whites in Reckit's blue to make them whiter, and stiffened them with a paste of flour and water. If it hadn't been raining, they would have hung everything on the line that stretches between the pear tree and fence. Instead they turned the kitchen into a steam room half-hidden behind racks of drying sheets.

Half way through the morning, Mr. Jones who delivers our vegetables came by to say his horse had fetlock trouble and there would be nothing until Wednesday. Julie groaned loudly. As she'd planned pumpkin soup for tonight's dinner, Ella was sent to the greengrocer to buy half a Queensland Blue.

The first break in the weather we headed for the shops, me pushing my chair, Ella walking alongside. Suddenly, a gap in the clouds and the sun shining through as if he'd never really intended to desert us.

We hardly spoke. My thoughts were filled with Felix Goldfarb. Why, with all the help Father was giving him, why couldn't he find work? Yesterday I overheard him tell Ella that he needed money rather badly. Yet each time Father suggests a career, he'll find some excuse for rejecting it. A few nights ago he replied to Father's question with, 'Looking at so many figures tires my eyes.' Then an acid, 'Accountancy? Surely not a gentlemanly occupation.'

Father was mildly taken aback at finding his own profession so maligned. 'I find it genteel enough,' he gruffly replied. 'Would you consider banking?'

Felix smoothed his little moustache, 'Dealing all day with money matters holds little interest for me.'

Other suggestions were Law, but for this Felix needs certain qualifications; Manufacturing, but for this he needs Capital; even becoming a shop assistant in one of our better stores.

Felix shook his head.

Finally Father cried, 'Many migrants travel into the bush peddling wares. My own grandfather realised that the real fortune was to be made in selling essentials to the gold-miners rather than looking for gold. He learned to love the bush and appreciate its true beauty.'

Felix sat down and carefully adjusted his trouser knees. 'Perhaps you are right. But I am told that your bush is mostly scrub. If one wishes for real beauty, one must travel to the European Alps.'

'Their charm is different,' Father cried. 'You cannot make a decision until you travel deep into the bush.'

In the following debate, Father quite forgot about helping Felix find an occupation. But how can Felix afford to lunch at the Windsor Hotel? Is Father's firm subsidising him? How can he afford to leave Sylvie in Zurich? No one inquires how he manages to pay rent. Whenever Sylvie's name comes up, he moans, 'But how can I send for her when I have no job and nowhere to live.' Nor, apart from boasting about the family's rich possessions, does he ever talk about his parents. Considering the news coming out of Germany – dispossession, labour camps etc. – why isn't he more concerned about their welfare? And why am I the only one to ask these questions? But like the Pied Piper of Hamelin, Felix manages to blind everyone with his unique mix of worldly sophistication and boyish charm.

ATTACK BY HITLER ON SPANISH LOYALISTS
25th January, 1938

In an address to the closing session of the National Socialist Congress today, the Reichsleader (Herr Hitler) made an impassioned attack upon the Spanish Republican government. Herr Hitler said it was ridiculous to regard Jewish Bolsheviks as the legal government of Spain ... Germany did not desire to play the part of an economic and political hermit. She was willing to co-operate with all countries that shared her views ...

18

Last night as we sat over a late supper, Felix entranced us with an account of travelling through Transylvania and falling into the hands of bandits. I couldn't help piping up, 'Transylvania. Isn't that where vampires roam?'

His olive gaze turned on me. 'Certainly Lilbet. We had many blood-sucking creatures to deal with.'

'So how did you escape?'

He helped himself to more shepherd's pie. 'Perhaps I will tell you. It is a very interesting story.' He chewed on a mouthful, then said 'I was returning from doing business with Count Anton Vladivostock. The roads were so poor, even my new Mercedes could hardly manage them. So much rain, I could hardly see through my windscreen. Lightning lit up the horizon and the thunder was deafening. Rounding a corner, I crossed one pothole too many, and my front tire blew out. The Mercedes skidded into a tree. Next I was surrounded by mustachioed men toting guns and knives and threatening to kill me if I didn't hand everything over.'

'How terrifying,' Julie breathed.

I glanced around the kitchen table. Though Julie makes the best shepherd's pie in all the world, even Father had forgotten to eat. 'So how did you free yourself?' Julie thought to ask.

'Oh …' Felix replied, off-handedly. 'That was easy. Before you could say Transylvania twice, vampires were attacking the bandits. In the melee, I managed to find a cave where I hid all night.'

Father's fork was poised in the air. He put it down. 'That must have been most uncomfortable.'

Orange hair gleamed under the strong kitchen light. 'Certainly it was. Particularly as I had to share it with a hungry bear. Only my small fire stopped that bear from eating me. I soon realised that I could not spend another night in that cave. Either that bear had to go or ...' he gave a little bow, 'yours truly. At dawn I crept out to look at what had happened to my car. Imagine my surprise to find that both bandits and vampires had turned into actors. Seems they were making a film called *Blood and Guns*. In the rain and confusion they thought I was one of them. Perhaps you have seen this film?'

We shook our heads.

"Tsk-tsk.' He shook his head. 'Though my role was small, both director and producer congratulated me on my acting and offered me a part in their next production.'

Father recollected himself. 'Perhaps we saw your next film and didn't recognise you. What was its name?'

'That next film? It never came to pass. Shortly after this I went home, saw what was happening and managed to escape through France and over the mountain pass into Spain ...'

A sigh went round the table. Poor homeless thing, everyone was thinking. He returned to his original story. 'So for the next two weeks I stayed with that film crew. When we finished filming, they helped me repair my Mercedes and I continued on towards Budapest ...'

And with this, we returned to eating pie and salad.

I'm sure he made it all up. I tell myself that it's his peculiar blend of sophistication and charm which stops them recognising his stories for what they really are. Yet I find myself watching the signet ring on his little finger, those fine gingery hairs on the back of his hands, and wondering what they might feel like on my skin? Then he catches my eye with a half wink, as if he knows my innermost thoughts. Other times I dream that his arms enclose me, and those lips – so full and red for a man – caress mine. His hands run down my thighs. As I roll against him, he whips off my night-dress leaving me as bare and rosy as a peeled orange.

It's then I wake, my heart beating in my ears and with an ache in my breasts and groin that no matter how much I rub *down there* never seems to lessen.

Ella and Felix spent most of Sunday together. Too much so, as he had offered to escort the family to the Botanical Gardens. Julie had too much to do and she kept me at home though she knows how I love to feed the ducks and swans and watch the eels wriggle in the lake. At the last minute Father changed his mind about going. So Felix and Ella went without a backward glance. I was left to help Julie prepare seven pounds of grapes for pickling. My only consolation is that once Sylvie arrives, Felix must leave Adeline Terrace.

19

Felix insisted that Julie's veal in mushroom sauce reminded him of a little café on the Parisian Left Bank. This cafe he said, was where he had met world famous artists, musicians and writers, and they had all become close friends.

I watched my sisters hang on his every word. 'Who do you know?' 'Who did you meet?' Even Father smiled and looked interested. Felix fingered the silver salt shaker – I have noticed how he loves to touch anything that glitters and shines – and said, 'Nancy Baker, the black singer. And Louis Armstrong the jazz musician. The artists Picasso, Miro and Chagall.'

Busy dishing out our dinners, Julie glanced at me, then paused ladle in hand to ask, 'What about writers? I know Lilbet would love to know if you have met any writers.'

'Why Ernest Hemingway. Marcel Proust. Flaubert.'

'But Proust and Flaubert are no longer alive,' I quietly protested.

His glance cut me in two. 'I didn't say that I had met them *in the flesh*,' he said reprovingly. 'But much of my time was spent reading their splendid works.'

'Which ones?' I persisted. 'Do you know *Remembrance of Things Past*? Or *Madame Bovary*? I would dearly love to discuss those with you ...'

But he was too busy complimenting Julie on the veal to bother answering.

Later when everyone was out of earshot, Julie took me aside. 'I don't know what's come over you, Lilbet,' she said crossly. 'How can you be so rude to Father's guest?'

I said, 'Do you really believe everything he tells you?'

She stared at me in dismay. This quickly turned to disapproval. 'What benefit would he gain from lying? Lilbet, Father has asked me to tell you to be careful where your tongue takes you.'

'I still think he's telling tales.' But I said this under my breath. They are so fascinated by his stories of meeting the rich and famous, nothing I say will make them change their minds. He sits at our dining table, the light falling on his coppery curls like a halo, and holds us in the hollow of his hand. Their waking hours are filled with him. Everything is 'Felix says', 'Felix likes', 'Felix dislikes', or 'Felix thinks …' He could tell them that he has been to the moon and met the goddess Diana and I know they would believe him.

But what if they are right and I am wrong? If this is so, how can I ever forgive myself for showing such distrust, to quote Julie, 'to a poor migrant'. If only there was a way to prove to my own satisfaction that he is not a rogue. Then I tell myself that if Father, who is usually so suspicious of strangers, does not question what he says, what right have I?

I cannot stop thinking about him. He is always on my mind. If Ella is falling in love with him as surely she is, perhaps I am too? But how can one love a man one has no confidence in? Altogether I have too many unanswered questions. My mind reels with them, but if I even attempt to broach them with Ella, she shrugs me off. How confusing it all is. How confusing to fall in love with someone I can't trust. Not even a little.

20

Last night Father detected an unpleasant smell in the living room. He dislikes cats and he's never had time for Motsy and Mitsy. Now that the poor old things are losing their hair, he can't stand them getting under his feet. 'Stinks like Mitsy's done her business in here,' he growled under angry eyebrows. 'Julie, first thing tomorrow this room must be spring cleaned.'

Ella sulked all evening in defence of her animals. But in fairness to Father, Mitsy hides behind the couches whenever we go out and in the past she's been responsible for several nasty messes. Breakfast over, the girls started pulling up rugs and taking them outside. There is order and method to Julie's cleaning. She gets Ella to move the furniture while I check that nothing has been left behind, then they tackle the area with dusters and brooms.

Often I try to imagine our house as a friendly animal. If the front door is its mouth; the passage, its arteries and veins; the kitchen its stomach and Father's study its brain; then the living room – with the upright piano, gramophone, wireless and dresser with the crystal and silver that Mother brought from England – is most definitely its heart. Ella would prefer a more modern house, one like Ruby Goldstein's with at least three floors, a wider sweeping staircase, an internal 'little room' beside each bedroom and downstairs, doors with mermaids and fish etched into the glass.

I agree with Ella that this house is dreadfully old fashioned. I would dearly love for Father to have a cistern built into our bathroom so that I did not have to ask for help when the back steps become too slippery to manage. But a modern house will not have our bay window looking onto the street. Nor will it have our high ceilings. The rooms will feel more cramped.

In summer the ivy hanging over our living room window turns the light to dappled shadows. It's then I curl onto the window seat and try to imagine a different life for myself. In my dreams I am always tall and strong; sometimes an Amazon minus one breast so I can throw a spear as accurately as any man. Other times Diana, the moon goddess, my shimmering gown lighting up the world. I once dreamt that I exchanged my poor legs for a powerful fishtail, and dwelt on a cluster of rocks far out to sea. There, I lured sailors to a watery death. Nor do my dreams always turn to legend and folk tale. Since reading *Gone with the Wind*, I have fallen in love with Scarlet O'Hara. However I must report that Rhett Butler has red hair, a pencil thin gingery moustache, soft white skin and wonderful olive-green eyes.

Once the rugs were up, Julie emptied all the shelves and between the three of us, we wiped and dusted at least two hundred books. Ella washed the larger pieces of china and I polished the silver platters Julie uses at Passover.

Sometimes when I feel particularly sorry for myself, I stop to wonder what it must be like for those poor people who lost their houses in the Depression. Each time Ella and I go into the city we see many beggars, and it is common knowledge that there are still not enough jobs to go round. And that even if there is work, it is poorly paid and often dangerous.

STAY IN STRIKE AT MINE
27th January, 1938

Thirty miners at Korrumburra last night erected barricades and began a 'stay in' strike with dramatic suddenness. The men held two meetings yesterday to protest against the alleged failure of the owners to observe the wage award which was to have become operative tomorrow ...

Only last month I answered the door to a woman with two small children. They were so thin, wild-eyed and bedraggled, my heart went out to them. I went to Julie to beg for food and money. She gave me what little she could spare. That poor woman sank onto her knees and kissed our hands. It was enough to make a strong man weep.

I would very much like to bring this up with Father. I admire his alert if somewhat bitter intelligence, but whenever I try to discuss the poor, he tells me they are mostly responsible for their own plight. 'Besides,' he growls, eyes darting about from under shaggy eyebrows, 'politics is men's talk and you mustn't worry your little head over something you can't change.'

It is easy to see how he can ignore their distress. On the whole, Melbourne is an orderly city. Only if you go into the working class suburbs such as South Yarra, Richmond or Collingwood, will you see the ongoing effects of the Depression. There are terrible reminders of the Great War. Too many men with lost limbs. Too many men wearing old army greatcoats dyed black that tell the world they were employed on government projects. Too many blind beggars. Too many men wearing signs saying 'Gassed in Flanders'.

Ella is equally indifferent. Though I remind her that, but for the grace of God, they could be us, she mostly tends to ignore human suffering. In her defense, she can't bear to see any animal mistreated. Not to so long ago, she threatened to report one of our neighbors to the police for tying up his dogs and leaving them without water. Nor can she bear to ignore any injured animal. In the past she has brought home several birds with broken wings and beaks and sometimes she has even nursed them back to health.

She used to pretend to tolerate my views, but lately she has no patience for any discussion. It's as if she has already left this house and all I have is her pretty shell. As for Julie – she is always in her own words, 'Far too busy to sort out the world.' Then she'll go on to warn me that if my political views are too open, that Father will forbid me to read the newspapers.

If only I wasn't a cripple.

If only I was a man.

If I were a man I would go to Spain to fight General Franco's fascists. What must it be like to be in a war? From everything I have read, it seems to me that no matter how heroic one seems, that war is a dirty, horrid business. But what else can folk do to preserve their life and liberty?

REPATRIATED TO AUSTRALIA.
30th January, 1938

Repatriated to Australia as a result of spinal injury suffered in a motor accident when coming out of the front line trenches in Spain. Mr. Ron Hunt reached Fremantle today in the Esperance Bay. He is the first member of the International brigade, fighting for the Spanish Republicans, to return to Australia ...

When Felix first arrived, I had hoped that he might share some of my interests. But when I tried discussing politics with him, he laughed and said, 'Lilbet, you're beginning to sound like a Socialist. I think it is much better if you stick to what you know.'

'I do that very well,' was my reply.

He smiled blankly. I didn't think that he understood me. Not one bit. But that night at dinner, he told us a complicated story about a would-be social reformer he once knew called Kominsky, an anarchist ...

Ella butted in, 'What's an anarchist?'

Felix smoothed his little moustache. 'Why, Kominsky was a Russian who didn't believe in following the laws of the land.'

I suspected that this story was being told for my benefit. 'What happened to him?' I asked.

Felix shrugged. 'For some reason Kominsky believed that the only way to better society was to blow it up.'

'But surely that has the opposite effect,' Father protested.

'Indeed it does. Only my intervention stopped there being a total massacre. The government was most grateful to me and awarded me a medal for bravery ...'

'A medal?' Ella cried. 'How wonderful. Can we see it?'

He gave her a modest smile. 'Unfortunately,' he gave his characteristic little shrug, 'one of the treasures I was forced to leave behind.'

'Oh!' You could cut their disappointment with a knife.

I said, 'What happened to this Kominsky?'

He turned to look me right in the eye. 'Lilbet, you do well to ask. He ended up in gaol and I doubt if he will ever get out. But it serves him right for meddling in politics.' Then he glanced at Father who grunted in agreement.

WOMEN'S PLACE IN THE NAZI SCHEME OF THINGS.
1st February, 1938

"You ask me what I have done for the women of Germany? Well, my answer is this – that in my new army I have provided you the finest fathers of children in the whole world; that is what I have done for the women of Germany.'"Herr Hitler.

In this installment extracted from *The House That Hitler Built* Professor Roberts tells of the Nazi idea of the part their women should play in the national life. Children, church and kitchen summarises their ideal of women's activities. The Nazis are raising a generation of blonde physical beauties,' says Professor Roberts ...

21

I woke feeling so low, I decided to lift my spirits by listing my better points:

My teeth are straight and white; though the eye-teeth are a little too pointy; as yet I have no fillings. My lips are thin, but one side turns down more than the other. And Ella says when I'm happy that my smile is infectious.

My eyes are a deep burnished brown, in some lights so dark their irises become almost indistinguishable from the cornea. A shame that when I feel unwell they are surrounded by purple shadows. My skin is clear if somewhat pale, and I rarely get blackheads or pimples. Sometimes when I walk a little further than usual, the exertion brings a faint flush that makes me look almost healthy.

My hands are narrow, the skin clear and pale. Ella files my nails to a point. If Father didn't dislike his daughters wearing make-up, they would look very good polished blood red. It's easy to imagine my hands going to parties and my right fingers holding a cocktail-glass, and in my left an ebony cigarette holder.

My hair is curly and disobedient. However, if I stand under a light, I can discern a faint reddish streak.

I like my neck. It's as long and white as Ella's.

My feet are small and ladylike. If I wore normal shoes, I would take a very narrow fitting. Probably triple A.

In the bath, I stay in the water until my skin feels dry and crisp and my toes and fingers wrinkle. I drum my feet, blow soap bubbles and run my fingers through them, stretch my good foot to touch the far end, drum up and down with my fists to create little waves. If I squeeze my arms against my sides, I can almost convince myself that my breasts and hips are full and seductive. Then I pretend that soon I will dry myself on a fluffy white towel, cover myself in costly French perfume – maybe Chanel – and slide into a black satin slip, black suspenders and long silk stockings. I try to imagine that my lover is in the next room waiting for me.

I wish that I did not always have to ask Ella to help me in and out of the tub.

I wish that she wasn't falling in love.

I wish that I could change places with her.

I wish, I wish, oh how I wish …

22

Early Sunday morning there was a knock on the front door. Father, still in his dressing gown, answered it. 'Felix,' he called. 'You have a visitor.'

Felix followed him into the hall. Who should Father usher into the kitchen but the Polish stall-holder from the market – the young man with the frizzy black hair and coffee bean eyes who quoted Keats to Ella. Still in his heavy European clothes, he looked as out of place in our kitchen in Melbourne, Australia, as an African tribesman.

The visitor looked nervously around. Later when we got to know him better, he confided that after only a few months in this new country, he knew the general attitude to migrants was 'Go back to where you came from.' But the day before he'd run into Felix who greeted him like a long lost relative. Even though he still had Felix's invitation ringing in his ears, plus his promise that Simon Marks's family was more than generous, he could hardly expect to be made welcome.

I watched Felix rush over and grasp his hand. 'Simon, Julie, Ella,' he cried, 'meet my blood brother, Yosel Cohen.'

'Pliz to meetcha,' Yosel mumbled. He was so tall, his head barely missing the overhead light, his shoulders as wide as the kitchen table, he seemed to shrink the room to half its size. I saw him catch sight of Ella, and his eyes visibly light up as he recognised the pretty girl he'd met in the market.

'Sit down, sit down,' Felix was saying. 'Have you eaten breakfast?'

Yosel shook his head. So Julie, openly impressed by how much food this massive frame must take to fill, fried four eggs, the same quantity of bread and tomatoes and poured hot water into the tea-pot.

Yosel mumbled 'Tanks'. While barely taking his eyes off Ella, he attacked his breakfast as if he hadn't eaten in a week.

Felix rubbed his hands. 'You see what a good fellow this is? He saved my life so that is what makes us blood brothers.'

I couldn't help laughing aloud. This little sparrow related to that giant? What nonsense was this! Felix shot me a sour glance and switched his gaze to Father. He pressed his fingers to his lips, then said, 'But if he is to succeed, he needs another name. What is Yosel in English?'

Father smiled and shook his head.

'How about Joseph?' Ella suggested. 'We could call him Joe for short.' She turned to Yosel, 'Does that name please you?'

Yosel was listening to all this very carefully. 'Joe.' He smiled. 'Now I am Joe. A goot name for a goot country.'

Felix nodded. 'And Cohen,' he added disapprovingly. 'What kind of name is Cohen?' On the tip of my tongue to mention Goldfarb was hardly King George's English. But Felix was already saying, 'Change one, change the other. Call yourself Joe Cowan.'

So he was Joe Cowan from then on. I watched him murmur the name to himself. I hoped he wouldn't forget it. Though his English was limited, and his accent appalling, I later found that he spoke fluent Russian, Polish, Yiddish, understood German, could read and write Hebrew and had more than a smattering of French and Italian.

We watched him take in our new 'Kookaburra' gas-stove, the kitchen dresser and ice-chest, and wondered what he made of us. That he was a good man, we knew instinctively. No matter that he was a migrant and spoke poor English.

Julie turned from the sink to ask, 'Joe, where are you from?'

Joe heaped several spoonfuls of sugar into his cup and carefully stirred it. 'Sokolka.'

'Where's that?'

'White Russia. Iz small village, but train stop two, mebbe three time a week.' He held up the same number of fingers.

'Oh, there,' said Julie. 'White Russia has the biggest settlement of Jews in a town called Bialystock.'

Ella laughed. 'Bialystock. How funny. Do you know where it is?'

Julie nodded. 'Northwestern arm of Poland.' At school she'd always loved geography, and spent hours poring over maps. Back then her greatest ambition had been to travel.

Father said, 'Thousands of small villages in Eastern Europe. No made roads. I imagine that when it rains, they turn into a sea of mud. Five generations ago,' he mused, 'our family came from such a village and travelled to England. That's where my wife was born.'

I looked up from my fried egg – eyes and ears agog.

'I met my wife in Manchester,' Father continued, 'where her family owned a small textile factory. It was several years before the Great War. I had sailed to England on business. And there she was, the most beautiful woman in the room.'

'Not as beautiful as Ella,' Felix murmured under his breath, and Joe's expression said he thought the same.

'More beautiful,' Father growled. He changed the subject to the one hundred and fiftieth anniversary of Captain Arthur Phillip setting up the first colony in Sydney and how expensive the re-enactment was.

AUSTRALIA CELEBRATES ITS 150TH YEAR.
26th January, 1938

Sydney was alive with the sounds of music, cheers and laughter as Australians celebrated 150 year of settlement. Festivities began with a re-enactment of Captain Phillip's landing at Farm Cove from a replica of his brig *Supply*. In the brightly decorated streets a million people turned out to watch a pageant of the nation's history pass by ...

I glanced at Father impatiently. I couldn't help wondering why this money wasn't being used to help folk still suffering from the Depression. I had read that some of the unemployed still relied on their Unemployment Organisations, and even their local councils. Aunt Amy had once taken Ella and myself to a Punch and Judy sponsored by the St. Kilda Council. 'Any child with unemployed parents gets in without paying,' she told me when I was amazed to see so many skinny white-faced children in raggedy clothes.

At the time I was so ignorant, I actually envied those poor children. Didn't Aunt Amy always say that envy would be my downfall?

I had almost found the courage to speak up, when Felix cut Father off in mid-sentence. We all knew how he hated any conversation to get too serious.

'What about all of us going to the cinema next Saturday? You too, Joe.'

Joe looked thoughtful. Shortly we were to discover that Saturday was his busiest market day. But at the time he couldn't resist this opportunity to be with Ella and get to know her better. 'Nex' Sat'day iz fine.'

'Wonderful,' Ella cried. 'That's something to look forward to. Will you come, Father?'

Father smiled and nodded.

23

This morning my entire left side was as stiff as a board and sore. I could no more get out of bed than fly to the moon and I had to ask Ella to help me out. She did this most unwillingly. These days she never seems to think about anyone but herself. Julie puts it down to heat, boredom and the wrong time of the month. But I know better.

Then elderly Dr. Williams arrived to give me my monthly check-up. With his thick white hair, bulbous red nose, overly flushed cheeks and bulging waistcoat, his appearance never seems to change. He took my pulse, listened to my chest through his stethoscope, and ran his fingers down my left side, in the process pinching me most painfully. Then he claimed I was losing too much weight and must take another of his evil tasting tonics. Though I protested very loudly, much good it did me. I once made the mistake of mentioning that I am sometimes constipated. The good doctor told Julie that if I didn't open my bowels every second day, that she should give me an enema; this entails Julie using a thin rubber hose to send a stream of soapy water into my insides. Then making me hold on until I'm fit to burst. The whole process is most demeaning. I sometimes wonder what Dr. Williams hopes to achieve. Perhaps he thinks that emptying my bowel will dislodge my spasticity?

Each morning Felix leaves shortly after Father. Though he doesn't get home until just before tea, he still has no proper occupation. Last week he turned up with several parcels from an expensive city store. When I asked him what he'd bought, he merely grunted and disappeared into his room. Mealtimes and after, he remains his usual delightful self, always ready to pull out a chair, or help Julie with the dishes. Felix, I might add, can do little wrong in her eyes, and she's always finding extra tit-bits – like the nose of the Shabbat chicken, or the crisp skin on the roast lamb – to pop onto his plate.

It's as if he's lived with us forever. What's more, he's got lots of spare cash. Not only has he paid his rent for the next four weeks, he added a little extra for what he calls 'hidden expenses.' Last Friday he bought lilies and carnations and an expensive double layered box of chocolate truffles for us girls. For Father he had a beautifully carved British pipe and three tins of tobacco. Julie told him that these presents were quite unnecessary, that he paid more than enough rent, but he insisted that nothing could ever cover all the care and attention he was receiving.

So after dinner, Father and Felix settle themselves in the living room and it's light and puff, light and puff, until the entire house is filled with a delicious smell. No wonder these days Father's moods are so much more pleasant.

As a boarder, no one could outdo Felix. He's become a fan of 'The Classical Hour' and 'Dad and Dave'.

IT'S DAD AND DAVE.
31st January, 1938

Dad and Dave have taken to the airways and it looks as if 2UW has a hit on its hands. "This is a human story of two typical Australians," the announcer says. "Their families, their lives, their hopes, their fear, their dreams and their triumphs …

Other nights if he's not telling us stories about the places he has visited and the famous people he has met, we group around the piano to play Schumann, Chopin and Mendlessohn. We usually end the evening with a sing-song around the piano. Felix and Ella's favourite song is Duke Ellington's *Body and Soul*:

> *'My heart is sad and lonely.*
> *For you I yearn, for you I'm lonely*
> *I tell you I mean it,*
> *I'm all for you*
> *Body and soul*

24

Ella and I spent most of the day polishing floors while I changed gramophone records. I always know when Ella is in a good mood because she'll tango to 'Jealousy' or waltz to 'The Blue Danube' using the mop as a partner until the boards are nicely buffed. But when life seems bleak, she silently shuffles around until we can't wait to start another chore.

This morning as we were putting things away, she cried, 'Ah Lilbet, if only there was more to life than polishing floors.'

I blinked uncertainly. I'd be grateful to manage a little housework myself. Besides, Ella could never concentrate long enough to learn shorthand or become a bookkeeper. She hates schools and is too impatient with sick people. Though she would make a fine veterinarian, Father would never pay for her to go to a university. So apart from a little housework, what else can she do until she marries and leaves home?

MARRIAGE LURES TYPISTS AT DARWIN FROM THE JOBS.
2nd February, 1938

So perturbed is the Northern Territory Administration at losing its pick their typists through marriage that it has been playfully suggested that all future female applicants should accompany their references with personal photographs ...

'What I'd really like is to be a film star,' she cried floating around the room while I sang 'Moonlight Becomes You' only slightly out of tune.

The front door burst open. Father stomped in. He took

one look at us, muttered, 'So that's how you spend your days,' and scowled his way into the kitchen. There I heard him ask Julie if she'd seen some missing papers. 'Can't imagine what I've done with that file.'

For Father to lose a file is like the sun forgetting to rise. Since Felix came to live here, everyone is behaving very strangely.

Tonight after tea he, Felix that is, suggested a game of cards and since then we have played *Twenty-One* non-stop, gambling for matches so wildly, you might think huge fortunes were at stake. I enjoy playing cards almost as much as filling in crosswords. Cards are a great equaliser. You have to remember every card and agonise over every throw. Most people can't be bothered to concentrate and that's why they lose.

Felix is equally keen. By Friday the others had to borrow matches from the two of us. Watching the others play tells me a great deal about them. Father and Julie's thoughts are too often elsewhere. Ella is too busy getting Felix to notice her. Even Felix – and how he hates to lose – grows impatient. I think that he knows I'm onto him, and sometimes I catch him watching me from under his eyelashes. Then he'll give me that slow half wink, as if he knows my thoughts are far less negative than I'd like us both to believe.

Between games, Felix regales us with stories about certain wagers he had seen in his travels. 'When I was in Marienbad …' In reply to Ella's questioning glance, 'Marienbad, a well-known watering place. Many a night I watched a certain English gentleman gamble a king's ransom on the toss of a coin.'

'How much did he win?'

Felix fingered his moustache. 'Did I say he won? Then another night in Monte Carlo, I saw an Indian maharajah throw his favourite concubine's necklace onto the roulette table …'

Of course Ella who loves jewellery almost as much as she

loves Felix's stories, demanded to know what that necklace was like.

His full lips under that pencil-thin moustache, twitched a little. 'Picture diamonds and rubies as big as ... as big as Mitsy or Motsy's eyes. But the central stone ... ah that was nearly as big as the Hope diamond.'

I glanced around. Everyone's eyes were out on stalks.

Felix picked up the cards and shuffled them so expertly they hardly seemed to move. 'However, seems that this necklace carried a curse ... a terrible curse.'

'What kind of curse?'

He turned to smile at Julie. Then gave a little bow before murmuring, 'Such a curse I could not repeat in the company of ladies ...'

And with this we had to be content.

But all in all, we are having so much fun, I must remind myself not to question him too closely.

25

MERCURY DROPS. RECORDS GO.
5th February, 1938
Melbourne's heatwave, which has not been exceeded for 40 years, ended at 12.26 p.m. today when the first refreshing draught of a cool change reached the city bringing the temperature down 10 degrees from 91.6 ...

Found Felix and Ella sharing the piano stool laughing over a Mozart duet. Felix called, 'Lilbet, tell your sister to behave. She won't play anything but treble.'

Ella giggled. 'That's all I can play.'

'Naughty girl.' He tapped her fingers. 'Playing bass will improve your sight reading.'

'There's nothing wrong with my sight reading,' she protested.

'In that case, change places with me.'

She shook her head.

'No? Then I will have to move you myself.'

'No, no,' she squealed as he pretended to push her off the seat.

I left. Why look like a spoilsport? They'll think I'm envious that they can play the piano and I can't. Of course I am, and not only for that. He has never been more handsome – fiery red hair, soft skin, wonderful olive green eyes. Nor she more beautiful – huge eyes, hair clustering around her cheeks, silky skin. Her lips are so soft, full and vulnerable I can hardly bear to look at them. Of course she will be hurt. I suppose I could warn Father and Julie, but they are so bewitched by him, they won't listen. My only consolation is that sooner or later, Sylvie will arrive and then he must leave.

I have just remembered that business with Ruby Goldstein. While Julie and Ella went along with Ruby's plans to marry Father, her manner towards me sent a warning prickle down my spine. As my conscience is clear about listening behind doors when things are discussed that might involve me, my efforts paid off. The following week I heard Ruby say. 'Simon, did you know there's an excellent place in Carlton just set up for spastics and the mentally retarded. Why not send Lilbet to live there? I'm sure she'd be happiest amongst her own kind.'

Just then Julie came down the passage and I had to pretend that I was heading for the bathroom.

The following Friday I followed Ruby into her kitchen to ask for a glass of water. I said, 'Ella's got a headache. She's probably going to have a fit.'

Ruby's chin dropped. 'What kind of fit?'

'Grand mal.' I bit my lip. 'Didn't Father tell you? Maybe I shouldn't have mentioned it. It looks so much worse than it is. After everything's over, she'll be fine. Don't say anything to her please … she gets so upset. We have to hold her down, make sure she doesn't swallow her tongue. All the Marks have some kind of epilepsy; it's in Father's family, but only Ella gets grand mal.'

Ruby slowly nodded. 'That poor girl. So pretty. What a shame.'

Over dinner, I remember Ruby's chicken soup wasn't as good as Julie's. But when Julie offered Ruby her recipe, Ruby said not to bother.

Not long after, we heard Ruby had married someone from Sydney. How Father felt, I never found out. Was he sad? Disappointed? Hurt? In the end I decided he looked relieved. He wore his new suit to the office and as far as I know, never mentioned Ruby's name again.

Joe turned up just before lunch with a bunch of violets for us girls. Julie decided that he looked half starved, so she piled his plate with rabbit cooked in her special wine sauce, then practically forced him to lick the surface clean. He showed us a cracked back tooth, and told us that he'd nearly cancelled our arrangement, he was in such pain. 'You haf not feltcher,' he said. Joe is so tall, he always tilts his head towards whoever he is addressing.

'Oh?' Julie filled a soup bowl with a double helping of lemon pudding. 'What's a feltcher?'

Joe reddened slightly. 'He pull tooth.'

'Ah.' Julie suddenly understood. 'In Australia, we go to a dentist.'

Joe nodded, and looked annoyed at showing himself up as a foreigner. But Julie handed him a glass of water and two Aspro tablets and told him to swallow them. Then she jotted down the name and address of Mr. Webster who has looked after our teeth since we were small.

At the last minute Father decided not to come with us to the theatre. Everyone was secretly relieved. It's always risky including him in any excursion. I remember him ruining our tenth birthday. Ella had pleaded for us to go to Luna Park. He needed lots of persuasion. 'Luna Park is where the riff-raff go.'

I don't remember where Julie was. Just that she wasn't with us. We caught the tram to St. Kilda, then strolled along the beach. Catching sight of the laughing mouth, Ella dropped Father's hand and ran inside towards the merry-go-round. At this, an old tramp squatting by the entrance called, 'That one'll lead you a merry dance.'

Father went straight into one of his moods. Nothing we did could charm him out of it. Come to think of it, interesting how Ella always creates the problem. Then she leaves Julie and me to cope.

But today's trip was different. No Father. Only grey skies and intermittent showers. Good reason to stay indoors. And no wheelchair, only Left and Right as my support. We took a tram to the Atheneum Theatre in the city. This time the effort of getting on and off those steps seemed insignificant. For once I could look the conductor in the eye without a flicker of nervousness. I think it was this new found confidence to handle climbing onto a tram that made me question if I could manage such a trip alone.

When we got to the theatre, Julie hates sitting too far from the screen, I dislike sitting too close, so we sent Felix to buy seats somewhere in the middle. First we saw a newsreel showing the Japanese advance in Manchuria. Though I had been following these events in the *Argus*, viewing it on screen brought home for me the unfortunate situation the Chinese were in. But whenever I have tried to discuss this with Julie, or even Felix, they look quite blank. Not that I expect them to be interested in world events – Julie is much too busy, and Felix refuses to take anything seriously except his own creature comforts.

Yet curious as to where the Chinese situation might lead, only yesterday I tried tackling the subject with Father. He garrumphed awhile, then said, 'Don't worry your little head about it. Events in Asia are far away and have little to do with us.'

I'm sure he must be right. But if Germany and Italy are a threat to world peace, how much closer to us is Japan?

JAPAN STILL ADVANCES. CHINESE DRIVEN INLAND.
18th February, 1938

The Japanese army in the north is driving the Chinese further inland. Japanese bombing raids continue, and planes have dropped leaflets on Chenghow (Honan Province) warning foreigners to leave the town before it is bombed ...

After the newsreel, the first half of the double bill was a British film, *Beloved Enemy*. The setting was Dublin, the story so moving, I couldn't help wondering if, like those lovers, I would sacrifice myself for my country.

When the house lights came on at interval, Felix laughed at our red eyes. 'It's only a story,' he cried, and he went off with Joe to buy everyone an ice cream.

'So generous,' Julie whispered. 'Such a lovely man.'

I stared at her incredulously. Didn't she notice in a particularly heart rending scene, Felix reach for Ella's hand? Didn't she see how Ella leaned against him? How can she be so unaware of what is happening in front of her eyes?

The second film was *Broadway Melody*. I thought the story predictable and the acting just so-so, but the others loved it and came out humming the songs. Just as Felix was suggesting the Windsor Hotel for afternoon tea, I heard a familiar, 'Yoo hoo, Julie! Ella!'

Daisy Aarons. In a blue hat worn over one eye, fox fur draped over a purple suit, and with Bunny Segal in tow.

The two men doffed their hats and there were introductions all around. You should have seen Daisy's eyes gleam on being with two such handsome specimens. Bunny's too, while he was being introduced to Joe. Was this because, to quote Julie, 'Bunny is a fairy?' What was it that made him like men more than women? If he found someone that he really liked, then what did they do? Surely it couldn't be harmful. Bunny is one of the kindest people I know, even if he is somewhat greedy and tells jokes I never quite understand. He always finds time to speak to me and even run little messages like fetching Left and Right, or helping me out of my chair.

Daisy demanded to know what the men thought of the film. Before they had a chance to express any opinion, she suggested that we all go to *Rocco's*, a city nightclub, for supper and dancing.

'Good idea,' Felix cried.

Julie glanced at me and shook her head. 'Lilbet's not used to staying out so late,' she murmured.

'*Rocco's*.' I felt the blood rush to my cheeks. 'But I've always wanted to go there ...'

'Of course not!' Daisy cast me a vicious look. '*Rocco's* is no place for Lilbet. She would feel quite out of place.'

Daisy is quite open about hating me. She'll do anything she can to put me down. She must be the most spoilt woman in Melbourne. My sisters are far too nice to her, much nicer than she deserves. Ella thinks Daisy's friendship might be useful and Julie ... well, Julie is always kind.

Daisy settled her fox-fur on her shoulder. I swear its button eyes glared maliciously at me. She said 'If we go to *Rocco's*, someone must take Lilbet home.'

Immediately both Felix and Joe offered to be my escort. I held my breath. A slight wind sprang up. Julie turned to button my coat. 'I have things to do for tomorrow,' she said briskly. 'Lilbet will come with me. But the rest of you must go.'

'We wouldn't dream of going without you,' Felix said hastily and Joe agreed. I felt Ella's eyes turn on me. If looks could kill, I would have been stone cold dead. In my mind I could hear her whisper, 'Oh Lilbet, why do you always ruin things for me?'

'We'll go to *Rocco's* another time,' said Daisy. Left unsaid was 'When Lilbet's not around.' Aloud she added, 'Bunny's so kind. He's promised to drive me to Flinders next weekend.'

'Where is Flinders?' Felix asked.

'On the Mornington Peninsula.' Daisy stared directly at him. 'Why not join us?'

Ella's gaze flickered between them, 'We wouldn't all fit in the MG, would we Bunny?'

Bunny stared at Joe, at his unusual height, broad shoulders, gentle face and that shock of frizzy hair. 'No trouble at all, darlings,' he murmured. 'Daisy's daddy will lend us his car.'

'But then we need two drivers,' Daisy cried. 'Felix, can you drive?'

Felix stroked his moustache. 'Not a problem,' he declared. 'I drive just about every make.'

But how skilful can he be? These days newspapers report so many accidents:

COBURG CRASH
19th February, 1938

Attempting to avoid a cycle yesterday in Sydney Road, Coburg, a motor-cycle and sidecar combination crashed into a stationary car. The car crossed the road, struck a motor-van and finally came to rest 60 yards away ...

All the way home, Ella couldn't stop talking about that proposed trip into the country.

'Not exactly country,' I couldn't help remarking. 'More like coastline. And we should be going to Portsea. Or Lorne. I'm sure they would be far more interesting.'

Felix turned to face me. 'Lilbet, why is that?'

Ella giggled. 'Portsea is where the rich build their beach shacks.'

'Really?' Felix's eyebrows rose. 'Sending me to look at

the wealthy? Lilbet, what is happening to your Socialist views?'

'Nothing to do with my *views*,' I said crossly. 'It's just that both Portsea and Lorne are surf beaches. And I understand that the road to Lorne has breathtaking scenery, not that I have ever been there ...'

But Felix wasn't interested in listening to any views – either personal or scenic. Something else had caught his attention. 'You say the wealthy live in shacks? This seems most extraordinary.'

'Not really shacks,' Ella hurried to explain. 'That's just what they call them. Some shacks are more like mansions. Our wealthy families spend much of the summer in them.'

'Just like the south of France. But in the English Home Counties the wealthy play polo.' And he stroked his moustache as if considering this information.

'Polo?' Ella gave her customary giggle. 'Here it's more likely to be ping-pong.'

WATER POLO IS JOLLY GAME TO PLAY.
15th January, 1938

This is a very fascinating game to play. All you need is a ping-pong ball or a balloon. Place it between two teams lined up on either side. At the word 'go' the sides must immediately try to get the ball into the goal at the opposite end by blowing it into the goal ...

Last night I dreamt that Father and I were holding a splendid reception for important dignitaries just like the one in *Beloved Enemy*. My eyebrows plucked to a fine line, blood-red lips, and hair caught in a smooth bun, I am straight and strong in a sleek white evening dress that shows off every curve. Father and I are welcoming our very important guests. As one bends over my hand, my heart beats in double quick time. I glance up to see Felix smiling down at me.

27

Because Felix and Joe paid for our cinema tickets, in return Julie cooked them a splendid French dinner. Chicken pâté as the hors d'oeuvres and then a proper French onion soup that was so rich, so filling, Felix insisted that it was better than any he had eaten in Paris.

Beef Burgandy followed, with all the trimmings. We finished with crème brûlée. This dessert is so delicious, I held out my plate for seconds. Father couldn't resist the opportunity to put me down. 'Next time Lilbet loses her appetite,' he growled, 'I expect she'll ask me to send her to Europe to recover it.'

I was too hurt to think of a reply. Ella came to my rescue. 'Only if I go too!' Everyone laughed. But I sat there fuming. Why must Father pick on me when other people are here? Ella would spring to her feet and slam out of the room. Then I pictured what would happen if I tried the same – Lilbet slowly clambers up, then takes hours and hours to limp away not even closing the door behind her.

Felix and Joe had brought two bottles of an excellent claret, and the men finished them off very quickly. By now, Father was laughing and telling stories. Even I could hardly remember how morose he used to be. Since Felix has come to live with us, Father stays in good spirits. Even though his cheeks are a little too flushed and recently he has started complaining about severe headaches. Last night Julie scolded him for working too hard. 'Looking at so many figures … no wonder your poor eyes are giving you trouble. That's why you are getting headaches.'

But tonight only Ella seemed low. Though she appeared to join to the fun, from the shadows under her eyes I could tell she wasn't happy. I believe she and Felix have quarrelled, and I can only guess as to the reason why.

Not that Felix gives much away. He is his usual entertaining self with a description of the first week he spent in Paris. He described a visit to the Left Bank, 'Where I met artists, gangsters and ladies of the night. You cannot imagine how exciting this was. Because my family has owned our factory for several generations, they can be so old fashioned. '

He pursed his lips and folded his hands to show us how proper they were, and we laughed loudly.

'So for such an innocent lad as I was once …' that characteristic little shrug, 'it could only be a delight to meet such raffish characters.'

He personifies all the elegance and worldliness that never reaches our little backwater. Though deep in my heart I know it's wrong for him to be here, I can't help wondering if it might not be better to make do with a little second hand sophistication, than have nothing at all.

Still, I do feel sorry for Joe. He never takes his eyes off Ella. In fact he reminds me of a lovesick dog. I half expect him to howl at the moon to get her attention. Ella of course, only has eyes for Felix. Meanwhile Father is preoccupied with playing host, and Julie continues in her usual calm way to look after everyone's needs but her own. As for myself? I am a turtle. A mollusc. A snail. Under my shell I creep along and observe those around me.

We ended the evening at the piano. Ella played Bach's *A Minor Prelude and Fugue*. As the music moved from one key to the next, the melodies turning themselves inside out and running against each other, I felt such envy, I could hardly sit still. Though my left hand is too stiff to stretch across the keys, why couldn't Father have let me learn another instrument? If I could play the flute or the clarinet, think what pleasure I might be giving others.

We called for an encore. Halfway through a Chopin Mazurka, Ella sprang from her stool. 'Someone else's turn.'

Father glowered at Felix. 'Right, young man, give us a tune.'

Felix sat down and played Beethoven's *Moonlight Sonata* with fewer mistakes than usual. Everyone clapped and Julie ended the evening with Cole Porter's 'Night and Day'. Though I pleaded for Ella's favourite 'Body and Soul', Felix joked the request away. 'Not that old thing. Your voice is so soft, we never hear if you sing.'

'I do, I do,' I insisted, but he had turned away to talk to Father.

ADV.   TOWN HALL. ARTHUR RUBINSTEIN
Thursday 6th February. 1938
Universally acknowledged as one of the Present day Giants of the Piano-forte. Program includes work by: Chopin, Cesar Franck. Ravel and Stravinsky.

28

Another scorcher of a day, and the iceman not turning up, made Julie rethink the evening meal. I met her in the kitchen, staring at the contents of our ice-box. Hearing me come up, she asked, 'Lilbet, what do I cook for tonight?'

What a person to ask! These last few days what with the heat and premonitions of great loss, my appetite is almost non-existent. I said, 'Why must you cook? It's much too hot to eat.'

'Not for everyone,' she said shortly. 'When the men come home, they are hungry.'

I didn't answer. With Felix as our permanent guest, I knew how she prided herself on producing as interesting and varied a menu as possible. No wonder. Felix was always so complimentary, wondering aloud why she wasn't cooking for the Duke and Duchess of Windsor, or even the King of England, or someone equally important. That man surely knows how to persuade the Marks to look after his every creature comfort.

But Julie was waiting for some response. I asked, 'What did you have planned?'

Her forehead crinkled in that endearing way. 'Potted tongue, a crisp salad and homemade ice-cream. Everything that must be chilled.' She opened the top of the icebox to show me where the ice-block had almost melted away.

The poor thing looked so tired, I pulled myself together and made an effort to be helpful. 'How about braised lamb shanks? And some of your tasty potato salad.'

'Clever you,' she cried and bustled away to write a shopping list for Ella.

It occurs to me that I have written very little about Julia. Though some might describe her as plain because of her strong features and the rather stocky shape she inherited from Father, her high forehead and mild expression prove to the world what a kind person she is. Her best feature is her hair, which is as black and thick as our mother's might once have been, and which she refuses to shingle. Instead she curls it into a bun she wears at the nape of her neck.

She washes her face with Velvet soap, never wears face powder or mascara, and only when we are dressed in our very best will she apply a touch of coral lipstick. I suppose that her other outstanding characteristics are her hands; strong and square, the nails clipped short, the skin dry and red from too much soap and hot water. Like their owner, they are never still. Every spare moment Julie can find from housework and cooking, she crotchets or knits – if not for the family then for some charitable organisation. My only disappointment is that she rarely reads, and when she does it is only the Women's Section of the newspapers and magazines. If ever I try to discuss some political event, or even a book in Father's library, she'll purse her lips – the only sign she ever gives of impatience – and say 'You're the reader in our family, Lilbet. Perhaps when things settle down and I can find a little time, you will tell me what to read.'

But sometimes in the middle of a busy day, I see her stop stock-still, and I know her mind is far, far away from Adeline Terrace. Do her thoughts ever drift to her ex-fiancé? If she had married Carl, now she would have been mistress in her own house. She would have had his children. Not so long ago we heard that Carl was doing well as a solicitor, and that he'd married an Adelaide girl and that they had two sons.

I thought back to when she cancelled their secret engagement. I knew about it of course, and so did Ella. I will never forget that evening. Ella and I came across Carl sitting on the nature strip outside our house. Though he had always reminded me of a busy bumblebee in that he never could sit still, that night he was so upset, nothing about him was humorous. Too anguished to go home, he confided to us what had just happened, crying, 'I will never forget her, never.'

Even back then, Ella was such a romantic, the thought of any unrequited love reduced her to tears. Equally upset, she murmured, 'But I don't understand why Julie did this.'

Tears fell unheeded down Carl's cheeks. 'Since Father has decided not to remarry, Julie sees it as her duty is to look after the family.'

Ella went back inside and tried discussing it with Julie. It was then I saw a side of my older sister that I'd never met before. Her face set in mulish lines, she very firmly told Ella to mind her own business. Both were so upset, I felt very sorry for them, and sincerely wished that I had been in no way responsible for Father's decision. But then, there are times when one must take one's own well-being into account, and I am sure that they would never have forgiven themselves if I had been sent to live in the Carlton House for Spastics and Retards. The truth is that without my family's protection, I would become as slight and insignificant as a passing shadow.

For Carl's sake, I hope that he is happy. For Julie, I'm sure that she found it best not to dwell on the 'might have been' and 'if only things were different'.

Halfway through the morning, she found me in my usual seat inside our bay window. 'Have you seen Ella?' she called impatiently. 'I need her to run these messages.'

I said, 'Did you look in the garden?' because Ella was probably in her favourite hiding place in the pear tree.

Julie frowned at my book 'What are you doing with those newspaper cuttings? What are you writing?'

She glanced over my shoulder. Father often comments on my poor penmanship, and I must admit that my writing slopes down the page like a mad insect's ramblings.

I held my book against my chest. 'Nothing much. Just notes for my novel.'

'What kind of novel?' And because she is always eager to encourage me in anything I can manage, 'Is it a crime story? Did you see the last edition of *Women's Weekly*? Some excellent stories. Even one by Agatha Christie. Why not write a short story and send it in? And the *Argus*. You could send it there. They often feature stories by unknown writers.'

I clutched my journal closer, and wished she would go away. I never intended to be rude, but Julie felt my irritation, because she said sternly 'Have you taken your syrup?'

'Later,' I murmured. 'I'll take it later.'

'I shouldn't always have to remind you,' she replied and hurried back into the hot kitchen. Poor kind, gentle, honest Julie. Ella and I are such a trial to her. I suspect that she often asks God why He had chosen to test her with two such difficult sisters. No wonder she often repeats how her married friends are delighted when they give birth to boys.

29

I cannot explain what prompted me to tackle this adventure. Perhaps it was catching the tram to the Atheneum Theatre and managing to get up and down those steep steps without any help. Perhaps it was Daisy's open contempt. Or even Ella's transparent unhappiness. But all this has made me realise that I must assert some independence or die in the process.

Yesterday dawned bright and fresh, not a cloud in the sky, a day to suggest the finest water-colour or oil painting.

> **SUNLIGHT IN PICTURES.**
> **23rd. February, 1938**
> Clear atmosphere and scintillating sunlight characterised Mr. Clewin Harcourt's work at the Fine Art's Galleries in Exhibition Street. Capable handling of oil colour is another feature in a world of painting in which there is much fumbling and technical affectation today ...

Straight after breakfast Julie busied herself wiping down pantry shelves. I told her that I felt strong enough to go to the park without my wheelchair. 'But I need Ella here,' she absent-mindedly replied, so I told her that I intended going alone.

She turned to me, worry creasing her mild forehead. 'You sure you'll manage?' Then she added, 'Lately Lilbet, what with all this writing, you are taking too much on yourself. Dr. Williams will not be pleased ...'

It was on the tip of my tongue to say, 'Please send Dr. Williams to the devil.' But as this would only upset her, I assured her that I felt strong enough not to need anyone's help. Ella was not the only one longing for some new experience. On such a fine day, the shores of St. Kilda beckoned.

Forgetting all about food and drink, I made sure that I had enough in my purse for fares, and set off for the nearest tram. My plan was that would take me to the second tram, which in turn would carry me to the beach.

The first part went surprisingly well. As I slowly made my way down Bridport Street, I could almost imagine that I was in a foreign country, perhaps France, and I carefully named some of the things I saw in that language: *l'arbre, les fleurs, l'herbe*.

I'd hardly waited five minutes when my first tram appeared. It stopped long enough for me to clamber on. The conductor took my fare and I sat back and stared through the window. Curious how, now that I was entirely on my own, how different everything looked. Finally I felt grown-up. In fact, I was so entranced by my grand adventure and by the houses and gardens passing by my window, I almost forgot to get off.

The conductor was a kindly man who helped me onto the road. I waited for the traffic to clear before crossing to where I must catch the second tram. Some cars and carts passed by. I felt their drivers stare at me, but I steadfastly ignored them. When the next tram turned up, I climbed on with a little help from the elderly conductor, and in no time I was being carried towards the beach.

Only when I got off and was facing the water did I realise that I hadn't eaten anything since breakfast. Light-headed with hunger, I thought that I might float away with the breeze. I took a left-hand turn and slowly headed into the tearooms at the end of the pier. I was already settled when I looked inside my purse. I hadn't brought enough money. When the waitress came up, I explained to her my mistake and very politely asked for a glass of water.

The manager was a big woman with the kind of yellow hair that can only come from a bottle. Thinking I must be a visitor and unfamiliar with our currency, she offered me a cup of tea and a scone saying visitors to our city, particularly those like me – tactfully, she didn't mention my disabilities – must always be made welcome.

I thought how Julie would never have allowed her to make this mistake. Julie is so honest she would divulge the truth and take the consequences. However, using my most refined tones, I told her that I was fresh from England and accepted her kind offer. She was so thrilled to meet someone from the 'Mother Country', she added another scone to my cup of tea, waving my thanks away, saying that she could hardly wait to travel Home.

Half an hour later and much refreshed, I settled myself on the sand. From here, the day was so clear and bright, I could see far out to sea. To my left was the faint outline of the Mornington Peninsula, on my right the ports of Altona and Williamstown. In front, children splashed in the water while their parents kept an eye on their activities. It seemed as if all my senses had never been this alert. Never had the sun been this hot or its light so bright. Never had the sand been this orange and grainy, the sea so blue, the air so filled with children's cries, cawing seagulls and waves lapping against the shore. Never had the smells of ozone and seaweed and frying food been this strong.

Two men sat further down the beach. Brothers I thought, admiring the affection they showed each other. One was stretched out on the sands, the other running his hand over his back, stroking him with strong sensuous movements.

I felt so envious as I sat watching. If only Father would sometimes treat me with similar tenderness. Then the stouter of the two turned around and I realised it was Bunny Segal! But Bunny has no brothers. Or does he? And what was he doing here? Who was that other man? A shiver of unease ran down my spine. Hadn't Julie called Bunny a fairy? Someone who prefers men to women? There was something in the way he stroked that man, something so intimate, that made me think Father would thoroughly disapprove of meeting him in these circumstances.

Almost the same moment that I recognised Bunny, he leaned forward to murmur something in his friend's ear. Then he rose to his feet and came towards me. 'Lilbet? What are you doing here all by yourself?'

I felt caught red-handed. 'Hum ... er ... wanted to see if I could manage ...' My voice trailed away. Then I wondered why I should feel so guilty. But given everyone's care and attention, it's hard to assert a little independence without feeling selfish.

'Ah.' He smiled and winked. I stared up at him. Only Felix has ever winked at me before, and even then I never knew what this meant. He said, 'Seems Lilbet, that we both have ...' he paused for a moment, ' ... other lives?'

Not knowing how to reply, I nodded.

He stared at me thoughtfully. Then stood up saying, 'This little meeting of ours ... If you say nothing, I will do the same.'

'Yes,' I murmured. 'I won't mention this to anyone.'

He seemed satisfied with this, and I watched him head back towards his friend, the sand so meltingly hot, he had to tip-toe. A few minutes later they both stood up and ran across the sand towards the street. As Bunny passed, he waved and I waved back.

Soon it grew too hot to sit without shade, and no doubt Julie would be wondering where I was. So I picked myself up and made my snail's pace way back to the tram. That trip went almost as easily, though it was already far too hot to be comfortable and I had a few problems getting off the first tram and onto the second.

I arrived home wet through with perspiration, extremely tired but triumphant.

Julie greeted me with cries of relief, and then a terrible anger. Seems I'd been away that bit too long. Fearing the worst she'd sent Ella to look for me. When I was not to be found, they'd decided that I'd either been kidnapped, or fallen sick and some kind person had taken me to hospital. Five minutes later and they would have gone to the police.

I assured them that I was fine. If I thought they would be pleased at my new found independence, I was sadly mistaken. Ella was so cross and upset, she could only give me that tight blank look. All Julie could say with tightened lips was 'What if something had happened to you?'

By now I was in floods. 'Why would anything happen to me?'

She shook her head. 'Father will not be pleased. Lilbet, you must never forget that you are different from other folk.' And again she reminded me, 'You test your strength enough with all that writing. Never forget that there are many things you cannot manage. You must promise me that you will never, ever do anything like that again. Promise?'

I dried my eyes and blew my nose. Then bleakly promised.

30

> **TOO DISCIPLINED FOR US**
> **28th February, 1938.**
> A teacher of German in Sydney, Miss R Hilliger, was a passenger in the *Lahn* from Hamburg which reached Melbourne yesterday. Miss Hilliger is returning from a holiday mostly spent in Germany, and she is tremendously impressed with the order and method that have taken hold of the country since her last visit. She said, 'Australians would never stand such discipline ...'

Took a few days after my little escapade for things to settle down. As if to prove Ella's point that very little of interest happens in Adeline Terrace, today we had the usual Monday morning miseries. Ella and Mrs. McInerny fired the copper, and while they boiled, rinsed, blued and starched, I helped Julie bottle plums. Julie was testing recipes from a book of Mother's. I was more interested in Mother's handwriting. She wrote her letters slightly above the line, small but perfectly formed, the capitals so ornate I think that she must have been very artistic.

Her alterations are interesting. Next to a recipe for apple chutney, she wrote 'Double the quantity of vinegar.' Here is a woman who never left anything to chance. I like to imagine that if she were still alive, she would advise her daughters not to act too impulsively.

This morning Julie took pity on my boredom. In spite of Father's strict instructions as to what I can and cannot do, and with many instructions so I shouldn't cut myself, she allowed me to chop up plums. If I hold the fruit with my left hand, and use my right to prise out the stone, this isn't too difficult. Though anyone tasting Julie's preserves always praises them, today's jam refused to set. Julie kept adding lemon and boiling up the mixture. By the time the jars were ready for labeling, we ate lunch in the atmosphere of a Swedish sauna.

The late morning post brought a letter for Felix. I examined the envelope. Sylvie crosses her sevens, places the number of the house after the street – GRANDVIEW STREET, 7 – and misspells MELBORNE. On the back of the envelope is GOLDFARB S., HONIGSTRASSE 299, ZURICH, SUISSE. The envelope has been handled many times, the stamps crisscrossed with markings. However, I finally worked out that the letter was franked on October 23rd, 1937.

So what have I learnt? That Sylvie Goldfarb actually exists. That she likes her husband well enough to write. And that anything from Switzerland takes a long time getting here. When I held the envelope to my cheek, I pictured someone in a slinky dress gazing at me through lowered eyelids, and talking in a husky voice about German Expressionism.

After lunch, Ella persuaded me to rest under the pear tree. From where I lay on my wicker chaise-longue, I could watch how the leaves cast dappled shadows on the ground. This is where our cots were placed when Ella and I were small. Nearly asleep, I focused on the northern wall where the passion-fruit blooms. Julie says she has never known the vine to bear so much fruit. From this angle, its greenish-purple spheres look like so many miniature globes. It struck me how this tangle of stem, leaves and fruit reflected the Marks family. Isn't this vine joined at the stem like we Marks, some of us aching to get away, at the same time knowing that without each other, it's doubtful if we can survive?

When I was little, I saw this vine as a forest where witches and wolves roamed, and where a fairy-tale prince would one day come galloping out of the foliage. Other times it was a magic bean-stalk which grew to the edge of the clouds, and I used to wait for a miniature Jack to climb up and fight the giant who always looked like Father. In my dreams I was always whole and splendid, proud and strong, swift and powerful – as far from my horrid disabled self as possible.

When Mother died, Father employed a wet nurse called Madge to care for us. Though I don't remember her at all, Julie tells me that her own child had been stillborn and she was very grateful to find two such hungry substitutes. Madge stayed with us nine months or so. Then Father became angry once too often, and she packed her bags and left. That afternoon Father's sister, Amy, called in. She took one look at two screaming babies and moved herself and her husband Bernard into the spare bedroom. These angels in disguise stayed until Ella and I turned ten. Aunt Amy loved children and was sad that she and Uncle Bernard had none. Uncle Bernard was a printer, but too often involved in get-rich-quick-schemes to support her. He liked nothing better than to swing Ella and myself around the room while we squealed with pleasure and fear. We adored him and though Father made scathing comments about his ability to lose money, in our eyes, Uncle Bernard could do no wrong.

Looking back, we were lucky Aunt Amy and Uncle Bernard lived with us for as long as they did. Then the inevitable happened. Uncle Bernard went into another of his get-quick-rich schemes. This time he might have gone to gaol if Father hadn't paid off his debts. There was a tremendous row, and Uncle Bernard moved Aunt Amy to Sydney.

Now Aunt Amy runs her own millinery business, and corresponds regularly with me. Sometimes I think her letters would make a fine novel if they weren't likely to upset her wealthier customers. She writes interesting gossip such as 'The Thomases are now the most influential members of Sydney society. Only because they have so much money. Their last ball, *A Night in Ancient Egypt*, was attended by more than six hundred guests. You have never seen so many Pharoahs and Cleopatras in all your life. Dina Thomas appeared as a Nubian slave which considering her colouring was more than appropriate. But I'm not complaining ... those headdresses take very little work and I was able to charge five guineas each ...' etc. etc.

I reply to her once a fortnight. Aunt Amy tells us about Uncle Bernard's latest schemes. If it wasn't for her, they might starve, but she still believes that he'll make his fortune. Even though Father says Uncle Bernard is vulgar and Aunt Amy far too bossy, they're the closest to loving parents I have ever experienced. Whenever my mind's eye pictures Amy, I see a stocky figure with strong features and bushy eyebrows like Father's. She's the only woman I know brave enough to stand up to him and I often wish that she still lived with us, and could help me achieve a little more independence.

31

WOMEN'S TOPICS: Eye Make-up is Important.
28th February, 1938
Eye shadow should be used and graduated lighter towards the eyebrows which must be kept well brushed and darkened. The eyelashes should be mascaraed and then combed with a tiny lash comb so they will not look gummed or sticky …

Just before supper, a breeze blew through the house reminding us that Indian summers never last. It rattled the windows, oozed its way down the chimney and settled on my shoulders. On my way to our bedroom to fetch a cardigan, I heard voices in the living room. 'Ella, my little Isabella. How you will take everything to heart. In the end, what does it matter?'

A murmur. Only a murmur. I peeped through the keyhole. All I could see was the couch. Then his light laugh. 'Of course I will respect you.'

Footsteps approached. I hurried??? down the passage. Two minutes later Felix sauntered by. 'Lilbet, feel like a game of cards?'

'Not tonight,' I said coldly. He gave me a teasing smile. He couldn't care less if I know what he's up to. He's too beguiling by half. I can see why every member of the Marks' family is caught by his charm. Without my help, how strong Ella must be to resist him. I wish she would confide in me. But Ella has always kept something back, nothing large, but a tiny part remains private. These days she rarely asks me what I am thinking. Perhaps she believes that she knows.

Only last night *he* entertained us with a story I will call the 'Table of Truth.'

We were finishing our lamb-chops, mashed potatoes and peas when Ella mentioned how Edward, now Duke of Windsor, had finally been forced to tell the truth about his relationship with the infamous Mrs. Simpson.

I took the opportunity to look meaningfully at Felix and say there was nothing more *precious* than Truth. Of course he had to bring this back to himself. 'As I have already mentioned,' he said helping himself to one of Julie's macaroons, 'My family has lived in the same chateau outside Frankfurt for several generations. Unlike this country where everything is so raw and new, each piece of furniture we own has its own history.'

'Really?' Julie said, entranced. 'Give us an example.'

'Have I mentioned the Truth Table?'

We shook our heads.

Felix nodded gravely. 'Our dining table is so old, it bears the marks and scars of many generations. It is said that this table exerts such magic, those who sit at it are compelled to only speak the truth.'

'We could surely do with such a table,' I said under my breath.

Nothing wrong with Father's hearing. 'What are you talking about Lilbet?' When I flushed and didn't answer he whispered, 'Best watch your tongue, my girl. I won't tolerate rudeness to any guest under my roof.'

Unfazed by this exchange, Felix continued, 'Mid-1913, a certain gentleman of Kaiser Wilhelm's court was present at our table. When asked if war would ever break out between the Great Powers, he felt compelled to reply that it would happen as soon as an opportunity arose. Even though he'd been sworn to absolute secrecy.'

Ella asked, 'Did this table always work?'

'Always,' he replied smiling into her eyes.

32

Another card night with Felix and myself fighting over a game of Twenty-One. After tea, Father went to his study. The rest of us stayed in the kitchen. I was not feeling the best. Half way through the game, I felt sick and dizzy so I closed my eyes. Next, head swimming, body lighter than air, I was floating towards the ceiling, up, up, now looking down at Felix who sat at one end of the table, his fiery hair paling everything else into insignificance.

Then the feeling passed, and I was back in my own seat watching him deal the next hand.

We'd started the game with eighty matches each. Ella kept on losing. By nine o'clock, she was forced to borrow from me. All evening Felix had been avoiding her gaze, and now she was frantic. Only Julie didn't notice anything untoward. Not that she didn't know Ella was upset – you'd have to be deaf and blind not to notice – but she probably put it down to one of Ella's many moods. Julie is so honest and straightforward, it would never occur to her that Ella might be interested in a married man or that a married man living under our roof would lead her sister on.

Felix dealt me a Queen and a seven. This move is tricky. A seventeen is mostly too low to win. Anything more than a four and I'd lose. The round played, the others eliminated, Felix looked at me. I nodded. He handed me another card, a two of diamonds. Nineteen points. I leaned back, tried to make him feel I was holding twenty-one. Did he realise that the real stake was more than a few matches?

Felix dealt himself a King, then a two. 'Well, Lilbet. All or nothing?'

'All.'

Slowly, very slowly, he peeled off a card. When he showed me his twenty-two, I threw down my hand, triumphant.

He shrugged. As I was returning the matches to their boxes, Ella jumped up from the table and fled.

I suppose I should have followed her. Instead, I helped Felix stack cards and box matches. Julie was preparing tomorrow's breakfast. I said, 'Let's drink our cocoa on the verandah.'

'You two go,' she replied. 'I need to mix this batter.'

'Come Felix,' I murmured. 'The winners will feast each other. But you must carry the tray for me.'

He followed me onto the verandah. Not a cloud in the sky, and a full yellow moon casting her magic glow. Settling myself on the chaise-longue, I left enough room for him to sit beside me.

Felix placed the tray on the seat next to me. I stifled a pang. 'You see,' I pointed to the sky, 'Diana is watching your every move.'

A long silence. Then a cautious, 'Who is this Diana?'

'The goddess of the moon.'

'The Moon Goddess.' He looked relieved. 'Off course. Lilbet, you have such strange ideas.'

I stared up at him. His lips were pink and full, his gingery eyelashes so thick, by rights they should be a girl's. I asked, 'Doesn't the goddess wonder at some of your actions?'

He shook himself and laughed. 'What an imagination. Lilbet, no wonder you wish to be a writer.'

'I do, I do,' I cried. And found myself confessing my hopes of one day completing my novel, sending it to a publisher, seeing my name in print …

Halfway through, I stopped. His eyes had glazed over. He gulped the rest of his cocoa, cried, 'Sleep well, Lilbet,' and went inside the house humming 'My heart is sad and lonely,' leaving all the important things unsaid.

33

> **SWIMMING TIME FOR YOU IS SNOW TIME IN SOME COUNTRIES.**
> **1st March, 1938**
> Here, while you are enjoying freezing ice-creams and spending days splashing in the sea, in Europe tens of thousands of boys and girls with gay scarves knotted under their chins and cosy gloves keeping their fingers warm, are gliding on skates over frozen ponds, or perhaps tobogganing down icy slops, and in the mountains thousands of people will be ski-ing ...

Sunday dawned bright and hot. After breakfast Father went to his study and Julie, who'd been up half the night preparing our picnic lunch, began filling a hamper. Felix was in an excellent mood. 'Dearest Julie, what did you pack?'

Julie wiped her fingers on a towel. 'Roast chicken, meat balls, asparagus rolls, dill cucumbers, potato salad, buttered scones and a chocolate honey cake.'

Ella was finishing off the dishes, her lovely face pale and withdrawn. I watched her make an effort to join in.

'What about something to drink?'

'There's four bottles of ginger beer and two with iced tea. Do you think that's enough?'

Ella swished a dishrag around the sink. 'Won't Father bring wine?'

'Father's not coming.'

'Why not?'

'You know he can't stand being near Bunny. Including Joe, we make seven.' Julie frowned. 'What if I boil some eggs?'

We giggled. Julie is convinced that it's up to her to make sure no one starves and she spends a lot of time making sure this doesn't happen. Felix said, 'Won't your friends bring provisions?'

'Of course.' Then she added a tin of macaroons in case they didn't.

A car pulled up. Bunny and Daisy in matching navy jackets and white slacks came into the kitchen. Daisy stood over me flicking cigarette ash into my hair. 'Daddy's being mean. He won't let anyone except Bunny drive his car.'

Dum-dee-dum. Bunny tried an awkward soft-shoe shuffle. 'No worries, darlings. I can manage.'

'Bunny, don't be stupid,' Ella cried crossly. 'There's Joe and all the food. And what about Lilbet's chair?'

'Why is she coming?' Daisy asked in a stage whisper. 'She'll only ruin our day.'

Ella's frustration boiled over. 'Daisy, don't be horrid. Of course Lilbet is coming.'

'Don't see why,' Daisy sulked. But under Ella's furious gaze, she quickly subsided. Even when we were little, Daisy hated having me around. Perhaps she thought my spasticity was infectious and that she might catch it. Once when Ella and I were quarrelling, Ella let fly that Daisy thought I was selfish.

My chin dropped. 'Daisy can talk. She's the most selfish person I've ever met.'

'Daisy says you always arrange our games to suit yourself.'

'I don't know what she means,' I cried, quivering with anger and disgust. 'She's just being horrid.' And though I didn't want to cry, I knew that I was, because I could taste salty water on my lips.

Ella cried, 'Isn't it mean to want everything your own way just because you're a cripple?'

My mouth dropped open. I could hardly believe my ears. Didn't I always put other people's needs, Ella's needs, before mine? My chest heaved, my head felt hot and feverish. Later, creeping out of bed to listen behind the door, I heard Julie say, 'You know Lilbet is more to be pitied than envied. Is it too much to ask you to be more thoughtful?'

'Why do I always have to give in?'

'We can't expect too much from Lilbet.' And picturing Julie's half frown and Ella's angry face, it was hard not to speak up and give myself away.

I snapped back to the present. Bunny was saying, '... Felix, you'll have to help me bring the other car.' The two men went off. Daisy demanded a cup of tea. Then Joe turned up with half a dozen bottles of beer and the biggest bunch of gladioli I had ever seen for us girls. Julie insisted that he try a slice of her apple cake. That man is the gentlest, nicest creature I have ever met. Why, if Ella *must* fall in love, why can't it be with Joe?

Twenty minutes later, Felix and Bunny returned with both cars. Felix and Joe packed the MG with Julie's hamper, the basket Daisy had bought from 'the *chickest* caterer in town.' Also blankets, towels, beach umbrellas and my wheelchair. Bunny said smiling, 'Julie, sure you haven't forgotten the kitchen sink?'

'Look who's talking.' Daisy poked Bunny's plump middle. He yelped and curled over. Daisy jumped into the MG and Felix started the engine. A crash of gears, and they roared down the street. The rest of us squeezed into Morris Aarons's Austin Ruby and set off after them. Crammed between Julie and Ella, what I mostly saw were treetops and telegraph poles. Half an hour later, we'd reached the fishing village of Frankston. Here, Felix took off in a cloud of dust. Soon as Bunny lost sight of his car, he worried the engine might overheat. He fretted so much, he might have ruined our day if Felix had not allowed him to catch up.

Here, I whispered to Julie that I felt squeamish and wondered if I mightn't vomit?

'Car sick!' Julie leaned forward. 'Joe, would you mind changing seats with Lilbet?'

'Stop ze car, Bunny.' We immediately swapped places,

and I decided Joe must be happy for any chance to sit beside Ella.

Now the trip was much more pleasant. At Flinders, Bunny parked at the top of a cliff overlooking the sea where we found Felix and Daisy giggling over something they refused to share, no matter how much Bunny sulked and complained.

Joe helped me out of the car. As I stared at the view in front of me, how I wished that I'd inherited Mother's artistic talent. Straight in front, a jetty dog-legged into a sea dotted with small sailing craft. The tide was out. Charcoal rocks edged into the water. Towards Cape Schank, a green promontory jutted into the ocean. Phillip Island was on the horizon, the day so green, golden and blue, it felt as if I could almost touch those trees and paddocks.

The girls carried the food hampers down a steep incline. Felix took my wheelchair, and Joe carried me onto the sand. Joe put up umbrellas and Julie spread blankets. What with Julie fussing that I was seated in the shade, that my blanket was clear of sand, and that nothing could bite me, it took ages to get settled.

Immediately, the others rushed straight into the sea. Soon we heard Daisy's shrieks as she jumped in and out of the surf. The tide was out and Felix wanted to explore the rock-shelf. But Bunny protested that he was absolutely famished. Felix opened several bottles of German *Liebfraumilch*. Everyone made a great fuss of the wine, saying how thoughtful it was of Felix to bring this along. I did too, even though it was far too sweet for me. And all the time Felix, Daisy and Bunny talked in riddles amongst themselves. I couldn't have cared less, but as I saw Ella get more and more upset, I had an overwhelming desire to hit Felix over the head with his own bottle.

Joe helped Julie pass around food and drink. But I'm not sure that he understood everything that was said because he listening gravely to everyone, no matter how stupid or trivial the conversation.

After lunch, Bunny suggested that we explore the rock-shelf.

'Per'aps Lilbet vill come?' Joe said softly.

'Only if not too much trouble,' I said, and I asked Ella if she wouldn't mind helping me remove my boots.

She was in the middle of stripping off her outer clothes to go with the others, and she turned impatiently. 'Why not later?'

I pointed to the incoming tide. So it was a pity Daisy and Felix refused to wait for Ella and chose that very moment to run down the beach. 'I say, old chaps,' Bunny called plaintively. 'Wait for us ...'

Ella stared after them, then turned on me to yell, 'Daisy's right. You never think about anyone but yourself.' She sprang to her feet and ran in the opposite direction.

I found it very hard not to cry. Julie took off my boots. I stared at my left foot. Never had the toes seemed so twisted, the scarring so evil. A few minutes later, Joe and Julie helped me to my feet, and as they supported me, the three of us explored the rocky ledge where tiny soldier crabs manage to live and breed and die, oblivious to the passion and pain we humans must endure.

Further out, the sea bubbled and foamed. When I closed my eyes, I heard the wind carry the voice of a thousand mermaids. Unbidden, these words came into my mind:

> Only Diana, moon goddess
> In her gentle passage over the earth
> Knows how our suffering legs and thighs
> Were once a fish's tail.

Julie felt sorry for Joe, what with the way Daisy poked fun at his English, Ella kept on ignoring him, and Bunny was uncomfortably attentive. I have noticed how she makes a special point of discussing ways and means of improving his little business. They began a long discussion as to the pros and cons of selling shirts in the country. Julie has a good sense of profit and loss. But as I watched the way she smiled into his eyes and hung on his every word, it was a shock to realise she wasn't helping him purely out of kindness, and that there was growing affection between them.

While those two talked amongst themselves, and the others were still away, I felt quite thirsty. Rather than disturb Julie and Joe, I reached out to help myself to some cold tea.

'Lilbet, no ...' Julie went to stop me. But she was just that bit too late, and the open bottle slid out of my hand to empty itself over Daisy's white slacks.

Julie held them up. Brownish stains covered both legs. I could tell it was an effort for her not to get cross. 'Lilbet,' she managed between my apologies, 'I know it is hard for you to do certain things. But if only you could be a little more careful, or ask someone else.'

What made things worse was that Daisy's slacks were the kind of woollen fabric that refuses to rid itself of any stain

'Salt, maybe get tea out?' Joe suggested, and pointed towards the sea.

Julie rushed the slacks into the water. But apart from soaking the garment right through and making it doubly unwearable, it made little difference to the marks, that looked like someone had had an accident with tan boot-polish.

THREAT TO WOOL
1st March, 1938

Artificial fibre has made serious inroads into the sales of wool of recent years, and members of the Australian Wool Board at a meeting in Melbourne today debated the best means of combating this threat to the Australian industry ...

An hour later, Felix and Daisy reappeared. They must have been wrestling because both were covered in sand. When Daisy saw the condition of her slacks – irrevocably stained and thoroughly soaked – she was so cross, she refused to talk to the others saying they were to blame for not keeping a better eye on 'that stupid cripple' and that she was sure I'd intended to ruin her clothes.

Even though I kept assuring her that I was really very sorry, and that I certainly hadn't spilt that tea on purpose, she refused to accept my apology.

After that, no one said much and we waited another half-hour or so for Ella to return. The wind turned chilly. Sand blew into our faces. A white mist like a shroud descended on Phillip Island. Seagulls rose, cawing like so many prophets of doom.

Julie sent Joe to find Ella. I could tell she was recalling other times Ella's temper has got her into scrapes. I told myself not to worry. Ella was big enough to look after herself. But the dreadful thing about being a twin is that you can never be free of the other. A little later they returned, Ella red-faced and Joe looking concerned. I heard him whisper to Julie that he'd found her teetering on a dangerous cliff and had to carry her down.

Then the long trip home. Before we left, Ella was so sunburned Julie had to smother her in butter to soothe her shoulders and legs. But we had nothing with which to soothe her wounded pride.

On the way home, no one said very much and I don't think Ella opened her mouth at all. As for Daisy ... still cross over her ruined slacks, as soon as we drove up to Adeline Terrace, she demanded that Bunny take her home immediately.

'I say, old chap,' he protested. 'Julie's promised this naughty boy a cup of tea and another slice of her marvellous cake.'

'You've had quite enough to eat already,' Daisy scolded. 'I want to go right now.'

Later, over a light supper, Father said to Felix, 'What do you think of our beaches? Aren't they equal to any in Europe?'

'They're good,' Felix agreed. 'But there is nothing to do but swim, walk and lie on the sand. Where are your hotels and cafes? These beaches are too wild to be compared to the French and Italian Rivieras.'

'Too wild?' Father looked puzzled. 'We don't want you chaps building dance palaces on the sand. We've room for those elsewhere.'

'Far too out of control,' Felix insisted, his gaze on Ella. I doubt that he and Father were talking about the same thing at all.

34

Spent most of this afternoon in the park rereading *Madame Bovary*. The similarities between Flaubert's Emma and my sister Ella are almost breathtaking. Both so needy for a romantic adventure. And both so heedless of where their impulses will lead them. What will happen to Ella if she is not a little more cautious? I think Father would kill her if he knew that she had fallen in love with Felix, who is after all married and his close friend. Isn't it my duty to warn Julie? But what will happen if I do? Will Julie listen? She can never believe ill of anyone, certainly not someone who is Father's guest.

My thoughts lead me nowhere and after a while I concentrated on my surroundings. Though the day was hot and dry, the roses were blooming very prettily, and the plane trees were giving splendid shade. Several old gentlemen wandered past deep in conversation. A lady rushed by leading a frisky young poodle, or rather the poodle leading her. Then two mothers pushing prams. They stopped long enough for me to clamber off my seat and come up to admire their babies.

The first was still quite young, fast asleep and very sweet. The other child must have been about ten, curled into the fetal position and sucking her thumb as she gazed vacantly about. 'Poor little thing,' I said to the mother. 'Does she talk?'

The mother – she was well into middle age – shook her head. Given my own afflictions, I thought it permissible to question her more closely. 'Will she stay with you?'

The mother sighed and nodded before she set off further down the path. As I watched them disappear around the corner, I wondered if I might not have been better off to be that young girl who was too brain damaged to know what was happening to her. In their case, it was more the mother than the child to be pitied.

Is this how outsiders see our little family? Do they feel sorry for Father and Julie and Ella because they must put up with me? The notion sent such a horrid shiver down my back, I tried very hard to concentrate on my surroundings. Observing nature reminded me of Ella, who is so keen on the naturalist, Crosbie Morrison, that she would never miss his weekly program on the wireless. She has also bought the first copy of *WildLife*, a magazine devoting itself to natural science which strongly advocates preserving some of our natural wonders as national parks.

Reminders of Ella led me back to Felix. Surely there must be some way to rid Adeline Terrace of his presence without appearing to be responsible. What if I was to hide some of Mother's silver in his drawers? If my handwriting was not so recognizable, I could post an anonymous letter to Father's office accusing Felix of some terrible crime. Or I could cut letters out of the newspaper to make up certain words. What might he be guilty of?

As I hurried??? home, I thought back to when Julie had suggested that I write a crime story in the style of Agatha Christie. In some ways, mightn't this be an even more satis-fying creation. But even if my reasons were exemplary, to go forward with this plan would take courage on my part. At present I wasn't quite sure that I had enough.

35

> **TEAHOUSES AMONGST THE HILLS**
> **6th. March. 1938**
> Dotted amongst the hills many little hives of summer industry in the shape of tea houses have sprung into being since the hot weather was last with us. And be they the humble wooden cottage with its neat little garden or more majestic structures of brick, they appear to be thriving with the exodus from the city …

Bunny enjoyed that trip to Flinders so much, yesterday he dropped in with an offer to do it again. 'Tomorrow,' he said to Julie over a cup of tea and a large slice of almond and apple cake. 'Any place you choose.'

Julie thought awhile, then suggested that this time we visit a farm. 'Eggs,' she said, ladling another slice of cake onto Bunny's plate. 'Much cheaper that way. Also a couple of roasting chooks.'

Bunny forked cake into his mouth. 'How about lunch?'

Even Julie, ever tolerant of Bunny's passion for food, had to laugh. 'Of course I'll bring lunch.'

I waited until he'd left to ask, 'Will Father come?'

She shook her head. 'With Bunny? Not likely.'

'So who will be with us?'

'Why, except for Joe who must work, the same as before.'

But at the last minute, it turned out that Felix wouldn't be coming. Nor would Daisy. 'Both have previous arrangements,' Bunny informed Julie. 'So we can't borrow the Ruby Austin. But the rest of us will fit into the MG.'

Just then Ella came into the room, so withdrawn and pale I nearly wept for her. No one should be that unhappy. Then to Julie's open dismay, after mentioning that neither Felix nor Daisy would be coming, she burst into tears and fled towards our room.

'Never mind,' said Julie who always puts a brave front on everything. I swear that if another war broke out she would see it as an excellent opportunity for us to band together. 'Means there'll be more space in Bunny's car.'

Bunny helped me into the passenger seat and Julie climbed into the tiny dicky seat in the rear. The roof down, we tore off in a cloud of smoke and dust.

The day was overcast, but as there was hardly any wind the drive was pleasant. It wasn't long before we left the suburbs. Now the road meandered through open paddocks dotted with small timber and iron roofed cottages. Bunny called over his shoulder, 'Julie, where shall we stop?'

'The first sign that says Eggs For Sale,' she yelled back.

Half a mile further we came to such a sign and Bunny drove off the main road onto a dirt track over a hill. A rough fence protected the farmhouse. Inside hens scratched up the dust, and I saw the remains of a rusty plough and an old horse trap.

Bunny beeped the horn, and a woman in a flowered apron emerged from the house. Bunny helped Julie out of the car, and the women spoke at some length while I sniffed the air that smelt of chicken droppings and dust. Finally Julie came back to tell us that the woman would sell her four dozen eggs and several chooks which she had offered to pluck and dress. While all this was being prepared, we would eat lunch at a shady spot by the river.

By now the clouds had disappeared and the sun was starting to burn. Bunny drove further down the track and parked in the shade under a river gum. Then he and Julie helped me out of the car, and I limped towards the river. Julie spread a blanket under a clump of willows where we could watch the sunlight dance over the water and glimpse small fish darting in the shallows.

As usual Julie had packed too much food. But as Bunny loves anything Julie cooks, he managed to consume it all. Since he and I have shared the secret of our meeting at St. Kilda beach, we are even better friends than before. I do enjoy his company, even though he will never talk about anything serious. Instead he spends his time telling jokes. Some I don't understand, though I never let on. He is always so cheerful I sometimes wonder what it would be like to have someone like him living with us rather than Father or Felix.

When we finished our lunch Julie repacked the hamper, then said brightly. 'Now Lilbet, you have not done your daily exercise. How about we take a stroll along the river-bank?'

'Not today,' I protested, rubbing my left leg. 'I'm much too sore.'

Her lovely forehead crinkled. 'But what's the point of coming to the country if we don't walk? After sitting in the car, I need to stretch my legs.'

'I'll stay with Lilbet,' Bunny hastily offered.

She smiled guiltily at him, then glanced at me. 'Sure you'll be alright?'

'What harm can I come to with Bunny looking after me?' I pointed out.

I waited for her to disappear behind some willows before saying, 'Bunny ... that time we met at St. Kilda beach ... who was that young man?'

He sat up abruptly. 'I thought we had an agreement ... Who have you told?'

'Why should I tell anyone? As you say, we had an agreement, and I have kept to it.'

He studied my face. 'Truly?'

'Truly. I'm not a child.'

He thought this over. 'Even though they treat you like one?'

I shrugged and nodded.

He chewed his lip. 'Rather annoying, what?'

'Rather annoying,' I pleasantly agreed, because what was the point of complaining.

'Can't you get them to stop?'

'How?' I demanded. 'Do you have any idea how?' As he had no answer, I felt I needed to offer one. 'They mean it for the best. Perhaps if I wasn't so crippled. So ...' I took a deep breath, 'That young man I saw you with?'

'A friend.' He sighed. 'Just a friend. But you have no idea Lilbet, how tenuous some friendships can be.'

'Tenuous,' I repeated. 'Does that mean he is no longer your friend?'

Rather than answering, he said, 'Did I tell you that I ran into Felix at *Rocco's* the other night?'

'Oh?' I said. 'Are you good friends with him, too?'

He tapped his teeth in thought. 'The chap's a bit of a question mark, isn't he?'

'Certainly is.' I used my driest tones.

'Still ... let's hope his business skills are above board, eh? We've all got quite a bit of money invested.'

'Was he at *Rocco's* alone.'

'No. Thought you knew. He was with Daisy. He's been squiring her round quite a bit.'

'Really? Daisy? I didn't know they were so close.'

'Chappie has a way with women, what?' And with this he lay back on the grass, and closed his eyes. Now several things – Felix and Daisy not coming with us today, Ella being so upset – came together. My mind was going nineteen to the dozen. Julie came back a minute later, and that closed my conversation with Bunny. Of course I couldn't mention these thoughts to Julie and Bunny, and on the drive home, both commented on how distant I seemed. To my annoyance Julie questioned aloud whether the whole trip had been too much, even suggesting that perhaps I shouldn't do it again.

When we got back to Adeline Terrace, I remembered to carefully thank Bunny for a delightful outing. He quickly promised to invite us to another one, and very soon. But who knows if this will eventuate. The news from Europe grows worse and worse ...

FOREIGN SECRETARY RESIGNS FROM
BRITISH CABINET:
21st February, 1938

Mr. Anthony Eden, the British Foreign Secretary, resigned tonight. The cause was a serious disagreement with the Prime Minister (Mr. Chamberlain) on the fundamental issue of negotiating with dictatorship countries ...

36

Two recent events deserve a mention. The first is that we now own a telephone. This luxury we owe to Felix. 'Simon, what if a client needs to contact you?' he cried, his fiery hair catching the light from our kitchen window, 'What if there's an emergency?'

Father scowled at the floor. 'I'm an accountant. I try very hard to avoid emergencies.'

'I cannot believe you're so old fashioned,' Felix persisted. 'How will I know if I have employment if a firm cannot call me immediately?'

All evening Father wouldn't stop muttering about extravagance and unnecessary expense. But early morning yesterday, two technicians arrived with a wooden phone and a black metal hand-piece. They drilled holes in the hall wall spreading dust and plaster everywhere. Mid-morning Julie called them into the kitchen for a cup of tea and a scone. As we're always curious about the world outside Adeline Terrace, she asked the elder, 'How long have you been putting in phones?'

'Twelve years. Only not during the Depression. Then folks could 'ardly afford 'em.'

'You were out of work all that time?'

'I were kept on six month doin' repairs. Then got laid off.'

Julie listened gravely. 'Do you have a family?'

'Too right!' He helped himself to another scone. 'Wife and three boys. '

'How did you manage?'

'We'd a bit saved up. That lasted till the wife was expectin' again, an' we 'ad to pay the old witch down the street to get rid of it ...' He reddened and changed the subject. 'We moved eleven times in two years to beat the landlords. Afters, we went up country.'

'I expect things were easier there.'

'Too right.' His grin revealed gaps instead of teeth. 'We ate lotsa underground roo.'

'Underground roo?'

'Rabbit.'

Everyone laughed.

'You was lucky to stay together,' his mate broke in. Light blue eyes, straw-coloured hair, lantern chin, quite nice looking, I thought he could be no more than twenty. 'My old man skipped home, and we ain't sighted him since.'

'How dreadful!' Ella exclaimed. Though I often talk to her about the disastrous effects of the Depression and how many people are still suffering the after effects, she needs real people to relate this to. 'How did your mother manage?'

He shook his head. 'Too many of us to feed. First she pawned the furniture. Me and me older brother Dick, we joined the Balaclava gang so's we could fill our bellies, but we was gettin' in more trouble 'n Ned Kelly, so Mum kept the littlest two, an' sent us to the orphanage.'

Not that the situation in 1938 is all that much better. The newspapers claim that only another war can provide full employment. Even more frightening is a 'Bulletin' editorial that argues that the Depression was all a Jewish conspiracy to take over the financial world. As a result only five hundred Jewish refugees have been allowed into this country.

Not that everyone is so openly anti-semitic:

JEW'S BLOOD FOR SCOT
30th March, 1938

Mr. John Adler had a bandage around his arm as he worked at his trade as a furrier in Capital House today. And a Scottish digger at Caulfield Military Hospital was feeling much better with a pint of new blood in his veins ...

However, when I asked Felix how he'd managed to gain an entry visa, all he said was, 'I'm here, aren't I?' Nor is Bunny interested in politics. While we were picnicking at the farm, he mentioned how some of his friends have joined the Socialist party. When I asked if he would do the same, he told me Karl Marx was an atheist. Then added, 'I'm in enough trouble already. What if I'm accused of not believing in God?'

'Do you?'

His gaze flickered away. 'Do I what?'

'Think there's a God?'

As Bunny never has too many thoughts, much less religious ones, he just laughed.

Soon as our new 'Magneto' telephone was installed, the older technician used it to talk to his head office. Julie was in the kitchen. She whispered to Ella to keep an eye on things in the hall and for once, after warning me not to drop the knives on my toes and hurt myself, she allowed me to dry the cutlery. Meanwhile the younger – his name was Bert – couldn't take his eyes off Ella and I heard him invite her out.

'No thank you,' Ella said politely. 'I wouldn't be allowed.'

'You married or summit?'

'I just can't. Thank you all the same.'

'Your bloke won't let you, huh?' And when she didn't answer, 'You girls're all the same. I'm just not rich enough for the likes of you.'

'Not at all,' Ella said hotly, 'I'm just not allowed.'

I walked into the passage. Ella's cheeks were scarlet. This was so different from her usual cool detachment, I assume this is because of other things in her life. Bert was flushed too. Only he was red with anger. Yet Ella was only telling the truth. Father would never allow her to go out with someone who works with his hands. Or someone who isn't Jewish.

Before Bert left, he rang someone called Olive and spent a long time talking to her, arranging to meet her after work. So it was almost lunch-time before we could test our new telephone. I wanted Ella to call Bunny to thank him for driving us to Flinders and the country. But Julie said firmly, 'Call Father first. After all, he will be paying the bills.'

'Let me,' Ella cried. She was dying to see how it worked.

But Julie shook her head. 'Father entrusted me with the installation.' We watched her lift the receiver and turn the handle. 'Y 693 please,' she told the operator. You could hear the ring at the other end. Finally Father's secretary answered and she went to fetch him. 'Father, this is Julie,' she said into the mouthpiece. 'I'm calling from home.'

A long silence. Julie listened, then replaced the receiver.

'What did he say?' asked Ella.

'Not much. To only use it when necessary.'

What an anti-climax. But now, each time I limp past, I am very proud to be part of this modern world.

As for the other ... Last night I woke with a terrible tummy-ache. 'Ella,' I called, for I needed her to help me onto the pot.

Ella's bed was empty. I managed to slide onto the floor. When I eventually climbed back into bed, I was shivering uncontrollably. I knew where she was. This was *his* fault. I accept that Ella is in love and therefore not responsible for her own actions. But I blame him for encouraging her. No, for nearly forcing her by clever conniving to do his will. What kind of a man accepts Father's hospitality and then sets out to seduce his daughter? And who is he anyway? He has lived with us these last two months, yet I know little more about him than the first day we met. What if he is planning to steal from us? I had noticed how often his eyes lingered on Mother's silver. What if I was to hide some of the more valuable forks and spoons in his cupboard? After all, if the longing is there, all I would be doing is acting out his fantasy and surely that is not a crime.

Then it struck me – perhaps he has been brought to Father's attention by some malevolent spirit. Perhaps he has been brought here to ruin our family before going on to his next victims. What if he had some ingenious plan to push us out of this house, and take it over for himself? What if we were just part of some devious plan, a plan designed to test our strength, a plan we cannot even begin to comprehend. I stayed awake until morning, my temperature rising, growing hotter by the minute, the air around me glimmering and shifting with wicked thoughts and intent. Only Father's voice in the kitchen complaining about his shirt-collar not being properly starched brought me to my senses.

But then there is Ella. Why don't I blame her for all this? I'd have to be deaf and blind not to understand her need to fall in love. Only two years ago when the newspapers were full of Prince Edward's abdication, I remember her saying that under the same circumstances that she'd do likewise. Not everyone agreed. Julie thought Edward was simply shelving his responsibilities and how she laughed when I found this little rhyme in the *Argus*:

> *Hark the Herald Angels sing,*
> *Mrs. Simpson's pinched our king.*

Not that the Duke is in any way to be admired for so easily dismissing his responsibilities, and the *Argus* reports that the Americans suspect his political leanings.

NAZI LEANING ALLEGED.
4th March, 1938

The belief has been expressed in the United States that the Duke of Windsor might cancel his visit because he is displeased with the American reaction, especially the description of the tour as a 'slumming party'. The *New York Post* has an eight column streamer heading on the front page "Pro-Nazis Guide Duke's tour," and alleges that the Duke is under fascist influence. It also adds that "A little Baltimore girl's ambition to swank about in her home country is mainly to blame for the visit's circus aura ...."

All that day I thought how this business with Felix would never have happened if Mother were still alive. After my restless night, the whole day passed as in a dream and later that night when everyone was in bed, though I slept very well, my sleep was filled with nightmares. I pictured the beautiful young woman in her wedding portrait seated beside me. Kneeling on the floor, I placed my head against her knee and knew a moment of true contentment. Then she led me to the chook house where the handsome rooster was straddling one of the hens. Whatever he was doing to her must have hurt, because the hen clucked loudly and tried to throw him off ...

A cry from the next room woke me. I glanced at Ella's bed – once again empty – then went back to sleep. Next I was in an operating theatre, and a doctor was cutting into my bad leg. I opened my mouth to scream. Felix removed his mask and slowly smiled at me.

I started up. Daylight was seeping through the curtains. Ella was back in her bed. During breakfast I stared accusingly at Felix, but all he did was continue eating his scrambled eggs on toast as if nothing had happened.

Ella has always shown too much interest in *that* side of life. Soon as we were old enough to travel around Melbourne by ourselves, I remember how under the excuse of looking for unusual fabrics, she took me to the unsavory parts of Collingwood. I remember how sorry I felt for those women, how openly they stared, how we pretended to mind our own business. I very much wanted to stop and ask them to explain what they actually *did*, but of course this was impossible. As we scurried away, one girl yelled at Ella, 'Ask 'er where 'er boyfriend goes at night'

In that act which occurs between a married couple, Ella and myself have been equally ignorant. Once dusting Father's study, Ella found a volume of 'Grey's Anatomy'. Though we studied the appendage between the male's legs, the text didn't explain its use.

Ella said, 'Polly Partridge ...' Polly was her particular friend at Cambridge College, 'says the man puts it inside the woman.'

I shivered. 'Wonder what that feels like?'

Ella returned the book to its shelf. 'Polly says it's rather nice.'

I shook my head. Hard picturing Father doing this to Mother. I can't imagine her actually enjoying it. Julie is equally useless. Only yesterday I heard her mention how Mrs. Maloney down the road is expecting again. As this will make this child their ninth, Julie said tartly, 'I know they're good Catholics, but surely it's time he took some precautions.'

'How would Mr. Moloney do that?' I asked.

Julie was peeling an onion. She concentrated on what she was doing. 'Lilbet. Have you taken your tonic today?'

I suspect that she knows as little as myself. Last week the *Age* reported that 'The police have taken a man in Richmond into custody for performing illegal operations.' All Julie could say was, 'That butcher is responsible for the death of three young women. He should be put in gaol and the key thrown away.'

'What do you mean?'

'Oh Lilbet,' she said sighing. 'Thank God you'll never have to cope with that kind of problem.'

'You mean I'll never have an unwanted child?'

She looked shocked. 'What do you know about these things?'

'Nothing. That's the whole trouble ...'

'So be grateful for small mercies,' she said tersely, and nothing I said or did would get her to say more.

37

For his twenty-fourth birthday Felix gave Julie a splendid excuse to produce a magnificent feast to which she invited Daisy and Joe. Then she insisted that Bunny receive an invite. She waved away Father's objections by saying 'He has been so kind to us. Of course he must come too.' It is so rare for her to argue with Father, for once he was left speechless.

Daisy declined as she was already committed to another dinner-party. What a relief! That girl hates me so much, she would only have made my evening miserable. But Bunny was so thrilled he turned up half an hour early sending us girls into a dither as we were in no way ready. Father was forced to offer him a sherry and make polite conversation while Ella continued setting the table and Julie busied herself in the kitchen.

I sat quietly by, watching Father attempt to find some way of entertaining his guest. Not that Bunny needs much entertaining, he is far too amusing for that. Anyway, soon as Father mentioned recent events in Europe, he flapped his hands and cried, 'Oh, I never bother this naughty old head with politics.'

Father's woolly eyebrows knotted in disapproval. 'Really?' He garrumphed a bit. 'Then what does interest you?'

Bunny opened his mouth and closed it. Fortunately Felix chose that very moment to come into the living room. Then, until Julie called us into the dining room, the time was filled by Felix telling the men about his meeting with a 'Prominent business man who assures me that the Flying Boat is the way we will travel to Europe in the future.'

Father asked, 'Do we have such planes?'

'Certainly,' Felix replied. 'My friend assures me that your overseas airline with its unusual name ...'

'... Qantas,' I quietly chipped in.

'... will soon be making these voyages,' Felix continued as I wasn't there, 'in maybe less than four days.'

LINDBERG GAPES AT 'FLYING BICYCLE'
5th. March 1938

BERLIN: Even Colonel Lindberg, the famous American air-man, gaped when a helicopter flown by Flight-Captain Hanna Reitsch, the only German woman flying captain, flew sideways at the Templehof Aerodrome today after hovering 18 inches from the ground. The previous day Captain Reitsch gave a demonstration of flying backwards in the machine which is described as a cross between a windmill and a bicycle ...

In celebration, Ella had threaded the chairs with ribbons and set the table with Mother's very best crystal and silver. Even the men 'oohed and aahed' as we walked into the dining room. After having sent Ella and myself to the markets to buy provisions, Julie surpassed even her own culinary achievements by presenting us with an Asian meal. We began with clear chicken soup containing tiny dumplings filled with spicy meat. Then fish cooked with ginger and shallots, strips of beef in black bean sauce, and chicken breasts cooked in a sweet sour mix. The dessert however, was totally European and as this was Felix's birthday, Julie served his favourite, almond and chocolate pudding with the passion-fruit and cream garnish.

Felix had never eaten Chinese food before, and he was so full of compliments, I am sure that Julie will never have to cook again, and he would still declare her the very best chef in all the world.

Bunny managed to stop eating for a moment to say, 'Chinese cuisine is almost as good as French. Felix, you ever eaten in Little Bourke Street?'

'Never.' Felix gave a little bow. 'Perhaps you will take me there?'

'Sure thing, old chap. That part of town … lots of things that might interest you.'

Both men laughed. Joe looked puzzled. Father glanced up and garrumphed disapprovingly. What was Bunny talking about? Having finished as much of the soup as I could manage, my gaze lingered on Felix's hands with their beautifully manicured half moon nails and the smooth white skin with the sprinkling of golden hairs. What would those hands feel like on my skin? I shivered and tried to concentrate on what was happening around me. Felix had been entertaining us with an account of Fashion Week in Paris. 'This is when the major couturiers host magnificent parades for the wealthy to enjoy …'

'And for them to buy,' Father tersely added. 'I'm sure they are expected to spend very freely.'

Felix smiled and continued, 'At Christian Dior, the theme was clothes to wear on your summer cruise.'

At this, Ella, who is seriously interested in fashion and an excellent home dressmaker, insisted that he describe every garment he saw in fine detail.

Felix was quick to oblige her. 'For daywear there were beautifully cut linen and silk frocks and slack suits …'

'Only loose women wear slacks,' Father growled.

Felix ignored the interruption, 'For evening, the mannequins wore silk dresses. The backs were very daring. Bare to here,' he pointed to well below his waist.

Ella frowned. 'What about necklines? Were they also low?'

He giggled. 'Some were quite naked. Those frocks left nothing to my imagination.'

Father gave his horse-laugh that displayed his large yellow teeth. Even Bunny seemed shocked. 'Bit much, what?'

'Perhaps.' Felix brushed an invisible crumb off his waistcoat. 'But only the bourgeois bother themselves with such proprieties. The end of Fashion Week, I travelled south to

Monte to stay on the Compte De Villiers' yacht. Such an assembled company, you wouldn't believe. Greta Garbo was there with Stokowski, the conductor ...'

At this Julie busy serving fish, looked up in surprise. 'You mean, Greta Garbo, the actress?'

'The one and only. Now she has given up making movies, she and Stokowski are very well known right through Europe. But only amongst what I call 'The Fast Set'.' Then he added very seriously, 'I would ask you not to repeat this as Stokowski still has a wife in America.'

Who would we repeat this to?

I piped up, 'Who else sailed with you?'

'Why, many members of the French aristocracy and some other film stars. Marlene Deitrich and Anna Neagle. Anna was in the next cabin. She mentioned to me that she intends to continue making films in Britain.'

'Tell us more,' Julie demanded.

He shrugged. 'What is there to tell? We sailed around the Mediterranean calling into Hydra in Greece, and Naples in Italy. We swam and sunbaked. A very nice time was had by all.'

'So that's all you'll tell us?' Bunny sounded unconvinced.

'Certainly there is more, but not in front of the ladies,' Felix replied. The men smiled amongst themselves and Julie went to fetch the beef.

As we sat very late over coffee and macaroons, the men with brandy balloons, I watched how the light focused on the assembled company's heads; Father's greying thatch, Joe's black frizz, Bunny's brown hair with its pale patch like a medieval monk. The women – Ella's soft curls and Julie's neat bun. Only then did I switch my gaze to Felix's fiery mop. How dull he makes us all seem. Even Bunny's constant jokes seem to pale in comparison with Felix's stories of the rich and famous.

Not that I believe him. Not one word. If anyone should be taking notes for a novel, it should be him. Everything about him except his physical presence is fiction. If only, like an unwanted character in a fairy story, I could banish him into oblivion. This latest piece I found in the *Argus* proves what a liar he is. Or does it?

GRETA GARBO IN ITALY
23rd March, 1938

The proprietor of the Hotel Belvedore at Ravello has confirmed that Miss Greta Garbo, the film actress, and Leopold Stokowski, the conductor of the Philadelphia Philharmonic Orchestra are staying at a villa nearby. He says that they keep to themselves and go for walks late in the afternoon so they will avoid meeting people ...

38

Ella behaves as if nothing unusual is happening. I'm wary of opening the subject. Who knows how she'll react? She has never been more beautiful; eyes huge and velvety, rosy cheeks, mouth a luscious strawberry, hair curling softly around her cheeks. Father scowls when he is with her, yet even *he* can't stop looking.

During the day, Ella and Felix treat each other in the same teasing way as always. A casual onlooker would suspect there is nothing between them. But there is a languor that hints at their being in love; a dreamy look in the eye, a looseness of limb, a dazed expression even in the face of being caught out. I try to imagine how they feel as they slide into each other's being and gaze at mirror images of themselves. At night, though I try my hardest to stay awake, my eyes refuse to stay open. She waits for my first snore, then creeps into his room. As the nights pass, she stays away longer and longer. Last night she didn't even wait for me to fall asleep. Could she mistake my silence for approval? And the truth is that when I consider the fine gingery hairs on the back of his hands, his olive gaze, that soft skin and pencil-thin moustache, his slim but strong body, how I envy Ella. How I want to be lying beside him, his smooth skin touching mine, our mouths joined in an endless kiss, our legs as intertwined as the stem and leaves of our passion-fruit vine.

What else does he do to her when they lie side by side? Surely it must be something to relieve that terrible longing that only when I rub *down there* until I shiver all over, do I ever gain some relief. Sometimes in the laundry when no one else is around, I smell his linen to learn more about him.

Only his expensive Cologne, and a certain musky odour. Is it his smell that so attracts Ella that she will defy everything to be with him? What do they do to each other when they are together? Sometimes when I wake in the middle of the night and her bed is empty, I lie there imagining that we have changed places, fingering my breasts and belly and running my fingers over my sides towards my thighs. How sensitive my skin becomes, how inflamed from this self-caress. Oh, why can't it be me in the bed beside him? Why does it have to be her? Surely I could love him just as much as she does.

I felt like a brittle shell lost somewhere in the bush yet surrounded by ants hurrying to feed their young, birds calling to each other, everyone occupied in a fertility dance. Only I am alone and invisible – a small mollusc lost under a shell until finally I will die and become one with the earth.

Last night listening for the slightest sound, I recalled our first years at South Melbourne Primary. What I mostly remember is Ella coming to my rescue. Day one, Aunt Amy had left us inside the gate, bags strapped to our backs, lunch-box inside. I stood in the yard, surrounded by boys pushing me with sharp cruel fingers ...

No, this must have happened some time later. We were in the playground. I remember the boys circling me. The ringleader was a boy whom everyone, including Miss Campbell our teacher, called 'Bluey'.

Bluey had ginger hair, green eyes, a thousand freckles and an angelic smile. He led a pack of boys who obeyed his every wish and command as if he was a young god.

Sometimes I thought he was a young god, the way he shinnied up trees, somersaulted across the yard, and straddled the fence like a tightrope walker. I watched him all the time. I couldn't take my gaze away. The offhand way he treated Miss Campbell stifled the breath in my throat – as if school and teachers were only to be tolerated until he was old enough to strike out on his own.

The yard was hot and dusty, the only shade to be found under the peppercorn tree. I remember Ella and some of the other girls skipping 'salt and pepper'. I was reading – I can't remember a time I couldn't read – and had settled under the tree. Suddenly a gang of boys had surrounded me. Bluey grabbed my book and yelled, 'Mum says you're a spastic, and you shouldn't be in school with us.'

'Please give me my book.'

'What you want this for, anyways? You'se only pretendin'.'

'I'm not, I really can read. Please give it back.'

He jumped on my book until the spine snapped. 'My mum says you Yids've got plenty of money.' He shoved a grubby finger at me. 'I'll give't back if you givus a penny.'

'Yeah,' another boy added. 'Givus all a penny.'

'We hates you,' Bluey coolly informed me. 'My mum says all spastics are stupid and should be put away.'

I burst into tears. It never occurred to me to say they were the stupid ones as they couldn't tell their B's from their D's, whereas I could read just about every book and paper I looked at.

Next, Ella waved her fist in his face. 'Leave her alone or I'll box your nose.'

'Yah, yah, try it,' he jeered.

She hit his face with my book. Blood spurted everywhere. Bluey screamed and ran away holding his bleeding nose. Miss Campbell made Ella stand in the corner and sent for Aunt Amy. Ella was forced to apologise. But from then on, I knew I could rely on Ella to protect me.

So why don't I return Ella's care and generosity? What is this feeling that so consumes me? Surely it can't be love. If it were love, I would do everything in my power to stop these nightly visits. If only she would come to me to talk things over. At the same time, she's so bewitched by *him*, she will surely view any comment on my part as interference.

I suppose I could approach Julie, tell her what's going on.

But she is sure to go to Father and then all hell will break loose. Knowing the way Father thinks, he will absolve Felix from any responsibility and Ella will receive the full force of his wrath. If only someone would tell me what to do. The only solution is for Sylvie to arrive in Melbourne. Why is it taking so long for her to get here?

To top everything off, today was unbearably hot. I spent most of the afternoon on the verandah. In the foliage under the steps, two fat frogs lay on top of each other. Blackbirds dug for worms to feed their young, flies crawled in pairs up the windows, and further up the street, a cat is on heat. The noise she makes is unbearable. I saw butterflies unfurl their wings in a delicate mating dance and bees dart between flowers. Even little sugar ants are on the lookout for crumbs to carry back to their nests. It's as if all nature is conspiring to exclude me.

Can something both attract and repel? Though I'm fond of Bunny, particularly since I share his little secret, even when we sit side by side, he never stops my breath nor constricts my stomach. Not like the young men I see loitering on street corners, or like those times Felix touches my arm or accidentally brushes too close. If Ella's body pulls her this same way, if he has drawn Ella into his net through her own weakness, my cause is hopeless.

I can only recall how in the past I have prevented us being separated. We were barely thirteen when Father arranged for Ella to go to a college in the country with a reputation for strictness. My planting a newspaper report '... boarding school a hotbed of unnatural vice ...' made Julie prevent Father from carrying this threat out. Even though the story was about an English college.

Another time when we were eight, Daisy Aarons invited Ella to spend the Easter break with her and her father in a rented beach cottage at Sorrento. At that time Aunt Amy and Uncle Bernard were still living with us. I said to Aunt Amy, 'Why can't I go too?'

She placed me on her knee before saying, 'You poor little dear. But they will have no one to care for you.'

'I can look after myself,' I said stoutly.

She sighed and didn't answer.

I worked myself into such a lather they sent for Dr. Williams. He stared at my mottled skin and said, 'Could be scarlet fever. Very infectious. Better not let either girl too close to other children.' So Ella had to stay home, too.

Another time, we were much older, fourteen. Polly Partridge invited Ella for the summer holidays to their property in Kyneton. 'No way,' Father growled. 'God knows what you'll get up to.'

'But Mr. and Mrs. Partridge will be there.'

'Julie needs you here to help her look after Lilbet. Your problem Ella,' he acidly added, 'is that you never think of anyone else but yourself.'

Ella came to me a little later to ask, 'Lilbet, what'll I do?'

'What if I come too? It'll mean less work for Julie.'

She shook her head. 'But you don't know Polly. Besides, you're not invited.'

'Do you have a better idea?'

Father finally agreed, and Ella was over the moon with joy. So it was a pity Polly cancelled at the last minute. Seems Mrs. Partridge didn't think she could manage two visitors plus a wheelchair.

39

WOMAN'S WORLD:
23rd March, 1938
FELICITY'S DAY AT THE SHOPS: 'Speaking of trimmings reminds me of the quaint little baskets of felt flowers I saw giving character to a dark brown afternoon dress. They were placed on each of the short sleeves and the front and back panels of the skirt, just above the hemline ...

Joe turned up tonight with a suitcase of pretty blouses. He aims to travel into the country to sell these to the farmers' wives and daughters, and has asked Julie to help him select his stock. She appears to be growing fonder and fonder of him, and is very patient with his poor English. These days she hardly ever wrinkles her forehead or thins her lips. After dinner those two spent the rest of the evening choosing colours, styles, and then toting up costs. I hope this is a success. Joe is such a fine fellow, he deserves every bit of luck he can get. Eventually Felix got bored with all this talk about blouses, and persuaded us to stand around the piano. We ended the selection with Ella's favourite *Body and Soul*.

Before Joe left, I said to him, 'I've always wanted to know ... That first time we met ... in the markets, where did you read that poem?'

He grinned hugely. 'In Cheder we read Talmud und Gemorras. At home we read oder t'ings.' His huge hand stroked my shoulder. 'No electric light, no running water, not much food, but like little Lilbet, we plenty, plenty read.

PARTY FOR AUTHORESS
27th March,1938

A delightful and original party was given for Miss Jean Campbell by Mrs F.A.Clement at her home in Malvern. The celebrations were in honour of Miss Campbell's latest book, *The Red Desert Wine ....*

40

Felix likes to reminds us that he 'attended an English Public School where I befriended many members of the aristocracy.' Though Father pretends that 'the goings on in high society' don't interest him, we girls often read the social news:

SIDELIGHTS ON SOCIETY
26th March, 1938

Introducing Mrs. Ian Mann, the daughter of Mr. and Mrs. Ernest Poolman of South Yarra. Although she has a wide circle of friends in Melbourne, Mrs. Mann has always preferred living in the country to the town. Her chief interests lie within the intimate circle of her home life – reading, music, gardening – while a 'pet passion' is her love of old furniture and china …

Only last week the entire family had been enthralled with Felix's description of visiting a castle in Devon. Tonight he elaborated on this, saying, 'My best friend, who also happened to be a duke's son and an earl in his own right, invited me to spend a weekend at his family's country seat.'

It was our usual dinner-hour. No matter how often Felix mentions to Father that 'To eat this early is appallingly bourgeois', Father still insists on dining at six-thirty.

As the late afternoon sun slanting through the window framed him in a halo of light, Felix said, 'A liveried footman in a smart trap pulled by two white horses picked me up from the station. Then I was driven through a splendid stone gateway down a drive twice as long as Grandview Street flanked by centuries old oak trees. When we reached the castle, I saw that it was so big ...' an expansive gesture demonstrated how huge this castle was, '... that it would take me all weekend to explore one wing. My friend ... I called him Tommy, though of course he has many more names ... met me on the castle steps and led me into a huge hall where several maidservants were lined up to take my luggage, show me to my room and make me comfortable ...'

By now Julie's eyes were round as golf balls. Father looked interested, and Ella, of course, hanging on every word. Just to irritate him, I played with my fork and yawned widely. I could tell it annoyed him that I refused to be impressed. The other day he said to me, 'Lilbet, your tongue is sharp enough to cut one in two. Why can't you be more like your two sisters?'

'You mean, more agreeable?' I said in my most pleasant tone.

'Yes, more agreeable. What is wrong with that?'

'But that would not be honest. Surely you regard honesty as important?'

'Of course, what do you think?' he said quickly turning away. I could tell I had him really confused, if not downright angry. Excellent, I told myself. He should know that even a 'helpless cripple' can sometimes outsmart even the most persuasive tongue.

Tonight Julie asked, 'Did you meet the duke and duchess?'

'That I did,' he replied. 'But not until tea. That meal is different from ours. They take tea at five in the conservatory.'

Julie asked, 'Don't they eat a proper dinner like us?'

Felix gave a little bow in her direction. 'A proper English breakfast at eight. Luncheon at one, and tea at five. Then a formal 'white and decorations' gathering in the dining room at ten. To this they invite their friends. Those three nights I stayed, it seemed nothing for thirty guests, each with a footman behind him or her, to sit down to a ten course dinner.'

'What did they eat?' Julie wanted to know.

'They began with several appetisers. Then soup, fish, potted pheasant, beef, duck, chicken, three desserts and a fine Stilton cheese with the brandy and port.'

Julie's mouth dropped. 'How many courses is that?'

Ella held up all her fingers.

Felix laughed. 'Between courses we were served various sorbets to flavor the appetite.'

Everyone nodded as if they knew all about this. Though I was sure that this was just another of his lying stories, I found myself asking, 'What was Tommy's family like?'

He stroked his moustache as he pondered his answer. 'Why, they were very pleasant, though perhaps a little eccentric.'

'In what way?' I demanded to know.

He coughed behind his hand before answering. 'The duke always took tea in his ancestor's full armour.'

As we tried to picture this, Father asked, 'Wasn't this a little awkward?'

'*Naturlich*. So the duke would get his duchess to lift the visor and pour the tea into his mouth through a watering can.'

I glanced at the others. So many mouths collectively open. So many silly fish gasping for air. I stifled a laugh and said, 'He can't have eaten much.'

Felix's expression didn't change. 'The duchess popped cucumber and water-cress sandwiches inside the visor.'

Julie giggled and said, 'Didn't anyone think this odd?'

Felix took the cigar Father was offering and bit off the end. This done, he said, 'I think they were used to it. The English aristocracy is so very inbred.'

'Did they do anything else extraordinary?' she asked.

'Off course. But it would not be fair to repeat it. I promised Tommy that my mouth would be forever shut.' And with this, and to my family's immense disappointment, he rose from the table saying that he had an appointment that he didn't dare miss as it might affect his entire future.

Even Father seemed astonished at this abrupt dismissal, though he didn't comment. We all wondered, what appointment at that late hour could involve a career. Then I overheard Father telling Julie that he remembered Felix saying that he had finally, finally managed to organise a meeting with an important Member of Parliament.

Julie's eyes widened. 'Who could that be?'

Father garrumphed in the way he has when he is unsure of what to say next. 'I did press him for more details, but he refused to divulge until he had something more concrete to relate. I'm sure we'll hear very soon.'

Though it is not in Father's character to question a fellow gentleman's veracity, I wonder if this mightn't be a mistake.

41

Last night I dreamt Ella and I were no more than ten or eleven and walking along a country lane with Aunt Amy and Uncle Bernard. Ella pointed to a blackberry bush. I don't know what made me wriggle inside – hadn't Aunt Amy always warned us to watch out for thorns? Next, I'd stepped into a bull-ant nest and the horrid things were running up my legs. I screamed and screamed, trying to brush them away.

I woke to next-door's dog barking loudly. A door creaked open. Someone called, 'Be quiet, Bruno,' and the dog whimpered and fell silent.

Almost immediately I fell back into a dream. Now I was strolling through a paddock. The sun blazed, burrs clung to my skirt and scratched my legs. I walked and walked until I came to a river shaded with cool, green willows. Dragonflies danced in the sunlight and small fish darted in the shallows. I took off my shoes – in this dream both my legs were perfect – and stepped into the clear cool water. But as I waded, the current turned scarlet. Suddenly I realised I was moving through blood, and that this blood was flowing from my own body ...

I woke and had to remind myself these were only dreams. A familiar throb told me that my monthlies had begun. Rather than disturb Ella, I waited for the dressing table and wardrobe to emerge from the shadows and the morning to begin. Meanwhile the magpies and wattle-birds outside our window sang so loudly, it was as if all God's creatures were performing for me.

Soon the sky clouded over and the singing ceased. I watched

the rain drip down the window and tried to make sense of my dreams. I remember Aunt Amy saying that to dream about blood is a bad omen. Right then, Ella sat up in bed and cried, 'Good morning, Lilbet.'

One might expect her to look jaded. Yet her eyes sparkled, her cheeks wore a healthy flush, her mouth was a tender rose. These days she parts her hair on one side. Soft curls frame her face. If anything, she is more beautiful than ever. Her whole bearing cries out that she is in love. During the day, though they pretend to ignore each other, she will find any excuse to be with him. When they think no one is watching, they reach out to touch each other. The family notices nothing. They are like silly starlings so absorbed in their own comings and goings, they forget to watch out for schoolboys who have come steal their eggs. It's as if I'm living with an African tribe speaking an alien language. The whole thing is making me quite ill.

Yet when it comes to yours truly, they never let up. At breakfast, Father saw me push my toast away and signalled to Julie. Instantly alert, she waited for the others to leave before saying, 'What's wrong, Lilbet? Aren't you well?'

'It's my time of the month.'

'Father worries too much about you,' she said reprovingly. 'Why must you always give him cause for concern?'

'If Father worries so much,' my tone was bitter, 'why does he never talk to me?'

She looked mildly shocked, as she does at any open criticism of Father. 'You don't understand how private he is. He could no more reveal his thoughts than fly to the moon. But sometimes to me, he'll let something slip.'

'He shows Ella plenty of love and concern,' I said sourly.

She puckered her lips. 'Inside, he worries terribly about both of you. He just doesn't know how to display it. It's as if losing Mother has removed his ability to show emotion.'

If this was really so, and Julie not just being kind, this put Father's behaviour into a different perspective. To have loved Mother so intensely made me wonder if Ella hasn't inherited her passionate nature from him? If so, this doesn't bode well for her future. And as Felix is still resident in Adeline Terrace, I'm convinced that sooner or later this situation must explode. Then I would prefer to be anywhere else but here.

But his stories of the rich and famous never cease. Last night he told us about a ball in Paris attended by the Russian Royals. How splendid they all were. 'Her Most Royal Highness wore a gown so covered in precious stones, the light glinting off the diamonds brought tears to my eyes.'

'Really?' Father's eyebrows shot up. 'Thought the Tsar and his family had all been murdered back in 1917.'

Felix looked annoyed. Then he recovered himself. 'Did I say this was the Tsarina?' He shook his head. 'I merely said a *member* of the Russian nobility.'

PRESSURE BY RUSSIANS
4th March, 1938

Russian airmen are believed to have had a part in the resignation of Madame Chiang Kai-Shek from the leadership of the Chinese airforce. Madame Chiang (who is the wife of Generalissimo Chiang Kai-Shek) will be succeeded by her brother, Mr.T.V. Soong. It is said that that the Russian airmen rebelled against taking orders from Madame Chiang. Also, that all foreign airmen fighting for China must wear a white linen badge which bears the flag of the National government ....

42

This morning, shortly after Father and Felix left, the telephone rang. I answered it. 'That you, Lilbet?' Daisy cried. 'Could I speak to Felix?'

'He's not home.'

'Oh! Tell him to call me soon as he gets in.'

'Certainly,' I said tartly. 'Any other messages?'

'No, that's all.' She rang off. But Daisy hardly ever understands my sarcasm.

Later, when I did happen to mention that Daisy rang, Ella said, 'Why didn't you call me to the phone?'

'She only asked for Felix.'

Ella's perfect forehead creased. 'Why did she call?'

'She didn't say.'

'Perhaps she's found him a job.' As she smiled at me in such a guileless way, I knew she was lying. But why lie about a thing like that?

Things continue with one exception ... Felix has started leaving the house straight after dinner. He hardly ever gets home until dawn. I expected Ella to get upset, but she tolerates his absences. Though her body floats around the house, her thoughts are elsewhere. She erases me like dust on a desk, or chalk from a blackboard.

Though Julie rarely loses her temper, she is becoming increasingly irritated with Ella. Yesterday my twin forgot to bring in the washing and broke three plates. When Julie warned her to be more careful, she laughed and carolled 'You won't always have to worry about three silly plates.'

What can this mean? Surely he's not planning to take her away. If he does, what will he do with Sylvie when she arrives? Surely he couldn't contemplate divorce. Then Ella would be named as a correspondent. Surely he knows that divorce would not only separate him from his wife but also from his friends. Though I smuggled a glass into our room and held it to the wall in an attempt to listen to what they say, they either speak too softly, or the walls of this house are too thick. I am very downhearted. We are two stationary shadows who can never meet. Or two icebergs floating side by side where one third is visible and two thirds hide our real longings. But where Ella's berg is crowded with seals and penguins, albatross and gulls, mine is windswept and barren.

Amongst Father's books is an anthology of Victorian poetry which once belonged to Mother. Yesterday I came across a poem by Christina Rossetti that explains how I feel:

> *Now all the cherished secrets of my heart,*
> *Now all my hidden hopes are turned to sin,*
> *Part of my life is dead, part sick, and part*
> *Is all on fire within.*

Nor does it help my mood that the news from overseas is equally gloomy.

NAZIS READY IN AUSTRIA
2nd March, 1938

Vienna: Thousands of Nazis are ready in Upper Austria and Carinthia to make demonstrations against the Chancellor, Dr. Schuschnigg. The police have been strengthened and they will take immediate action if trouble threatens …

I clipped this from the *Argus* only last week. But how quickly things can change. Two days ago, there was a failed attempt to keep the Naxis out of power in Austria. Hitler's troops entered, and the next day the country was declared part of the German Reich Auschluss. What can happen in Europe now?

This morning there was another envelope from Suisse, the sender Goldfarb, S. Exactly the same address, but the date too smudged to read. What's more, the phone is running hot. All the calls are for *him*. Sometimes I pick up the receiver. Very often Daisy is on the other end. Sometimes it's Bunny who always chats a while before he asks to speak to Felix. But lately, the calls are from strangers. All men. No names. One rang long distance from Adelaide. Though I hung around to hear who it was, all I got was 'Hang on, old chap. Haven't I promised to send it in the very next post?'

Silence. Then the click of a receiver being replaced.

Another silence. Felix stared absentmindedly at the wall. No one else was around. I stood behind him so he couldn't escape. 'Felix.' I cleared my throat. 'Felix, I need to talk to you.'

He spun around. 'Oh, Lilbet.' He seemed relieved to see me. 'I didn't hear you come up. What were you saying?'

'I … er … wanted to talk to you about Ella.'

'About Ella?' His smile broadened. 'What do you want to say about Ella, little sister?'

What did I want to say? He was so handsome, his ginger hair so fiery in the half-light, his very presence so exciting, my resolve faltered. 'It's just that I worry about her ...'

Before I could say more, Felix drew me close enough to study each hair of that little moustache, and look deep into those olive eyes. For a moment I marvelled how we were almost the same height. Then he leaned over as if to kiss me. Dear God, all I can say was that I must have gone completely mad. My body afire, before I knew what I was doing my arms reached out to hold him.

Before anything could happen, he stepped back and laughed. 'You see how it is, little Lilbet? None of us are free from certain longings.' And he turned on his heel and left.

Now I know that we are sworn enemies. I will never forgive him. Never. Not for anything. How quickly my love has turned to hate.

Last night I was walking along the shore, my bare feet stumbling over pebbles and coarse sand. As I looked towards the horizon, I saw a white crested wave rolling towards me.

Instead of ebbing at the shore, it defied nature by rising higher and higher. I waited, unable to move as it rose and engulfed me, filling my mouth with water and flowing into my throat and lungs until I could no longer breathe.

It was then I woke in a cold sweat. It took me a long moment to realise that this was yet another dream.

What could all these dreams mean?

What adds to my discomfort is that last night when Ella and I were taking our nightly bath, a shadow passed by the window. 'Ella, someone's out there.'

She leaned over me to shift the curtain. 'Only Father.'

I sank further under the water. 'Why does he keep watching us?'

She continued drying herself. 'What make you think he's watching us?'

'Why otherwise would he be looking through the window?'

'Oh Lilbet, you see shadows everywhere,' she said impatiently. 'You know Father stays outside to smoke his cigar when it's hot. Anyway ...' she swiveled her hips in a mock Charleston, 'Don't you know how men like to stare at women's bodies? That's why they go to the Old Tiv.'

'You mean, like Judy Moloney?'

'What a child you are, Lilbet. Of course just like Judy.'

Though the temperature in this room was close to steaming, I suddenly felt cold. If Father was spying on us *that way*, no matter what Ella says, it just didn't feel right.

43

> **DANCING AND DANCE BANDS**
> **18th March, 1938**
> At the Kingsford school:
> Private tuition daily. Single lesson: 5/-. Five lessons: 21/-.
> Teachers dance with all pupils. Refreshments provided at all classes ...

Two days ago Morris Aarons caught a train to Ballarat to complete some urgent business for Aarons and Marks. Yesterday morning Daisy phoned to invite Ella and Felix to dine with her. Not that I expected an invitation knowing how much Daisy despises me, but not a mention of Julie, though Julie is really Daisy's friend.

I waited for Ella to leave the room before asking, 'How come Daisy didn't invite you?'

Julie was kneading pastry for tonight's dinner. 'Oh,' her mind on her task, 'she knows that I must look after Father and how I hate to say no.'

Julie has an excuse for everybody, no matter how evil. I think she would even excuse Genghis Khan for his murderous habits. So much kindness can be infuriating. How I want to shake and shake her until she sees the world for the low conniving place it really is.

Anyway, as there are so few trams at night, Ella and Felix set off before sunset and didn't get back until after midnight. I stayed up in bed reading until well after ten, and still they weren't home. This morning I followed Ella into the laundry and started to quiz her: 'What did you eat?'

She looked up from brushing black polish into my left boot. 'Fish and chips.'

'I thought the Aarons employ a cook. Is that all she can make?'

'Oh,' she said airily, 'It was cook's day off. So Daisy took us to a little café on the Esplanade. We then went onto the Palais.'

My jaw dropped. 'Felix was happy to go?'

'Why wouldn't he be?' She spat into the polish to make it go further. 'You know how interested he is in visiting the demi-monde.'

The Palais de Dance at St. Kilda. Another place forbidden to 'Yours Truly'. A knife-pang ran through me. 'If Father knew,' I remarked. 'He would never approve of you going to a dance hall.' Then curiosity overcame even envy. 'What was it like? Who was there? What music did they play? How much did you dance?'

She giggled. 'I danced all night. I barely managed to sit down.'

The laundry chair has rickety legs. Very carefully I settled myself on it. 'Two women to one man? Surely not.'

'Why ever not?' She inspected her work, then picked up my other boot.

I felt myself grow hot. Why did I have to drag everything out of her? How I hated this nonchalance. I could imagine my hands grasping her neck and squeezing so hard her eyes bulged and her cheeks turned purple, so she would finally tell me what I wanted to know.

She said, 'We danced all night. You know how Bunny loves to dance.'

My eyes widened. 'Bunny? Bunny was there? You didn't say. What dances did you do?'

'Fox-trot, tango, Pride of Erin, and we finished the evening with a waltz. There was a competition for who could Charleston the longest ...'

'Thought Charlestons were old hat.'

She studied my old boot. 'Bob Gibson's band didn't seem to think so. Mickey and Mascot Powell performed for us.'

'Lucky you,' I managed, having long wished to watch these well-known ballroom-dancers. The *Sun* often describes their act, so I know it is performed on a gleaming floor bordered by illuminated glass bricks, his black tails flying and her sequins flashing in the light. I asked, 'What does the Palais look like?'

'Very big, and for the final waltz, they dimmed the chandeliers.' She smiled a cat smile to herself. 'It was very romantic.'

'Was the floor crowded?'

'Crowded? Very.' Another cat smile. How I hated her for it.

'Tell me more,' I begged. 'What did you do after? Did you catch a tram home?'

'Oh Lilbet, nothing is ever enough for you.' She stretched and yawned. 'You always want to know everything. We had a good night. What else can I tell you?' With this she handed me my boots, now all spotless and shiny. Then she slid the polish and brushes into their drawer, and turned to leave.

I gritted my teeth. How unfair she is. She knows how trapped I feel, how I need her to be both my ears and eyes. Once she wouldn't have thought twice about telling me everything. Once we would have reflected, questioned, laughed and cried together. But since Felix has come to Adeline Terrace, everything is changed. He has turned her into a total stranger. How I loathe him for what he is doing to our safe little world. How I long for revenge.

I limped after her saying, 'You know Father would never approve of you frequenting dance-halls.'

She paused in mid-step. 'Father need never know. Not unless someone tells him.'

The warning was perfectly clear. I replied, cool as anything, 'Now why would anyone do that?'

44

After that business with the Palais, it came to me that I now had *carte blanche* to handle my affairs as best I could. Not that I *wanted* to blame Ella for being thoughtless and conniving. No, the real culprit was Felix. And this meant that I must find some way to rid us of his presence before something irrevocable happened.

Never before had I felt quite so helpless in the face of looming disaster – if not for the entire family, than certainly for myself. What good could come of this romance? And more importantly, what could I do to stop it?

I was so angry and frustrated, in the end I resorted to what others might see as childish actions. I spat into his glass of water, and hid two slugs in his luncheon salad sandwich. When I found a shard of broken glass in the street I waited for his splendid Italian shoes to appear in the laundry for their regular brushing and slid the shard into a toe. However my timing was out, and it was Ella who cut her finger when she went to clean our shoes. Julie tut-tutted loudly as she bandaged Ella's finger. 'How could this have happened?'

No one had any answer. Though Ella glanced at me, I met her gaze with total composure.

It was more than difficult. Anything I could manage must look as if it had nothing to do with me. Or like the business with the shoe, as pure accident. Once or twice I caught Felix watching me oddly, as if he suspected that my bland face and pleasant manner hid something more unpalatable. But I was careful to ensure that there was nothing he could accuse me of, except perhaps a failure to be as enchanted with him as the rest of my family. At the same time, there was something so toe-curlingly seductive about him, something that made me want to ask him to wrap his arms around me and carry me into his room, and there do whatever he did to Ella, that churned my stomach and made me feverish. But like a spider lurking in a dark place, I knew to bide my time and wait for an opportunity to prove to everyone what stuff he was really made of.

Things went on like this for the next three days. Then Friday evening he came home late to report that there was a concert at the Melbourne Town Hall the following night that we Marks simply must attend. 'Bach and Beethoven,' he said waving tickets in our faces. 'You can't possibly miss such splendid German composers.'

He was quick to add that those tickets had been expensive. Though I couldn't hide a smile, he pretended not to notice. I suppose he thought that he could hardly leave me out. What he didn't realise was that I was smiling at what I saw as his blind spot for anything German. I wonder if he ever remembers that his splendid home country has also managed to confiscate his family's property, lose his family and finally expel him?

'Not me,' said Father. 'I've an appointment I can't break.' Felix managed to look disappointed. 'Your presence will be sorely missed.'

Ten minutes later Julie also changed her mind about going. 'Too much to do,' she said regretfully. 'Maybe if I'd known a little earlier …'

Felix coughed apologetically behind his hand. 'Next time, I promise, I will give more notice.'

'What about those tickets? Can you return them?'

'Of course,' he cried, though that left only Ella and myself. 'We will go earlier and return them.'

I could barely contain myself. I even told myself that if Felix included me in *some* of his activities, then I could almost forgive him *some* of his sins, that I could stop trying to get rid of him. But my life is such that I never rely on my body not letting me down. So much excitement resulted in a sick headache, and this quickly developed into a raging migraine. Praying no one would notice, I limped into the outhouse where I threw up everything I'd eaten that day.

One look at my pale face, and Julie ordered me straight to bed.

I could tell Felix was furious, and that he didn't quite believe me. But he hid his temper, and said to Father, 'Now Simon, what do I do with these tickets?'

Father looked uncertain. Then even he had to agree that it was a shame to waste all five. So with his permission Ella and Felix set off to that concert together, Ella in her new 'waltz' frock of parchment taffeta with its full skirt and fitting bodice. She wore this with a matching cocktail hat, and no one meeting her would have guessed that her outfit hadn't come from an expensive Collins Street couturier.

Though I tried staying awake until they came home, I fell asleep shortly after eleven and still they weren't here. Over breakfast next morning, Father commented on how late they'd been. Felix raised a gingery eyebrow. 'But Simon, they did Beethoven's Ninth with a full orchestra, soloists and choir. You know how long that symphony is.'

Rather than admit his ignorance on musical matters, Father hastily agreed.

I waited for everyone to leave the kitchen and Ella to start the breakfast dishes before saying, 'Did you enjoy the Bach? Didn't you find the Beethoven too serious?'

Ella glanced over her shoulder and giggled. 'Felix will be so mad if I tell you ... But they don't play Bach or Beethoven at the old Tiv in Bourke Street.'

I chewed my lower lip. 'So all five tickets went back. I suppose you enjoyed seeing more of the demi-monde?' My voice dripped gall.

Ella pretended to ignore it. 'We certainly did. The Tivoli Theatre is such fun.'

'Really?' If I was seeking information, I had to *pretend* to be pleasant. 'What did you see?'

'Lots of girls dressed in very little ...'

'How little?'

'Bare from here.' Ella pointed to the top of her thighs. 'And the living statues naked to below the belly button.'

I pretended not to be shocked. 'Was Judy Moloney there?'

Ella frowned slightly. 'I thought I recognised her. But those chorus girls wear such elaborate headdresses and make-up, it's hard to tell who's who.'

'What else did you see?'

Ella laughed into the sink. 'Ventriloquists. Contortionists. So many acts, you wouldn't believe.'

'And the music? Was it just a piano accompaniment?'

Ella shook her head. 'A full blown orchestra. They ended with their version of the *Swan Lake* ballet. They call it 'Silver Swan' and wear high-heels instead of ballet slippers. So funny. I laughed and laughed.'

'Did Felix enjoy it?'

She blushed a little. 'He didn't like some of the acts and he finds Roy Rene appallingly vulgar.'

'Didn't he want to leave?'

'Yes. But I made him to sit through to the end. He thought some of the acts very tasteless,' she reluctantly admitted. 'Of course he has seen the best ballets and operas in Europe. But he did agree that it was entertaining.'

Huh, I thought. Of course she'll forgive him for anything, even for being rather pompous. I smiled sweetly at my twin. 'So with Julie and myself safely at home, you had a good night?'

'That we did.' Her smile was equally sweet.

MORE THEATRES AND 'BIG STAGE PLANS'
23rd March, 1938

New theatres are to be built in Sydney and Melbourne. Attractions of all kinds will be provided, and stars will be imported to appear in the productions. Mr. Frank Neil, the director of Tivoli Theatre Circuit Ltd will go abroad next April to book attractions and take a more personal interest in the musical and dramatic productions on offer in New York, London and continental cities ...

45

UNIVERSITY RENAMED
22nd March, 1938
The Frederick Wilhelm University, which was named after Wilhelm 111 of Prussia has been renamed the Adolf Hitler University ...

Thank God, this farce with Felix is over. Well, almost over. Fridays we light the Sabbath candles and eat in the dining room. As this was also Joe's twenty-third birthday, Julie spent the afternoon cooking his favourite dishes. While Ella set the table, I peeled vegetables, and Julie prepared the almond and passion-fruit tart we know the men adore.

We were seated around the table, Father carving the chicken, when Felix suddenly cleared his throat. Though we half expected him to entertain us with another of his stories about the rich and the famous, what he had to say was doubly surprising, though far more sobering.

'Simon,' he said in rather subdued tones. 'Yesterday I received a letter from Sylvie. She writes that she will be joining me in Sydney in ah ... less than two weeks.'

Father's knife stayed in midair. Julie nearly dropped a platter. Ella flushed scarlet, then went dead white. I thought she was going to faint.

'I didn't know you were going to Sydney,' Father said once this news had sunk in. 'I thought you were settling in Melbourne.'

Felix looked embarrassed. 'It is true I had intended making our home here. However Simon, as you know, I cannot find any reasonable kind of employment, no matter how hard I try. Also, I hear Sydney is more of a metropolis, and though your Melbourne is most agreeable, and I could find no more *gemutliche* friends,' he bowed to Julie, 'Sylvie is used to living in a big city.'

Another stunned silence.

In that space of time which seemed to go on forever, we listened to the clock in the living room chime the half-hour. Cars travelled past our fence. A wattlebird called to another.

Joe finally broke the impasse. 'Ve hope you will be fery happy.' For a moment I thought he was going to pass out, his cheeks had gone so white. To our consternation, he hid his face in his hands. No one knew what to say. When Joe finally looked up, his cheeks were like red danger zones. 'Dis is not de time to … to mention such matters,' he managed to get out, 'But Felix, you haf borrowed much … yes much money from me. Vit'out dat capital, I haf no more business. You vill pay me back soon, yes?'

Another long silence before Felix drew himself to his full five feet four inches. 'Of course you'll get it back,' he said indignantly. 'Only not right away. ' Then aware of all our shocked faces, he quickly added, 'However, I will not disturb the Marks with any more coarse talk about trade.'

'You borrowed from Joe? From Joe as well as me?' Father's eyes under their shaggy brows bored into Felix. He turned to Joe. 'How much did you give him?'

Joe was nearly in tears. 'Three hundred and forty pounds. Eferyt'ink I safe since I come here.'

'You loaned him three hundred and forty pounds?' Father flushed scarlet and garrumphed awhile. 'In that case, what happened to our investments?'

Felix gulped. 'I had a little problem with ah … that company I recommended. Though I thought them perfectly safe, seems that its directors disappeared with ah … all the money …'

'Really?' Father's tone was incredulous. Cheeks now mottled red, he said, 'Let's not ruin Julie's delicious dinner. But when we finish eating, there is business that must be discussed.' Though his heightened colour gave his true feelings away, he made a big effort to look calm and return to dissecting the chooks. Julie ladled out vegetables. Everyone kept on cutting, forking, chewing and swallowing, even though Julie's delicious dinner might have been cardboard for all the good it did us.

Father didn't wait for dessert. Still dangerously flushed, he beckoned a very pale Felix into his study. The rest of us didn't dare look at each other. Ella's cheeks were a distinct shade of grey. She looked like she was about to vomit. The atmosphere was as thick as a London fog. We heard angry shouts from Father's study. Ten minutes later Felix stormed out. We heard a door slam, another bang open. Next the unmistakable clatter of boxes and cases. Felix was packing up to leave.

The strain became too much. Ella jumped to her feet and ran into the back garden. Julie gave a half-strangled cry. Joe whispered in her ear. I grabbed Left and Right, and made my slow way through the back door towards the pear tree. 'Ella,' I called. 'Come down.'

No answer. Only sobs like a puppy whining. My heart felt ready to break. Surely no one should be this unhappy. 'Ella,' I called once again. If she stayed up there, Father might start asking questions, and with Felix in Sydney, Ella would be bound to carry the full brunt of his wrath. 'Ella, come here. If Father suspects something is wrong, you know what he's like.'

No answer. A slight breeze blew up. Towels on the clothesline twisted and turned. What could I say to bring her down? 'I will never forgive Felix,' I said firmly. 'Never. I have always recognised him as an opportunist. But you are my sister, my twin. That means I will do everything I can in the world to protect you.'

All I heard were more sobs. 'Don't you see,' I insisted, 'If you don't come down, Father will get suspicious. He'll know there's more than money to discuss. Come down. Let's start the dishes. Make everything look ordinary.'

A few leaves landed on my head. Ella slid down the trunk and stood before me, head bowed in shame. Heart filled with exultation, I placed one hand around her waist, and we slowly headed back to the house. I peeped into the kitchen. There were Julie and Joe. To my astonishment, they were locked in a fierce embrace.

Only later that night did I remember watching two policemen carry a drunken Aboriginal from the steps of Flinders Street Station. We rarely see any Aboriginals, and I reflected on how dirty and hopeless he seemed, how condemnatory the crowd, how hopeless that poor man's situation. What made me think of this? Surely here was nothing to compare. Surely Felix deserved every punishment he got.

ABORIGINES' CRUEL PLIGHT
17th March, 1938

In an address to the Anthropological Society last night, Professor Wood Jones of Anatomy at the University of Melbourne, disputed the suggestion that the white man found a dying and degenerate race when he came to Australia. "That is the humbug with which the white man has always guided his extermination of native races ...'

46

It's nearly a week since Felix left for Sydney. Shock waves have rung through this house. Father hid in his study, only coming out for meals. He hasn't uttered a pleasant word to anyone. Not even to Julie. He seems to hold his family responsible for his own lack of judgement. He won't tell us how much he loaned Felix to make 'a secure investment'. But from his grim demeanor the sum was certainly princely. Seems that not only had Felix borrowed heavily, but he'd also promised Father a handsome return if he put lots of money into some little-known company, and of course Father did. Now it seems that the directors have fled leaving no forwarding address, and every investment is now lost. As I have so often said, it was as if Felix had bewitched us, and now we must pay and pay for all our foolishness.

Julie remains her usual good and calm self, but every so often she'll pause and frown, as if deep in conversation with an invisible opponent. I think she finds it hard to take everything in. And when I think of all she doesn't know, my head feels ready to burst.

Ella is hardest hit. Yet neither Father nor Julie notice anything unusual. It's true that for this last month, Ella was in such a dream, to the casual eye nothing has changed. But one can see that she's stopped eating, her face is drawn, that she tosses and turns instead of sleeping. I talk to her for hours, try to show her where she was mistaken. But no matter how logical I am, her loyalties are still with him. She claims that he is only waiting to settle Sylvie into a flat before he'll send for her.

I think she's made it all up. Even as a child she refused to admit when she was beaten. Any spare moment, she sits at the piano to play *Body and Soul* over and over again until I could scream. It's as if she has a dreadful illness and cannot get over it. Yesterday, even Julie lost patience with her. 'Next month is Passover,' she declared. 'Ella, time to make us new outfits to wear to Synagogue.' She emptied her purse. Coins rolled onto the table. I stared in amazement. Even Ella's lethargy vanished. She cried, 'Where did you get all that?'

'Saved it, of course,' Julie replied.

'Doesn't Felix owe you money?' I asked.

'Course not,' she said indignantly. But all week Bunny has been hot on the phone. Julie and yours truly must be the only people from whom Felix hasn't borrowed or persuaded to invest in some company that has gone bankrupt and its directors nowhere to be found. When I asked Ella what this firm was all about, at first she refused to answer. Only when I persisted did she tell me that she believed it was to manufacture a new form of light aircraft.

Enough said that the firm does actually exist and is listed on the stock-market, so Felix hasn't actually stolen from anyone, only recommended badly and borrowed heavily and is now unable to pay off his debts. So now he can't return to Melbourne without being torn apart by angry creditors. Bunny claims Felix must owe at least fifteen hundred pounds. All in three months. Not only does he lead an expensive life style, he's also a chronic gambler. Those nights he went out were spent in illegal two-up schools. What he didn't lose in those alleyways, he gambled in gentlemanly bets with his fellow Masons. What makes things worse is that Ella didn't warn anyone. Not even Joe. 'How selfish,' I said indignantly.

'Maybe,' she admitted. 'But it was the only way we could make any money. At first Felix won five hundred pounds. Then he wanted to make more, and lost the lot. So he had to keep on borrowing from everyone to try and win it back.'

That girl was so taken in I could almost believe Felix cast

a spell on her which still exists. Because whenever I try and reason with her, she puts her fingers in her ears and closes her eyes.

Back to our new outfits.

'Three pounds, fifteen shillings and four-pence.' Julie counted it again, then sent us to Ball and Welch to buy the fabric. I chose five yards of fine wool in a rich shade of mulberry. Then Ella went to work, cutting and fitting. I ordered a pleated bodice to give my figure more fullness, and the skirt to be topped by a short jacket and matching beret. Julie promises I can wear Mother's pearls with this outfit.

Still, life is dreadfully dull. No more stories. Or card games. Or sing-songs around the piano. Though part of me is so very relieved that Felix is no longer with us – after all, didn't I work very hard to rid ourselves of him – another unexpected part mourns the loss of the fun he brought into this house. I find myself remembering his stories and laughing aloud. He certainly had a talent for interesting narrative.

His very last story, the one he told just a few nights before he announced that he was leaving had us nearly splitting our sides laughing. Seems that he was in the audience at a West End Theatre when Noel Coward first sang *Mad Dogs and Englishmen*.

Julie is a great fan of Noel Coward. 'Lucky thing,' she said enviously. 'Can you remember it?'

Felix nodded. So she settled at the piano. Felix struck a pose and pretended to be Noel. It was so funny, even though he couldn't remember half the words, how we laughed and laughed.

Surely I should be relieved that someone I loved and hated in almost equal proportions is no longer here to distort my emotions with his presence. Too much grief and pain can break the strongest heart in two. Oh to be as carefree as Motsy and Mitsy. They spend all day lying in the sun. Yesterday Motsy caught a blackbird and brought it inside. I scolded her for killing a wild creature, but she seemed very pleased with herself. How I envy their simplicity, their ability to live in the here and now. Animals have no troublesome passions to deal with. Last night a sudden storm filled the night, each flash lighting up our back yard and storming across the sky towards the city. Thunder filled our streets with noise, and sent the animals scurrying for cover. Lightning speared our hearts like the memory of lost love.

My mind insists on playing games with me. Sometimes limping down the corridor, or entering the living room, I hear a voice with a slight inability to pronounce the letter 'V'. Does our silver reflect a flash of red hair? A glimpse of olive eyes? A pencil thin moustache? All I want is to forget him. Let someone else tinkle Mozart and Chopin on our piano; let someone else tell stories that make my eyes widen; let someone else tighten my stomach and stop my breath; let someone else disturb the even tenor of my day. Yet a voice in my mind keeps on singing 'I'm all for you ... body and soul ...'

47

GOVERNMENT OFFERS HELP
28th March, 1938
The Federal Government has set aside 1,720 pounds for relief work for 2,500 unemployed men ...

The days are still warm with hardly any rain, though the nights are turning cooler. Joe is still in Gippsland selling blouses. Considering how Felix went off with all his money, that he has anything left to sell is little short of a miracle. However, the manufacturers are so impressed by his honesty and hard work, they have allowed him to work on commission. Once he's built up some capital, he'll start his own business. He will soon ask Father's permission to marry Julie. Whenever he is in the city, he joins us for dinner. The other day he brought me several country newspapers. It saddened me to read that many farmers are still suffering from the after effects of the Depression. Though we are better off financially, in some ways I suspect that our lives are far grimmer. I read a great deal, listen to the wireless – the overseas news gets worse every day – and play Patience. Each time a game turns out, is a symbol of how quickly Ella will forget Felix. One winning hand is worth a month. So far this week I have won two games.

We are all very serious. Even Bunny has become almost terrifyingly serious. His gossip consists solely of who is owed money, and how much it is. Felix of course, owes him a great deal. He called in yesterday, and over our usual tea and scones, confided that he has been left in such a financial mess, he might have even to sell his precious MG. I think he would miss his car even more than he would a person. As he sadly admitted, 'A car can never deceive you.'

Hard to see plump, jovial Bunny looking so miserable. I said daringly, 'And your friend ... the one I met at St Kilda. Surely he can offer you some consolation?'

'Ah ... him!' Bunny smiled wryly. 'Lilbet, you'd be surprised at how much love money can buy. And if the money is no longer there ... how little.'

Only Father and Julie continue to behave in much the same way as before, even if their thoughts are very different. I think this business has shattered Julie's faith in her fellow man. And Father so hates to waste money. So yes, perhaps their thoughts are very different to what they were. I doubt that we will ever fully recover.

If ever I recall my trip to St Kilda beach, that hard won moment of independence, I can hardly believe that I am still that same girl, so much has happened to me since. At least I am fortunate in that I can use these notes to pursue my emotions. There is a lot to be said for putting down one's thoughts on paper. It is the most reliable form of confession. But I am starting to wonder if this book should ever be published? There is too much in here that others must never know.

48

Last night, Joe was back with more orders than his manufacturer can fill. Seems country women are totally charmed by his bad English, huge frame and bashful manner. In celebration, Julie cooked goulash. I don't think Joe's ever tasted goulash. When I asked what he ate in Poland, he said, 'Black bread. Herring. When t'ings are goot, chopped liver and gribennes.'

Julie was ladling meat onto Father's plate. 'What are gribennes?'

'Onions fried in chicken fat.'

We all shuddered. Joe looked distressed – he so hates being seen as a foreigner – and hugged himself. 'Iss very cold in Sokolka.'

After dinner, Joe followed Father into his study. When they came out, Father informed Julie that Joe had asked for her hand, and that he had given them his blessing.

Ella and I kissed the newly engaged couple. Even Father smiled dourly. They will marry at the end of the year and live with us. Father offered them his bedroom, but Julie insisted that her room is large enough for two. She knows how inadvisable it is to disturb Father's routine, how even the tiniest change can reduce him to unswerving bleakness. Then I turned on the wireless, Ella mimed to George Formby's *When I'm Cleaning Windows*, and everyone joined into the chorus.

Next morning, Ella and I went into the city. Ella wanted ideas for Julie's trousseau. But I think it's an excuse to get away. It's almost as if her lethargy has been replaced by an inability to sit still. Last night I heard her throwing up. Also, her appetite is peculiar – one minute she feels too sick to eat, next she's searching the pantry for leftovers. Anything sweet or pickled.

Have I mentioned before how she loves to tease? Two years ago on April Fool's day she had Julie convinced that Sunday was Monday and time to fire the copper. Last year she crept out of bed and set the clocks two hours forward. But this year, nothing. She complains of a dreadful tiredness. I think she can't shake off this influenza. I keep telling her to stick to dry toast, but she craves dill cucumbers, pickled onions and sweet biscuits.

Just as we were settling into some routine, a letter arrived from Aunt Amy. She's her usual chatty self, but this time I read what she had to say with particular interest. In part she said, 'Your former lodger Felix Goldfarb and his wife Sylvie, came yesterday to order new hats. Seems that the Thomas's have invited them to lunch at Randwick. Sylvie mentioned that she had a letter of introduction from Dina Thomas's cousin Maria who now lives in Zurich. The result is that the Goldfarbs are cutting quite a swathe in Sydney society. I suppose you're curious to learn what this Sylvie is like? Well, she's small and plain and has a very large nose. Felix is completely under her thumb. Her great attraction is her money. She doles this out rather meagerly. I heard him complain of having no cash for their taxi. I had to stop myself from saying 'how wise.' They were both very friendly until I introduced myself as Simon Marks's sister and your aunt. Then he could hardly wait to get her out of here. I heard him tell her to try another milliner. I wonder how he will explain it away? And now we know how he managed to gain an entry into this country. Seems Dina's cousin sponsored his arrival. I did question Dina as to why he stayed so long in Melbourne. She couldn't answer this, but I'm guessing that he felt he would be unable to move about as freely in Sydney.

'Your Uncle Bernard sends you all the love he can spare

from me. He is interested in buying land at Whale beach. Thankfully, we have no spare cash.

Darlings, do look after yourselves,
A million kisses and hugs ...' etc. etc.

49

Not a cloud in the sky, a cool breeze, the trees turning lovely autumn shades of red, yellow and brown. I decided to spend my afternoon in the backyard reading. Who should I find behind the pear tree? Ella. She'd been throwing up.

I said, 'A flu that doesn't go away? You must see Dr Williams immediately.'

She mopped her face with a hankie. 'Oh Lilbet,' she sighed. 'You're such a child. Don't you realise that I'm pregnant? I'm expecting a baby.'

I could hardly open my mouth to speak. 'What makes you so sure?' I managed at last.

'That!' She pushed the vomit under some leaves. 'Plus, I've missed two monthlies and I'm getting fat.' She showed me how her skirt waistband wouldn't do up.

All I could think was, 'Father ... He'll never cope.'

Ella went even paler. 'Think I don't know? I'll have to get rid of it.'

'Whatever do you mean?'

She explained briefly.

But all I could think was – get rid of it? Surely she's talking about a baby. A baby boy or girl. What might it be like to hold a child, hear him laugh and cry, watch him run on sturdy little legs? I pulled myself together. 'How do we do that?'

'Other girls fix things ...'

'But other girls aren't you,' I cried. I wanted to wring her lovely neck. How could she have got herself into such a mess? As we stood under the tree where we'd spent so much of our childhood, I remembered Mary Moloney. Didn't

Mary have to go a Home for Unmarried Mothers? Wasn't she forced to give up her child for adoption?

My mind darted from one idea to another. Of course Ella has no option. I recalled the two telephone men, the elder talking about 'the old witch down the road'. I reminded Ella of this and then added, 'Maybe we can find her?'

She stared at the ground. 'Isn't this very dangerous?'

I sank to my knees. 'Not if we go to the right person.'

Ella squatted beside me. 'Who do we ask?'

'Daisy. Or maybe Bunny will know?'

'I'd rather die than tell Daisy or Bunny.' She burst into tears. 'I wish I was dead. If only I was dead.'

I nearly died myself. 'Shouldn't Felix be told? After all, it is his child.'

Ella sobbed even louder. She no longer believes Felix intends to leave Sylvie. I told myself that he probably never did, but what's the point of rubbing salt into a wound? For the first time in months, the talk between us was honest. Ella admitted to slowly coming to the realisation of how foolish she'd been. She said, 'It was as if I'd been taken over by someone else.'

I tried not to show too much curiosity. 'But surely you enjoyed what ... whatever you two were doing in there?'

'I would have walked from here to Sydney just to be with Felix,' she said fiercely. I waited for her to say more. She said, 'All I could think about was him. It was as if I was in the desert dying of thirst and he offered me a drink.'

'Yes? And then ...?'

She fell silent.

'But ... you still haven't said what you did in there.'

'Oh Lilbet,' she sighed. 'Just be grateful you'll never have to fight those feelings in yourself.'

I swallowed and looked away. To be told again and again that certain experiences are forever denied one is always hard to accept. But once I recovered we talked and talked. It was as before Felix came between us. Once again we were two sides of one coin. We were twins again in every possible way. In the end Ella cried, 'I got myself into this mess, so I'll get myself out.'

'Of course,' I agreed though I couldn't think how. Then I remembered Julie. 'She'll have to be told.'

'What if she goes to Father?'

'We'll beg her not to.'

Ella didn't answer for a while. 'Yes,' she sighed. 'I suppose we must.'

50

Six o'clock and Julie was busy preparing dinner. Five minutes later, Joe turned up. Ella had no chance to talk to Julie until next morning when she caught her in the bathroom.

I settled into my usual place behind the door to listen in. 'What do you mean, you're expecting a baby?' Peering through the crack, I watched the tendrils of Julie's hair frizz in disbelief and a red spot like on a china doll appear on each cheek. 'You're not even married.'

It took a while for this to sink in. Then she questioned Ella very closely, wanting to know names, places and dates, dates in particular. 'Does Felix know?'

Ella shook her head.

'Then Father will have to be told.'

'Please don't tell Father,' Ella pleaded. 'He'll kill me.'

For someone who is usually kindness itself, Julie could be unrelenting. 'You should've thought of that before. How were you planning to keep this from him?'

Ella clenched her eyes as if she couldn't bear to see what was happening around her.

Julie's lips were now the thinnest line. She wrung her hands. I suppose she knew that Father would hold her responsible. 'It's all my fault,' she cried. 'I should have been watching you more closely.'

She hurried away. Ella sank onto the bathroom floor where she cried so hard she made herself vomit.

'Isabella!' boomed from the study. Ella flushed the vomit down the basin, and walked out of the room like she was going to her own execution.

'Close the door,' Father ordered.

The door clicked shut. I limped down the passage and listened. Father's voice rose. He went on and on. Eventually I pulled myself together and went to the phone. My hands shook so much, I could barely hold the receiver.

A woman's voice said, 'Number please.'

'Long distance, please.'

I listened to the wind whistling down the wires, and repeated the number in my mind. Please God, I prayed. Don't let me get this wrong.

'Long distance operator,' someone said at last. 'State city and number.'

'Sydney, SD 489.'

I heard a long ring and several clicks. A man said, 'Madame Amy's Millinery Salon. To whom do you wish to speak?'

'Madame Amy, please.'

'Whom shall I say is calling?'

'Lilbet Marks. Please hurry. I'm phoning from Melbourne.'

Aunt Amy came to the phone. Tears rolled down my cheeks. I opened my mouth. Nothing came out.

'Lilbet! What's wrong?'

I pulled myself together. Aunt Amy listened. She was always a good listener. 'Only one thing to do,' she said after I finished the whole sorry saga. 'Your Father'll be too concerned about any scandal to be of much use. Tell Ella not to make herself ill. She's not the first young girl to land herself in a family situation. Leave it to me to contact Felix.'

We said our good-byes and hung up. I limped down the corridor and opened the door to Father's study.

That was all he needed to turn savagely on me. 'Lilbet, can't you see we're busy?'

Knees shaking, I said, 'I've just spoken to Aunt Amy. She's going to contact Felix.'

I closed my eyes and waited for the ceiling to cave in.

Father took a deep breath and closed his eyes. 'Perhaps you're right,' he finally managed when he reopened them. 'My sister deals every day with clever rich women. Surely she will know how to handle such a situation. He gerrrumphed a little longer. 'At least one of you shows some sense. Did you tell your aunt to call me back?'

I shook my head.

Father glanced at Ella, now snivelling on the chair in front of his desk. He said, 'I'll ring her from the office.' With this, he walked into the hall, took his hat and set off for his offices in the city.

51

It strikes me that Father is quite extraordinary. How can he manage to go to his office, to behave as if nothing unusual is happening when such a family disaster is about to fall upon his head? Perhaps it has something to do with working in the city. To bear out my argument that Melbourne is truly a city of the future even if at times we seem a little dull, I found this clipping in the *Age*.

THE CITY OF DREADFUL NOISE
7th April, 1938
EDITORIAL: It is a strange fact, and little known, that the Noise Abatement League of Melbourne gave the world a lead in the suppression of public noises some 10 years or more ago. The league was short-lived, but it set an example which was followed with success in other parts of the world.

52

All morning, Ella and I mooned uselessly about. After lunch Julie decided that we'd be best off re-establishing Felix's bedroom as Ella's sewing place. I was no help moving the machine, but at least I could fold materials and slip bobbins into boxes. Though Ella and I hardly exchanged a word, being together gave us strength. We are the Marks twins, I told myself. No one ever again will disrupt our twinness. We belong together like bread and butter, buttons and bows, sugar and spice. From now on our twofold existence is as fixed as the stars, as constant as the rising moon.

When Father came home, he went straight to the bathroom. Julie waited for him to come out to ask, 'Did you speak to Aunt Amy?'

'She'll ring after dinner.'

Just as we started eating, the phone rang.

Father put down his napkin and walked into the hall. We tiptoed after him. He picked up the receiver. 'Amy? What did Felix have to say?'

A long silence.

'Let's get this straight. He insisted that his wife stay with him?'

Another long silence. Father's face reddened. 'He suggested that Ella marry Joe?' His voice rose, 'Did you tell the little rat that my daughter won't be palmed off at his convenience?'

He replaced the receiver and turned, his complexion livid, a vein beating visibly in his forehead. Ella was standing in front. He raised his fist. 'No Father, no,' I cried as Julie rushed to protect her.

Father put his hand on his forehead and slowly sank to the ground.

Everyone froze. Julie knelt on the floor. 'Father,' she said clearly. A little spittle trickled from his mouth. 'Father,' she cried. 'Can you hear me?'

Ella shook herself like a puppy. 'What's wrong with him?' she whispered.

'He fainted,' Julie whispered back.

'What if he's having a heart attack?'

Julie's eyes rolled in fright. 'What should we do?'

I pulled myself together. 'Call Dr. Williams.'

Father moaned slightly. His breathing became more laboured. Julie and Ella seemed rooted to the spot. For the second time that evening I went to the phone. It took ages for Dr. Williams to answer. 'Could be a stroke,' he said after I told him what was going on. 'Cover him with a blanket, and I'll call an ambulance.'

Ashen faced, we sat on the floor watching Father's face first turn blotchy. Then pale as death. The minutes ticked by. Father snored softly. I waited for him to open his eyes and abuse us. To see him like this made me feel quite ill. At the same time a wicked little voice whispered, 'Serves you right, Simon George Marks. Brought this on with your own foul temper.'

Then all I could think was, my only living parent was about to die. Now he would never be the Father I'd always needed. Now he would never look at me as he did my sisters with pride and admiration. Ella whispered through cracked lips, 'Is Father going to die?'

Julie shook her head, but I think this was more to comfort us than what she truly believed. Someone came to the door. Behind the lead glass I recognised Joe's towering outline. 'Thank God,' I muttered. No one moved. I managed to heave myself up and let him in.

At the sight of her fiancé, Julie burst into tears. It was also the signal for Dr Williams to arrive. The ambulance turned up minutes later. Under the good doctor's supervision, Father was lifted onto a stretcher and covered with blankets. Julie and Joe climbed into the ambulance and they took off down the street. Only when Father disappeared into the night, did I dare properly breathe. I turned to Ella and said, 'Let's clear the table.'

53

Father is still in hospital and though it was touch and go, Dr Williams now thinks that he will live. Though conscious, he has no speech and Dr Williams says that he may never regain the full use of his left side. I can't help thinking how ironic of fate to give Father, always so impatient of my disabilities, a similar affliction.

Julie and Joe spend all day with him in hospital while Ella and I keep house. Ella cooks, and I must say her food is quite tasty. In the middle of all this, a letter arrived addressed to Miss E Marks of 'Adeline Terrace' etc.

The writing was unfamiliar. I might have guessed it was from him, but there was no sure way of knowing to whom this letter was addressed. Dr Williams's nurses change so often I never recognise their handwriting, and they always refer to me as Elizabeth. I slipped the letter into my pocket. Then Morris Aarons turned up to inquire after Father and I forgot all about it.

This morning when I woke my body was very sore and my left side stiffer than usual. After lunch, Ella went to buy chicken carcasses to make soup for Father. I told her to leave me in the gardens and collect me on her return. Only after she disappeared down the street, did I remember the letter.

I tore it open. A train ticket and a check for twenty pounds fell out. Also this message:

> My Darling Ella,
> I cannot tell you how much I long for us to be together. Yesterday your aunt, Madame Amy, informed me that you are expecting our child. I had

no idea. Tears of joy filled my heart. Because Sylvie was there, I could not show how moved I was. Though our situation, yours and mine, is not that of a married couple, I believe that in God's eyes we are meant for each other. Last week at Randwick, Lady Luck smiled on me, and I won enough for us to be re-united. Next Sunday I will be waiting for you at Sydney's Central Station.

All my love, my love.

I'm all yours, body and soul.

Felix.

PS. I pray that you have not changed your mind.

I reread it. All my love, my love? I'm all yours, body and soul? I sniffed in disbelief. Felix has a nice turn of phrase. For a foreigner, that is. But what about the next time he runs out of cash? Or his horse turns out to be a donkey? I can just imagine how loving he'll feel then. And a baby to be fed, clothed, cared for.

Ella's voice broke into my thoughts. 'Lilbet, what are you reading?'

I slid the letter into my pocket. 'Oh … ah … a letter from Aunt Amy.'

'What does she say?'

'Just that she's very busy and Uncle has another hare-brained idea for making money. He wants to buy land at Whale Beach. Can you imagine? I read it to you last week, don't you remember?'

Ella frowned. 'I thought a letter came in yesterday's post.'

I rubbed my eyes and openly shivered. Ella was instantly concerned. 'What's wrong, Lilbet?'

The letter was burning a hole in my pocket.

'I feel a bit cold,' I admitted.

'You mustn't get chilled,' she scolded and pushed me home. By the time she'd settled me on the couch and unpacked the groceries, she had forgotten all about the letter.

Not that I like being forced to lie. But when the lie is for some-one else's good. What alternative is there.

I stayed awake half the night and mentally stood in Father's shoes. I tried to view things from his perspective. How hard it is to interfere in another's life – even if it is in that person's best interests. What if Felix was to give up gambling and his expensive tastes? Could he reform enough to look after a wife and baby? Can a profligate turn into a solid citizen? Can leopards change their spots? Only when dawn began seeping through a crack in the curtains did I manage to doze off.

All morning my head swirled and I avoided any conver-sation. 'Lilbet, you are definitely catching a cold,' Julie declared, and she forced me to take more of Dr Williams's evil tonic.

This afternoon Ella was alone in the sewing room. I went to give her the letter, then talked about everything else. The longer the letter stayed hidden, the harder it was to hand it over. Could I pretend it had fallen behind a bush? Or the post-man had forgotten to deliver it? The stamped date on the envelope is clearly visible. In the end I stuffed it under my mattress. When everyone else went to visit Father, I pleaded a migraine and stayed home. Then I picked up the telephone.

'Oh Lilbet, it's you. I was expecting someone else.'

Daisy didn't bother hiding her disappointment.

I had decided not to hedge. 'Daisy, I'm in trouble. Women's trouble. Can you give me the name of someone who can help me out?'

A stunned silence.

Then, 'What did you say?'

I took a deep breath. 'I need the name and address of someone reliable.'

'Wonders will never cease.' Daisy laughed for a very long time. 'Who was it?'

'Never you mind,' I said tartly, a little too tartly, for she cried, 'Say who, or you'll get nothing out of me.'

'Bunny Segal.'

'Bunny Segal, that fairy?' Daisy laughed even more. 'No way. I'll bet it was the charming Felix. They say he's into everything. But I never thought he'd stoop as low as a cripple.' I gritted my teeth. There was a long silence, and then she said, 'All right. There's a man in Sydney I can personally vouch for ...'

'You mean ... you've visited him? For the very same problem?'

'How otherwise would I know,' she said impatiently. 'And he's safe.'

'But ...' I hesitated. 'How can I get to Sydney? No, it has to be in Melbourne.'

'Hmm, that makes it hard. The police are far more active here. I'll give you an address, on condition you keep mum about everything I've just told you. Agreed?'

'Agreed.'

'I'll have to make another phone call.'

'Right,' I said and hung up.

Daisy was as good as her word. I waited in the hall for the phone to ring, and five minutes later it did. I jotted down the address. Then questioned her very carefully on what must be done and the dangers this involved. Finally, she told what it would cost. I thanked her profusely and hung up.

I waited for Ella to come home. Then we opened Father's study door. Though we knew Father wasn't there, and that he couldn't scowl or growl at us, years of habit made us creep inside. In his desk we found the tin box where he keeps his cash and a large bunch of keys. Eventually I found one that would open the lid. Inside was a roll of five and ten pound notes. I removed three ten-pound notes and returned the box to where I'd found it.

All this time, Ella wouldn't stop crying.

Poor Ella, I thought tiredly. By now she has wept enough tears to fill the sea.

54

Ella told Julie she needed more bobbins. These can only be bought in the city. By the time we set out, Ella pushing me in the wheelchair, it was well after ten. We caught two trams to Brunswick and it was exhausting getting the chair up and down the steps.

Where was Fortescue Street? Ella stopped to ask for directions. The lady's shabby coat and shapeless cloche had seen better times, as had her manners. Without answering, she waved vaguely in a north-easterly direction and scuttled away.

This area has never recovered from the Depression. We walked along cobbled streets lined with tiny wooden cottages and saw front doors opening onto the pavement. Ella glanced inside. 'What's in there?' I asked her. 'What do you see?'

She shivered. 'Broken walls. Torn lino. Old mattresses.'

'Poor things, ' I said.

She nodded wordlessly.

Snotty-nosed children stared open-mouthed as we passed by. Their mothers only stopped gossiping long enough to gaze stonily at my wheelchair. Here the visible signs of the Depression have never been removed. I could only wonder at the poverty and misery that surround these ramshackle buildings.

The further we went, the more we changed personalities. I became braver, Ella more cowardly. She said, 'You sure you know ...'

'... where we're going? Daisy said 3 Fortescue Street.'

Fortescue Street ran alongside a factory belching black smoke. In the foul stench, my new-found courage quickly disappeared. I signalled for Ella to stop.

'What's wrong?'

I gulped. 'You sure you want ...'

'... to go through with this? What choice do I have?'

At number 3, an old woman in a grubby dressing gown opened the door. She focused a bleary gaze on Ella. 'What youse want?'

'You..ah ... ah..' Ella was left speechless.

'Pretty little girl in trouble, eh?' The woman's smile revealed a lonely tooth. 'Like's of you always need Ma Harrigan. You got thirty nicker?' Ella nodded. Then the old woman pointed at me and spat. 'Whatchya bring her for? She'll givus the evil eye.'

Suddenly a voice, it must have been mine, spoke up clearly. 'Thank you, but we've changed our minds.'

The old woman stared. 'Whatchya saying?'

I cleared my throat. 'We won't be needing your help, after all.'

'Huh!' She slammed the door in our faces.

'Lilbet, what have you done?' Ella whispered.

'Dirty old woman. Did you see her fingernails? Black as coal. Daisy should've known better. She told me how dangerous this was, how some girls die after their abortion. That old woman would more likely kill you. No, you're going to have this baby. Julie must marry Joe as quickly as possible.'

She stared at me as if I'd lost my mind. 'What's their marriage got to do with this?'

'Then they can say that this baby ... that he is theirs.'

'How do you know it's a boy?' And when I didn't answer, 'Julie will never agree. Besides, Father will never allow it.'

'Julie can be talked into it. And now Father is so sick, he can't do anything to stop you.'

'No, don't suppose he can,' she said wonderingly.

'And one more thing,' I fiercely added as several buffoons passing by made the usual loutish comments about what they'd like to do to a girl in a wheelchair. Perhaps it was meeting old Ma Harrigan that inspired me to say, 'Serves that Sydney bugger right if we hang onto his baby.'

A little colour came into her cheeks. 'Serves those Sydney buggers right,' she echoed.

Last night I had a dream ... such a dream.

In it Ella and I were sitting in a boat far out to sea. Night. Only the ocean and a vast wheeling sky studded with stars and a swollen moon rising over the horizon – that moon so close I could see her valleys and mountains almost as clearly as if I was flying into it.

Hardly any noise. Only water lapping against the sides of the boat and the wind's gentle susurrus. Sea birds flew overhead. They swooped and dived, then flew up and vanished into the distance.

A movement made me look down. Felix was lying on my lap, moonlight catching his olive eyes and gingery moustache. He smiled as we cradled him between us. Far out to sea mermaids beckoned me to join them. I shook my head.

A baby's cry pierced the night. I glanced down to see that Felix had gone and I was holding a baby. The baby smiled a gummy smile and blew milky bubbles. Ella picked him up and put him to her breast. As we held the baby between us and watched him suckle, we knew true contentment.

55

> **NEW FLYING BOAT SERVICE IS UP AND AWAY**
> **5th July, 1938**
> Australia's rapidly expanding aviation industry made a big advance today when Qantas Empire Airways began its regular flying boat service between Australia and England. Several hundred people gathered at Rose Bay just after 7a.m. to watch the flying boat *Cooee* set off for Southhampton ...

Weather, cold, wet and thoroughly miserable. I settled myself in the living room to read my notes and clippings for the very last time. I felt so calm and contained. It was such a relief to no longer feel the need to pour out my heart on paper. I realised, I could never send these pages to a publisher. There are too many secrets in here, too much that must not be revealed. Anyway, who has the energy and patience to waste time writing novels? Mostly bored young women I suspect, who have too little to fill their hours and are looking for some activity. Though this might once have been my fate, I felt that in the future, that my life, that all our lives would be far too busy.

Not long ago, both my sisters had encouraged me to write. But where Ella wanted a romance, Julie had suggested a mystery. What would they have said if they'd known that I was tackling a family saga? I am sure that they would have wanted something more thrilling. And more importantly, something far less revealing. In some ways it is highly ironic that these last few months have held more than enough excitement to fulfil any writer's, or reader's, needs.

My thoughts turned to the latest events at Adeline Terrace. Julie had taken some convincing to accept Ella's baby as nominally hers. Originally she had planned to have the child adopted out. 'That's what Father would have wanted,' she insisted. Only Joe saying, 'Ella's baby alvays velcome, no metter who ze fader ...' convinced her to change her mind. Joe's plan was that they would marry as early as possible. Then present Ella's baby to the world as theirs.

Thus six weeks ago to this very day, Joe and Julie stood under the canopy at the East Melbourne Synagogue with just a tiny gathering to watch them 'tie the knot'. Because Father was still too incapacitated to give Julie away, Morris Aarons stood in for him. Bunny and myself acted as witnesses, and Ella and Daisy were Julie's bridesmaids.

Ella sewed all the wedding outfits and all three women looked wonderful in a mix of cream and violet satin and lace. (Violet is Daisy's favourite colour, and she insisted that Ella use it.) Though I would have loved to be one of Julie's bridesmaids, Daisy pointed out that having me in the wedding party would only ruin the photographs. She was so keen on everyone looking their best, and she made such a fuss about the wedding pictures, saying how she intended sending them overseas to some cousins living in America, Julie gave in just to keep the peace. So it was a great pity that just before the photographer turned up, I stumbled against Daisy, accidentally ripping her dress across the bodice so the lace had to pinned together.

Joe smashed the wedding glass under his foot in that age-old Jewish ritual. We all shouted 'Mazel-Tov', and thus Julie and Joe are now man and wife. Then Bunny and Morris drove us all back to Adeline Terrace where Julie had prepared a wonderful buffet lunch with all our favourite dishes, including her special almond chocolate-rum cake with the cream and passion-fruit sauce. Halfway through the meal Morris presented the toast to the bride and groom and Bunny told stories at which everyone laughed and that I am just beginning to understand. Everyone agreed that though these nuptial celebrations were small, that everything went off splendidly.

Since Ella's condition has started to show it has been agreed that both my sisters will stay out of sight until the baby is born. This way no one will know which sister is actually pregnant. Then the little boy – for some strange reason we are all convinced that this baby is a boy – will be presented to the world as Julie and Joe's.

Now that Ella is over the worst of her morning sickness, she is waiting the birth with less anxiety than anyone might have expected. The entire experience has sobered her up considerably, and she is no longer the same flighty girl she once was. Sometimes I catch her looking pensively into space. But then she always smiles bravely and tells me how lucky she is to have such a close and loving family.

The baby's welfare is uppermost in our minds. Julie makes sure that Ella drinks lots of milk so that the baby will have strong bones. Every spare moment Ella can find, she sews baby nightdresses and knits layettes. I am sure that this child will enjoy being read to and I have searched out those books I loved as a child. I have also suggested to Ella that the baby be called Max. Or Maxine if it's a girl. This much at least we owe Felix. After all, the baby's ancestry is German and Max is a good German name.

Four weeks after Father's stroke, he came home from hospital, though with hardly any movement in his left arm and leg and still speechless and incontinent. Julie keeps saying, 'It'll take a big effort on our part to keep him comfortable.' And, 'The doctors at the hospital say it's far too early to hope for a complete recovery.' We have been instructed to massage his stricken limbs daily and to make sure that we only feed him on food that can easily be chewed, swallowed and digested.

I am looking forward to keeping him abreast of world affairs. I never give up hope that he will regain enough speech to discuss these with me. So much has been happening overseas.

Britain and France had agreed to the German annexation of Czechoslovakia. More young men from all over Europe and even Australia have gone to Spain to join the Republican push against General Franco. The Japanese are doing far too well in China. Almost every newspaper predicts that these actions could only be the prelude to another world war.

As for Aarons and Marks, Morris Aarons had promised to keep the office running, but it was too much for him to manage alone and he needed someone to fill Father's shoes. Bunny Segal has offered his services. As a trained accountant and now desperately short of money, it seems the ideal solution. Of course Bunny will have to be paid a decent salary, and the firm will have less cash. Though Daisy hates housework so much and she made a big fuss about having to give her cook notice, this doesn't bother the Marks sisters. We are quite used to living simply and doing for ourselves. Julie has promised that I can help her with the housework when Ella is occupied with the baby and there is too much for one person to manage. Besides, we have faith in Joe – faith that his business will succeed and that one day we will be quite well off.

Since, I have found out lots more about Felix. Mostly from Daisy. Of course she and Bunny know about Ella's condition, but they have been sworn to secrecy. I am sure that they will keep to their word, if only to ensure that *their* little secrets are equally safe with me.

Seems everything Felix told us about having wealthy parents was false. Daisy said, 'His parents owned a little tailoring shop and could hardly make ends meet. Felix was the fourth of seven children. They're a religious family who utterly dislike Felix's lifestyle. They refuse to have anything to do with him.'

Soon as I could get Daisy alone, I asked, 'What do you know about Sylvie?'

'Only that her first husband owned steelworks outside Frankfurt. When he died, she sold up and left most of the money in a Swiss bank. If she can keep Felix away from those accounts they should do rather well.'

'Where did he meet her?'

'In Baden-Baden. At a roulette table. She's at least fifteen years older than him.'

I blinked incredulously. 'You mean, meeting Hitler, travelling around Europe as a big time businessman, all those resorts and restaurants and castles and film-making, meeting all those famous and noble people, they were just a pack of lies?'

Daisy laughed. Since *that* phone-call, she has decided to ignore the number of times I 'forgot' to deliver her messages to Felix and Ella. As she put it, 'Anyone prepared to look after a sister as you did, can't be all that bad.' Sometimes I wonder what Daisy would say if she knew how far my actions have taken me. 'Tell me more about Felix,' I pleaded.

'He's a ne'er-do-well.'

'What about him going to school in England, and the Sorbonne University?'

'All stories, lies.'

'But he behaved like a gentleman. And he spoke so many languages.'

'They were all learnt around gaming tables. He has a very musical ear.'

'Not bad,' I agreed, remembering his performance on their piano. But that had been much like Felix himself – lots of bravado to cover his technical weaknesses.

Something else was bothering me. 'Why did you tell him where to find those two-up schools?'

Daisy reddened slightly. 'I'm always short of cash. Anyway, how was I to know he was gambling with other people's money?'

'Yet he was always the perfect gentleman.'

Daisy's yawn showed several gold-filled teeth. 'Parrots can be taught to speak and mime. Ever since Felix came to Australia, he's been making the most of people feeling sorry for him.'

233

I nodded sadly. How typical of Daisy to see things in black and white. But haven't I always accused her of lacking imagination?

One evening in mid June, I opened the door to a man in a brown suit and black homburg. His words slid out like in a gangster film. 'Felix Goldfarb 'ome?'

I shook my head.

The man wiped his mouth on his sleeve. 'Give 'im a message from Big Ted. Tell 'im, where's our money.' This delivered, he took off down the garden path.

That night there was several phone calls for Felix. Both times I answered the phone. Both times the caller only left a message. The voice seemed familiar. I was sure it was the same man. Though I was tempted to tell him where Felix was, something stopped me. Though Felix was a gambler, a liar, an adulterer, I sometimes wonder if he was as much an opportunist as I once thought? Whenever I recall the way his gingery hair caught the light as if he commanded more air and space than ordinary mortals, his olive gaze, the golden hairs on the back of his hands, that pencil-thin moustache, my stomach tightens and my breathing quickens.

Felix brought glamour into our dull suburban lives. And he taught me something about love ... even unrequited love. He showed me how love can be so close to hate; how one cannot be experienced without the other; and how it is better to experience both rather than nothing at all. He taught me something about myself, and for this I will always be grateful.

In the end I saw him as a man trying to pull himself into a better existence. And as time goes on and I consider what his fate might have been if he hadn't left Germany. It's hard to blame him for trying to make the most of every opportunity that presented itself.

His major flaw was that he stayed on in Adeline Terrace. In an effort to save his own skin, a true scoundrel would have fled. The newspapers are full of such stories – detailed accounts of confidence men that disappear into the night. So why didn't Felix? Surely he must have realised how hopeless his situation had become.

I think that he stayed on because of Ella. He never expected to fall in love. For love her, he surely did. His letter proved this to me. But how long this love might have lasted, given making a living etc. is problematic. Whereas once I saw him as merely self-advancing, I now admit to myself that I was wrong. Perhaps his real problem lay in an all-consuming weakness that forced him to always look for easy solutions.

Sometimes I ask myself what might have happened if he had indeed been stronger and, like Edward and Mrs. Simpson, openly stated his feelings? Of course that would have meant divorcing Sylvie, settling into domesticity and taking on an everyday profession. Could he have done this? Maybe this was too much to expect from someone with his expensive tastes.

I rarely feel guilty for not passing on his letter. It's true that sometimes when I look at Ella's pretty face, that I do feel a certain remorse. To counter this, I picture my sister living with a chronic gambler, growing wrinkled and old and sour before her time. Surely both she and the baby are better off in the bosom of a caring and loving family.

So the Marks family remains intact, soon to add a baby to its ranks. If ever I recall that blue and golden day on St. Kilda beach, I experience a momentary sadness for that lost freedom. How wonderful it was to do anything I liked without having to ask for help. Or being told that 'This isn't suitable conduct for a cripple'. But before my spirits fall too low, I focus my thoughts on this new babe and all the delights that this new life will bring us.

If I glance at the scene outside our bay window, all I see are bare branches and grey skies. Now that autumn is over, I like to reflect on how bountiful it has been. The apple and pear trees carried heavy crops and we have more than enough produce to lay down dozens of jars of pickles and fruit.

Midsummer was when I first decided to cut clippings out of the newspapers and use them and my family as the basis of a novel. Back then I never suspected how events might turn out. All in all, I am relieved to no longer be writing. Yesterday, when Ella asked if she could read a little, I quickly shook my head. 'It isn't quite ready.'

I pray that Ella will forget all about it. And if she doesn't? Well, then I will have to pretend that I have destroyed these pages. I wonder at my ability to stay this calm; as if all the passion I recently experienced has fled leaving me with a new understanding of myself and others; as if all envy and hate have disappeared; as if my external self may look no different, but deep inside there's a rainbow day, and truly I am reborn.

These days Daisy often visits us. Last night over dinner she asked, 'Lilbet, how can you stand never having any fun?'

'Depends what you call fun,' I replied, thinking how I have never expected much of interest to happen to my external shell. My true excitements are those of the spirit, and I hope that one day I might, to quote the poet Yeats

> *...pluck till time and times are done*
> *The silver apples of the moon*
> *The golden apples of the sun*

Once I used to imagine that in my next life I will return as a beautiful insect – a ladybird, a beetle or a dragonfly. But why wait for then? Even now my dull exterior hides my true self. One day I will emerge from this cocoon. Then I will flutter my gossamer wings and skim over the valley high into the air, well beyond the rising moon.

If you enjoyed this book, join **Indra Members** at

www.indra.com.au

and tell us whether you would like to receive:

- invitations to book launches
- special offers on Indra titles
- information about new releases